Loose Ends

Copyright © 2012 Tom Woodward
All rights reserved.

ISBN-10: 1-4783-7378-4
EAN-13: 9781478373780

Loose Ends

A Collection of Short Stories of a Mysterious Nature

Tom Woodward

2012

Dedication

To Diane, the Love of my life;

And to all the people in my small hometown

who meant so much to me

when I was growing up.

(After reading the stories,

see if you can you guess

the name of my hometown.

The fewer stories you need to guess

correctly, the better detective

you may make.)

"Love often comes with murderous intent."

Unknown

Table of Contents

I'd Rather Be Lucky	1
Loose Ends	27
Gas Pains	43
Mountain of Regret	71
The Good Doctor	93
A Quick Study	107
One More Statistic	137
The Naked Banker	145
Witness Protection	173
Princess Pamela and the Blind Hog	189
The 3000 Eyes	223

I'D RATHER BE LUCKY

He appeared in the doorway of the detectives bullpen just as the telephone number I'd dialed began to ring. As I stood at my desk watching him across the tops of the cubicles, a knot formed in my stomach. His very presence irritated me so much I almost didn't hear the small voice answering at the other end of the phone line. "Medical Examiner's Office."

"Call you back," I whispered without taking my eyes off the cheesy grin he was wearing, a smirk that always meant a headache for someone else. As I hung up the phone, I watched his bodybuilder bulk, with his close-cropped black hair, pale skin, and disturbingly green eyes, make its way through a maze of cubicles. Even his walk revealed the arrogant attitude that dominated what passed for his personality. I sat back down at my desk and returned to the stack of burglary reports I'd been working on all morning.

He stopped just outside my workspace. He didn't say anything, simply waited for me to acknowledge his presence. This was a power thing. And I would rather have crawled over two miles of broken beer bottles on my hands and knees than to give him the satisfaction.

Finally, "his highness" spoke. "Sorry to disturb your slumber, Woody."

"I've told you before, only my friends call me 'Woody.'"

"You've got friends, Woody? Or should I call you by your true first name?"

My irritation grew at this remark. I have never liked my true first name. "What do you want, Fraser?"

"That's 'Sergeant Fraser' to you," he said in his best remember-who-you're-talking-to voice.

2

He'd risen to the bait, so I jerked the line. "What do you want, Fraser?" The voices in the nearby cubicles, going about their normal routines, suddenly became quiet as they waited to see where this was going. The others recognized the tension between us. They didn't know why it was there, but knew it was always just below the surface.

I think Fraser started to say something fairly ominous, but decided otherwise. Instead, he tossed a stack of reports on the corner of my desk. "More burglaries reported. Same circumstances, same M. O. Why don't you do the taxpayers a favor and earn your pay on these, before the perpetrators hit every home in the county?"

My frustration and anger rose, but I held fast. The storm passed. Through a weak attempt at a grin, I shot back, "Instead of truly *earning* my keep, maybe I'll just get lucky and stop the guy for a routine traffic violation and find the stolen goods on the back seat of his car." My voice dripped as much sarcasm as I could muster.

With this, his face turned a deep red, and his beefy hands became menacing fists. Before I could stand to meet what I took to be a challenge, he turned and left the bullpen area very quickly. He didn't leave because he feared me, and I knew it. Right on cue, those other voices returned to the dull roar of their routine.

Don't you love watching professionals at work? I knew the outrage my last comment was certain to bring. Okay, okay, I also knew the whole thing was childish, but there was a history between us. And as I watched Fraser stomp away, that history ran through my mind.

Only a little over a year earlier, Jay Fraser and I'd been uniformed officers, assigned to routine patrol, on the police force in our county in the suburbs of Washington, D. C. At the time, each of us had just scored very well on the sergeant's examination and was hopeful of promotion. With just a little less time on the force than I, Fraser was fairly sharp at his job, though not always too swift on the uptake. Some guys laughingly claimed it was caused by the steroids he must've taken to get the mass of muscle he wielded. Whatever the explanation, I suspected Fraser wasn't as dull witted as some thought, only slower at getting the brain cells engaged. Methodical, some might have called it.

Well, one day Fraser was out on patrol when he made a huge cocaine bust at a local gas station just off the interstate highway. It turned out to be the largest coke bust ever in this area and one of the biggest ever on the East Coast. Soon the DEA was involved big time, but the individual glory was all Fraser's. Before the hullabaloo died down, a large, newly formed drug ring had been broken up.

Fortunately for Fraser, the arrest he'd made immediately preceded one of those get-tough-on-drugs policy speeches that emanates from our nation's capital occasionally. So when the story hit the papers, Fraser was invited to Capitol Hill to serve as part of the backdrop for the speech. Of course, the publicity-savvy PR types in our department made the most of it, taking every opportunity to use it as an example of the diligence and expertise of our police officers. Meanwhile, notwithstanding our pride in the recognition of our police department, the rest of us sat back and wondered what the hell had happened with Fraser and how. Despite whatever talent he had as an officer of the law, this plainly didn't sound like the Jay Fraser we knew, and it didn't add up.

The answers weren't long in coming. At the last minute, I was volunteered to drive Fraser's collar, named Haverd, a rodent-faced man with a jagged profile and a unibrow, to the feds. Normally, Jay would have had the privilege of the "perp walk" in full view of the news media, but he was busy being congratulated or decorated or something somewhere. In any event, while I was driving into DC, we passed a police officer with a motorist pulled over. I made some offhand remark about cops catching the bad guys in the act. Haverd laughed sarcastically and muttered something about the dumb luck of some cops. With a glint of expectation, I looked in the rear-view mirror at him. My curiosity was immediately aroused, so I asked Haverd what he meant. At first he clammed up. His tiny, close-set eyes darted from side to side, avoiding looking in my direction. Then, after some time of quiet contemplation, he commented that he'd been caught red-handed and had already admitted his part in the conspiracy, so what the hell.

Haverd's voice cracked thin and high as he told me that he was only a "mule," hauling the cocaine on Interstate Highway 95 to his partners farther up the East Coast. He had pulled off the highway and into a service station for gas. When he did, a cop, Fraser as it turned out, pulled in behind him. Because Haverd was part of a group of freelancers trying to make some big money quickly and it was his first run as a mule, he panicked, assuming he had been spotted somewhere along the highway. He got out of the van and lay on the ground with his arms spread so as not to be shot by the police. When Haverd freaked out, Fraser noticed the bundles on the front passenger seat, partially covered by a bed sheet. The bundles were cocaine. Lots of it. And lots more in the back of the van. Later, while he waited for backup, Fraser told him he had only stopped to tell the driver his brake lights weren't working. Haverd was not smart enough simply to determine why the cop had stopped, take a traffic ticket, and move on.

As a result of his lucky break and the accompanying media coverage, Fraser was leapfrogged to sergeant and made deputy chief of the burglary division over other more experienced, more senior officers. These actions were unprecedented. The press he'd received further inflated his already considerable ego. Although he believed a mere burglary division was beneath him, the department brass was willing to go only so far in rewarding Fraser's exploits and bowing to the media clamor. Even the promotion and the deputy division chief's job he received were too much for some on the force. Especially now that I knew the truth of his "drug bust," I was on that list. He walked around as if he had solved the disappearance of Jimmy Hoffa single-handedly. Within the department, I'd kept what I'd learned to myself. For whatever reason, I'd never confronted Fraser with Haverd's version. I would just drop occasional hints about what I knew as he went through life living the myth. I have never begrudged anyone's success earned through hard work and determination. But, to me, his story was different.

Now, I was working *for* him and dealing with his highhanded attitude daily. God, I couldn't stand the sight of him. Fraser displayed just such an arrogance that I wanted to let the air out of his balloon at every opportunity. And he would not let up on me about this series of residential burglaries I'd been working. These damned burglaries. Nearly all the property taken in the break-ins had been recently purchased, high-end electronic equipment: big-screen televisions, stereos, computers, and the like. Although the burglaries were spread across the county, I had worked the angle of a common denominator because there had been so many of them in a short period. However, the electronics had been bought from many diverse stores, including big box specialty stores, department stores, and so on. Additionally, different salespeople, with no known connections among any of them, were involved in the purchases. And, finally, a few victims had used cash, some purchased with credit cards, others bought on a payment plan, so there was no common link there. As hard as I worked, I was at a loss for answers. Beyond just the political heat involved, it was becoming a matter of pride to get these cases solved.

I redialed the number I'd called a minute earlier. Again, the same voice at the other end of the line answered, "Medical Examiner's Office. This is Dr. Pirkle. How may I help you?"

"Hi, Diane."

"Was that you who called a second ago? I didn't recognize your grunt."

"Yeah, sweetheart. I'm sorry I had to hang up," I pleaded quietly, close to the phone.

"Fraser again." This was more a statement than a question. Sometimes I was convinced she should have been a cop instead of a forensic pathologist.

"Yeah. He just really irks me sometimes with his—"

"You give him too much power." Silence. It drove me crazy when Diane said things like that. Mostly because she was right. After letting me stew for a short time, she continued, "You know you do." Another pause. "But I'm on your side, you know."

I was embarrassed by my shortcoming but her voice was so disarming in reminding me of it. "You're right." She just knew what was good for me. Awkwardly, I tried to move on to another subject. "So how's business in the 'tomb'?"

"The usual. Just dead," she responded, relishing every opportunity to use her morgue jokes. "I was just laying out some work for tomorrow," she giggled.

Relieved to move on, I laughed delightedly as if I hadn't heard this a dozen times before. Her giggle always made me smile. Actually, the sight of her merely walking into a room made me break into a wide grin. I had it bad.

"Are we still on for dinner tonight?" she asked.

"So long as nothing else comes up here unexpectedly. I need the diversion of you."

"Am I just a 'diversion'?" she taunted.

"You know that you're more than that to me."

"Just checking."

"See you at Lindy's at 7:30." I hung up the phone and, again, returned to reading through the stack of burglary reports.

Seven-fifteen that evening found me ensconced at a table toward the rear of Lindy's Restaurant, our favorite place, a Cuba Libre firmly in my grasp. This one was not my first. Shortly after seven-thirty, I looked up to see Diane wending her way through the other diners toward our table. I broke into that broad smile.

Diane and I met a while back at a house where a grisly multiple-victim murder had taken place. Not your usual answer to the "How did you two meet?" question. Responding to the 9-1-1 call of "shots fired," I was the first uniformed officer to arrive at the location. Having found the bodies, I confirmed the situation to dispatch. Initially, I secured the crime scene and started a crime-scene log, noting everyone who entered the area marked off with the yellow crime-scene tape. Other uniformed officers began to arrive. Dr. Diane Pirkle appeared at our location shortly thereafter to act as the representative for the Medical Examiner's Office. Normally, in our jurisdiction, the ME's office sent an investigator to the scene to make any death-scene examination they needed in conjunction with their autopsy report. On that occasion, Diane had happened to be nearby, returning from an aerobics class, when she heard the radio dispatch on the police scanner in her car and took the call.

At the time, Diane was new to the area and was the first female forensic pathologist we'd ever had. She was still unknown to most of us on the police force. So, when she got out of her car in workout clothes and walked to the tape, another uniformed officer stopped her with a condescending remark about woman having no business there. Somewhat indignant, Diane flashed her credentials at him and identified herself. The officer was Jay Fraser. As I listened to him stumble through an apology, I realized that I might well have received her response. "But for the Grace of God," as they say. Although I'd like to think that I would not have been so disdainful, given her obvious physical allure even in her sweat clothes, I was glad it was not I. Fraser's inept apology only made things worse as he again referred to her gender. Diane quickly reminded him that Ginger Rogers had done everything Fred had, only backward and often in high heels. It appeared that such inane remarks had been cast her way before, and she was prepared with a riposte. She left Fraser standing in stunned silence.

Diane then proceeded with clipboard in hand to my location to have me note her entry into the site. She was all business at that point. Thank you, Fraser, I thought. Since no detective had arrived on scene yet to take over the case, I explained what I'd found after responding to a neighbor's call about shots being fired. Apparently, she immediately saw my discomfort with what I had found and was describing. I have to admit that mine is not the strongest of stomachs when it comes to the blood and gore of some crime scenes. She smiled at my uneasiness. Later she would describe it as "surprising but sweet." But for me, as a somewhat burly police officer, it's been a constant source of embarrassment.

Anyway, Diane waited for the detectives to arrive at the scene and for them, finally, to give her the okay to enter to do her job. After she had completed her tasks there and I was relieved of maintaining the log, she asked me if I wanted to get a cup of coffee. Because my shift had ended while we were at the crime scene, I gladly accepted. I was just relieved that she wasn't hungry, considering how my stomach felt at the time. I had been instantly struck by her hazel eyes, intense and yet, at the same time, soft and comforting. Her dark hair set off a mischievous smile on a captivating face. Something inside told me that my getting to know her in any serious way may be a long shot, but I was up for the journey. Over coffee that night, I apologized for Fraser's behavior. Diane dismissed him out of hand, saying that her opinion of men in general had already been tainted enough before she ran into his wretched sexist butt. She opined that he was just a guy who only wanted a woman willing to play second fiddle to his daily, self-centered barbell workouts and was merely one of many men who likened women to pianos: if they're not upright, they're grand. Wow! I thought that was perceptive for such a brief encounter. Insight like that can be very intimidating.

She immediately softened and changed the subject. She explained that she was a newcomer in the area, didn't know anyone yet, and would like someone to show her the sights. Again, I gladly accepted the undertaking, a term she found hilarious when I used it at the time, given her profession. We hit it off immediately and things had progressed from there. As it turned out, she was the funniest, most intelligent person I'd ever known. She always had a comeback to my smart-aleck remarks and never let me get away with anything. I responded in kind. We had evolved a way of teasing each other to a point where other couples might have felt uncomfortable. But not Diane and I. And our common interests seemed to know no bounds, from music and food to old movies. I grew to love her very much.

Diane and I met and started seeing each other about four months before Jay's big "drug bust."

I rose as Diane reached our table.
"Always the gentleman," she teased, as she settled in.

"Just a southern upbringing," I smiled. "You look great!"

"You look terrible."

"Thanks. I love you, too."

She ordered a drink, and, as the server walked away, she asked, "So how was the rest of your day? Did you and Jay play well together this afternoon? Or did the teacher have to separate you two?"

"C'mon, Diane. Please, let's talk about something else. I'm just sick of the guy living off dumb luck."

She didn't seem to have heard me. Then she looked deeply into my face and said, "Sure. Only, know that I care very much about you, and I hate to see you let something like this guy and his attitude keep eating at you. You just need to rise above him."

"Thank you, doctor. And your college minor was in psychology, right?" I realized that my words had a harsher effect than intended as I saw Diane's face redden slightly, so I quickly continued, "Seriously, Babe, I know you're right, and I really do appreciate your understanding and your counsel. I'll work on things. I promise."

Diane leaned forward with an elbow on the table and her chin in her hand. "Speaking of luck, didn't you tell me once about a very lucky break you caught on a car-theft case?"

Diane had a memory like the well-known steel trap. What she said was true. Several days before Fraser's big incident, I'd been on evening patrol, driving through the parking lot of an apartment complex, when I found a vehicle that had just been reported stolen earlier that afternoon. The area was what we refer to as a "high crime area," involving everything from drugs to robberies and so on across the spectrum of criminal behavior. Our vicinity had recently been subjected to a massive and unrelenting higher-end car theft epidemic, which the brass assumed was the work of a single ring of thieves. But knowing about the ring and catching them were different matters. They were smart and crafty. Anyway, when I found the car, I didn't know whether this culprit was part of the ring, but wanted to get him, whoever he was, wherever he was. And the thief could have been anywhere in the large complex, although my hunch was that he was in the apartment building in front of which the car was parked.

I sat in my patrol unit and confirmed the status of the stolen car on NCIC while trying to think of some course of action. About the time the confirmation on the car's status came through, my attention was diverted to the blare of fire engine sirens coming into the complex from the main road. Although I didn't know where the fire or emergency was, I immediately ran to the building where the car was parked, started banging on doors, and yelling that there was a fire and all the vehicles needed to be moved so the emergency vehicles could do their job.

With that done, I waited and watched the short time until a mope came tearing from an apartment, jumped into the car, and started it. In the excitement, he didn't even see me walk up beside the car where I reached in and turned the engine off with whatever type key he'd been using. To my amazement, he *was* part of the theft ring. He had merely stopped off to get something to eat before delivering the car to his pals. The suspect quickly spilled his guts on the delivery location and his fellow conspirators. Although this led to a major bust and did bring me a measure of recognition within the department, the case was quickly lost in the banner headlines that accompanied Fraser's accomplishment. Drug busts are always a sexier story than the breaking up of a theft ring. But I *had* been fortunate. And so Diane was right. As usual.

I flagged down our server in time to get another drink at the same time Diane's first one arrived.

"*Can ly!*" I said as we raised our glasses.

"What?"

" 'Cheers!' Vietnamese," I answered, finishing the drink I'd had before me when she arrived.

I picked up my most recently arrived rum and coke and proposed, "*Budem!*"

"Now what?" she said as she sipped her chardonnay.

"A Russian toast."

"Well, at least that year sailing on-board freighters wasn't totally wasted. How many foreign languages can you make a toast in?"

I grunted. "Enough to put me under the table."

"Great!" she said sarcastically, rolling her eyes. "Next subject. Is your Mother still coming for a visit next weekend?"

"Yeah," I said, finishing my drink. "She'll be here that Friday night, and then leave Sunday morning."

Watching me quickly finish my drink, she asked, "Do you drink like this in front of her?"

"Are you kidding? She's too much the old-fashioned, southern lady. She wouldn't tolerate it."

Diane swirled the liquid in her glass and frowned slightly at it. Then she set her glass down without drinking from it further. "Am I supposed to tolerate it?" she asked, half in jest and half in earnest.

"Diane, you know I don't normally drink like this. It's just been a very rough day in a very tough week. These burglaries I've been dealing with just keep happening, and Fraser won't ease up on me about solving them. I just can't get a lead on them. But, please, I want to forget them for tonight."

"Okay, let's not talk about your work."

"Well, let's not talk about *your work* either if we're going to eat," I quickly added.

Her laugh lightened the moment, and she moved on to another topic. "I picked up my new stereo system this afternoon. Are you still going to help me put it together?"

"Uh-oh. Yeah. Well, I was hoping you'd wait to get it after these burglaries have been solved."

"Sorry, big boy, but I wanted to get it playing while my CDs are still on the charts and not gone the way of the eight-track tapes you probably have squirreled away somewhere."

I always loved her playful nature even when it was at my expense. "All righty then." I raised my glass. "Live to serve you ma'am. The assembly will be done as promised. When do you want me to do it?"

"If you're going to spend a lot of time with your mother next weekend, I'd like to have it set up before then."

"Well, I'd like you to be with Mom and me at least some of the weekend. It's up to you, Diane."

I realized Diane was studying my face, smiling softly. "That's great. I'd love to meet and spend time with her. That just sounds like a big step for you. Am I to read it that way?"

"I'm not afraid of commitment, if that's what you're getting at. I've told you that I just want both of us to be certain before we make any big decisions. I've made an impetuous leap before, and as Jimmy Buffett said, 'It cost me much more than a ring.'"

"Yes, but, from the talks we've had, the time we've spent together, and the way we feel, I think we're both as sure as any couple can be. Besides, you were too young to get married when you did the first time. She got you when the grapes had just been made into wine. Now, that wine has had time to age to perfection. And, as Frank Sinatra said, 'It was a very good year.'" Her warm smile enchanted me every time.

I feigned a wince as I responded, "Somehow being compared to a bunch of grapes just doesn't give me a warm and fuzzy feeling, you know?"

When the server returned to take our dinner order, I put my palm over my cocktail glass, declining any further adult beverages. I didn't want to push on *that* envelope too much.

Later, as we ate, another thought occurred to me. "Speaking of meeting my mom, Diane, there's something I need to mention. As I said she's always been something of a delicate, southern flower. Mom's led a somewhat sheltered life, protected as she was from everything by my 'old-school' father. As a retired schoolteacher, Mom's classroom is about as far into the world as she's ever ventured. I simply don't think we should get into what you do for a living too much at all."

"Is that for her benefit or yours?"

"No, seriously, it just might upset her to hear about … well, you know."

"Okay. I'm sure she and I can find plenty of other things to talk about." She paused before continuing, "And just so you know, those of us from Pennsylvania do know how to treat a genteel lady."

"Yes, dear," I said sheepishly, sounding as though we were married already.

"Dinner will be ready in about five minutes. Making any headway, sailor?" I was sprawled on Diane's living-room floor with wires running everywhere, trying to set up her new stereo system two nights later. Diane was calling to me from her kitchen.

"It's coming together with what I'm sure you'd deem a surprisingly slow pace."

"I *did* think you'd have it done by now," she said as she came into the room. "Sheesh! Didn't you tell me you worked with electrical wiring in the engine rooms on those freighters?"

"Well, yeah, I did, but I don't recall ever wiring a stereo system in a boiler room." I held up my hands in mock fear as she entered. "Please don't hit me."

"A flogging should be the least of your worries, sailor. Not having completed your assigned chore, I shouldn't even feed you. But wash up, sparky."

Later, after dinner, the stereo was ready for its trial run. I gave Diane the owner's manual and all the accompanying paperwork and cleaned up the mess left from the installation. Then, we put on some music and relaxed with a bottle of wine, with me sitting on the floor leaned up against the sofa, and Diane curled up on the sofa behind me. Diane had an armed draped over my shoulders and was playing with one of my earlobes. When I didn't say anything for a few minutes, she asked me what was on my mind.

"Sorry, Babe. I've just been retracing the steps I've followed in trying to track down the perp or perps in this rash of burglaries. There was another one last night."

She snuggled closer. "Still no leads?"

"No. But I have to believe that there's a common element."

She squeezed my arm. "You'll find it. If anybody can, you can. I know it."

I loved her for saying so, but only wished I shared her confidence. With that, Diane went to the kitchen for another bottle of wine. When she returned, she curled up on the settee across from where I was sitting. She was snuggled up with an afghan throw. After a few minutes, Diane slid a bare calf from under the throw and gave me an enticing smile. Her hair fell loosely around her shoulders. I was beguiled anew.

16

Later in the week, I was out interviewing burglary victims when I decided to track Diane down during the lunch hour and confirm our plans for dinner with Mom on Friday night. I went to the Medical Examiner's Office where the autopsy area was adjacent to the offices. While standing in the passageway waiting for Diane, the chief medical examiner for the county, Dr. Saul Bizar, trudged wearily down the hallway, his big rounded shoulders holding up a pair of bright red suspenders, which in turn sustained a pair of jeans. The suspenders were undergoing a stress test on a thick middle, owing to too many years of Jewish desserts. Like their owner, the jeans had seen better days. His rolled-up shirtsleeves revealed wiry black hair covering his arms from the backs of his hands to his elbows. Smelling vaguely of formaldehyde, Bizar was a soft bear of a man with baby-fat cheeks, thinning hair parted on one side, and small light eyes. He casually carried clipboard on one hand and a partly eaten sandwich in the other. The sandwich was tuna judging from the aroma wafting my way as his intentionally exaggerated hand motions threw the thing closer to my face.

I laughed. "Judas priest, Doc! Are you selling used cars in that getup? Just call BR549?"

"What's the diff, detective?" he grinned. "The customers don't seem to care. Their next *ride* won't be that important to 'em." With the back of his sandwich hand, he smoothed the top sheet on the clipboard. "By the way, are you involved with that triple murder-suicide from the Belmont Apartments? I was just pulling the slugs out of one of the victim's intestine, and … . Oh, wait! That's right! Your forte is burglaries. Sorry." His grin expanded as he gave me a little verbal twist of the knife in return. Suddenly, the doctor's recounting his latest foray into human remains coupled with the bouquet of his lunch caused me to nearly double up in revulsion, as I suspect he saw reflected in my face. Doc Bizar smiled and shuffled off to his next "appointment." Recovering and smiling as I watched him move away, I knew that, no matter what else he was, Doc Bizar was quite a character.

Diane finally appeared. I offered to take her and Mom to a fancier restaurant for the special occasion of "my two girls" meeting. Diane said she didn't care for those places where the servers hovered in red vests and clip-on ties. If Lindy's was good enough for us, she was certain it would be good enough for my mom, too. Live to serve you, Ma'am.

I picked up Mom at Reagan National Airport on Friday afternoon. After a short visit and an opportunity for Mom to rest, we met Diane at Lindy's for dinner. Diane was already seated at our table when we arrived. She apologized for having to meet us there, explaining that some work had kept her longer than she'd expected. I gave her a look of concern about avoiding the subject of her work.

"Woodrow tells me you're a doctor," Mom said, her face beaming and her voice full of liveliness, as if Diane were the first doctor she'd ever met. "You know," she went on, "Woodrow Senior wanted our Woodrow to go to medical school and become a surgeon like Senior had been planning to do before the war changed his life forever." I gripped the edge of the table at the sound of my first name, anticipating what might be coming. The irony of my long-lost, potential "career," combined with my squeamish stomach, was not lost on Diane. Fortunately, before she could respond, our server arrived and made the obligatory greeting, including a recitation of that evening's special menu offerings. She finished her spiel with an inquiry about something from the bar.

Although I was ready for a drink at this juncture, I said, "Thank you, no. We'll just—"

"Wait, please, Woodrow," Mom interrupted. "I don't know about you two, but I could use a bracer myself after that flight."

My face must have shown my shock as I said, "Mom, you can't mean you—"

"I'll have a Long Island iced tea, please." Mom ignored my protest. "Oh, and please have your bartender make it with Coca-Cola and not actual tea. Thank you." Satisfied with her order, Mom folded her hands before her on the table and turned to Diane and me. "Something for the two of you?" Mom was beaming. Diane glanced sideways at me in unmitigated amusement.

Still stunned, I spoke before Diane could place her order, "Mom? Long Island iced tea? That has rum, vodka, gin, uh, triple sec, and—"

"And tequila. Oh, my, yes." Mom enthused. "And I love them all! This way I can have all of them in one glass at the same time!"

While Diane, trying in vain to hide a huge smirk, ordered her chardonnay, I sat back and tried to take in this turn of events. My Mother, my sweet, unadulterated, proper Mother drinking a powerful cocktail disguised as iced tea. I came back to the conversation as Mom was explaining the finer aspects of the drink. " ... and I've actually known some people to make it with tea. But Coke really does it right!"

"Mom, I cannot believe what I'm seeing and hearing! *You* ordering a *drink* like ... like a *sailor?*"

"Now, Woodrow, there's no reason to make it sound so vulgar! And, of course, I mean no denigration of that time you worked on those big boats."

"Ships, Mom. They're called ships."

"What? Oh, yes, dear, of course. Ships."

The steadfast server took my drink order and departed. Diane was still grinning broadly as she injected, "Mrs. Bradley, I think you just caught Woodrow by surprise. That's all."

Aside from relishing the obvious shock I had just received, Diane was enjoying using that name, free of any objection from me. The name was a "gift" from my parents, and I dared not protest out of respect for them. But, years ago, it had kept me in fistfights from elementary through middle school. So, ironically, it had made me tougher than I might have otherwise been. All astonishment aside, I, too, had to smile at the evolution of my mom from the staid schoolteacher I had known all my life to the seemingly cosmopolitan woman before me. Fortunately, I was not too stunned to order my supper with the ladies. I may only do a few things in life well, but eating is one of them.

After a brief conversation between the two women, during which they referred to me as if either I wasn't there or was an infant in a bassinette over which they stood talking, our dinners arrived. We settled in to enjoy a pleasant meal. Suddenly, as luck would have it, a thought seemed to return to Mom. "Now, Diane, what type of medicine do you practice?"

Diane glanced in my direction before answering. "Well, actually, I'm a forensic pathologist in the medical examiner's office here. Are you familiar with the work we do?"

"Oh, my, yes. You perform autopsies! It has to be fascinating work! You must see many intriguing things. Would you tell me about some of the more interesting cases you've handled?"

My knuckles, already gripping at the edge of the table, grew whiter still. "Mom, you don't want to hear about that during a meal!" I objected in the lowest, kindest yet most forceful tone I could gather.

"Yes, Mrs. Bradley, I think that maybe I should wait until after we eat." Diane halfheartedly joined my protest, nodding in my direction as she spoke. She covered one of my hands that had returned to the table, resting. Diane smiled sweetly, knowingly. I read her face and was grateful for her understanding.

Mom glanced at Diane's tender caress, smiled knowingly, and then returned her attention to her. "Nonsense, dear. Being a police officer, I'm sure Woodrow sees and hears about these things all the time, and I'm fascinated! I would love to hear more about it. I assure you that whatever you say will not bother me in the slightest bit. And I have some questions about the forensic aspects of autopsies. One sees stories about these things all the time on television and at the movies," she continued, "but one never knows if it is reality or just literary license employed by an author."

As I sighed deeply, Diane gave me a knowing glance and shrugged. "I'll be very happy to answer any questions you may have."

"Well, on television, they always talk about using the stomach contents of the deceased to establish the time of death. How is that possible?"

In exasperation, I dropped my fork, which unintentionally crashed against my plate with thunderous results.

Mom looked at me with surprise and stern maternal disapproval, "Woodrow! Do be careful!" She turned back to Diane and continued, "Is that really something you can do?"

Diane hesitated, during which time I suddenly felt the urgent desire to leave the table, to possibly join the scrum at the bar for the length of this conversation, but I remained at my place. And, what with Mom's obvious enthusiasm for learning about the process, Diane felt compelled to respond, "Please understand, Mrs. Bradley—"

"Oh, please call me Margaret, dear!" Mom acted as if she had found a kindred spirit.

"All right, Margaret. If we don't have an actual eyewitness to the person's demise, a statement as to the time of death is usually a best-guess estimate based on several factors. And yes, stomach content is one of the factors."

Mom leaned toward Diane to get every morsel, you should pardon the expression, of her lesson. Simultaneously, I leaned as far away as I could and tried to go to a happier place in my mind.

Diane lowered her voice. "If we can learn the time of the person's last meal and what that meal was, it will *help* determine the time of death. The stomach usually empties itself in about four to six hours, depending on the type and amount of food ingested."

Both women continued to enjoy their meals as they talked. I sighed in exasperation as I realized that my stomach contents may well be emptied in a much shorter duration if this conversation continued. Nonetheless, I braced myself.

"If we find that the small intestine is also empty, death probably occurred at least twenty-four hours after the person's last meal. If the colon is empty, no food has been ingested for about forty-eight to seventy-two hours before death."

"How utterly fascinating!" Mom enthused as she cut into her steak, grilled to her specifications: blood rare.

"But, Mrs.—, uh, Margaret, just to make it clear, these times depend on a number of factors, such as how heavy the meal was and whether the meal was rich in fat and protein versus one that is high in sugars and carbohydrates. There are other factors to be considered, too."

"Oh, that answers my question, Diane! Thank you! Isn't that fascinating, Woodrow?" I smiled weakly, gingerly as Mom continued her inquiry, "What about the organs that are removed and weighed, et cetera. What happens to them?"

Diane decided she'd had enough fun with me on this night. "I'll tell you what we'll do, Margaret. Since I'm not on call this weekend, why don't we plan some time together while you're here? And I'll answer all your questions then. Maybe, if you like, we could even go to the morgue for a quick tour."

"Oh, that would be marvelous! You wouldn't mind, would you, Woodrow?"

Did I *mind?* At this point, I was ready to *insist* on it! "No, Mom. In fact, I may have to go to the office for a short time, and that would be the perfect opportunity for the two of you to get to know each other better."

Mom gave Diane a perceptive smile, reading in my response the advanced stage of our relationship.

The meal progressed nicely, but the damage to my appetite had been done. As I left the table, I realized that this probably had been the best chicken marsala I'd *never* eaten.

Sunday night I stopped at Diane's place after depositing Mom on her flight home.

"Well, did your mom catch her flight all right?" Diane asked as I came in.

I laughed, "Yes, and none too soon. If I had to listen to one more anecdote you shared with her about your work, I might have told her the truth about my queasy stomach and gotten it over with. By the way, what's this about the most important piece of advice you'd give to someone entering your line of work?"

"Oh, she shared that with you, too?" Diane was pretending to be dismayed, but I knew better.

"Oh, yeah. I got to hear that your number-one tip for new ME's is the same as for new plumbers: don't lick your fingers on the job. And I heard this over breakfast, no less." My stomach was distressed at merely repeating her words. I pretended to be upset with Diane as she feigned embarrassment, but neither of us could hold the pretense long enough to pull it off. We erupted in simultaneous laughter and a hug. I held Diane at arm's length and relented, "Seriously, thank you so much for spending time with her and dealing with her questions. She thinks the world of you." We embraced and I smelled that delicate scent of her hair I'd grown to relish. "It must run in the family."

Diane snuggled her head against my shoulder. "It was my pleasure. She's a wonderful lady and is so different from what I expected after your descriptions of her. We hit it off very nicely. We're going to get along great. Besides, most of her questions made more sense than the ones I get from attorneys in the court room. *And* she had some very interesting anecdotes to share about you, too."

"I'm very happy you two got along so great! But I'm not so sure I'm crazy about her telling you stories about me."

Diane eased back to a place on the sofa and patted the space beside her. "The damage is done now, big boy. I read in the paper this morning about another burglary in the exclusive Belvedere Estates community. Man, *there's* some money. Were you called on it?"

I sat next to her and sighed. "Oh, hell yes. Detective Harless was on call and went to the scene to handle it. But his report will be on my desk in the morning. No leads. Nothing. Same as the rest."

She put her hand on my shoulder. "I know you've followed every possible lead you could think of. But may I offer an idea that just occurred to me in the last couple of days?"

"At this point, I'll take anything," I said as Diane handed me a postcard size piece of paper. Suddenly, a possible solution to this whole series of burglaries opened to me.

The next morning, I sat at my desk and picked up the telephone receiver. Having spent the previous night going over the burglary reports for details, I had already made a number of phone calls to the victims to ask a few more questions regarding their stolen items. The cases started to make sense. It added up. I dialed a number, listened as it rang, and looked at the piece of paper Diane had given me the night before. I read the words at the top of the document, "Product Registration Card," as a female voice at the other end answered, "Postal Inspection Office. May I help you?"

That started the resolution rolling. With the extraordinary help of Postal Inspector Berry, the burglary ring was broken and the culprits, one by one, arrested. We were even able to get some property back for the victims.

With all the work involved in closing the multitude of burglaries, I didn't get an opportunity to see Diane again for two days. We finally had a chance to meet at Lindy's for dinner. Diane was at a table when I arrived.

I kissed her and eased into my chair. "Sorry I'm late, Babe. I had to stop off somewhere."

"Is your being late the thanks I get for 'saving' your career?" she teased. "Where did you have to go that was so important?"

"Well, you gave me a piece of paper that made a big change in my life. I thought I'd return the compliment," I explained as I handed her an envelope.

Puzzled, her eyebrows knotted slightly as she accepted my offering. As she opened the envelope and removed its contents, her dancing hazel eyes filled with tears and she broke into a beautiful smile. She looked at me in utter astonishment. "Does this mean what I think it means?"

Tears filled my eyes, too, as my love for Diane filled my heart. "Yes, it does. Of course, it's only a sample I picked up at a store. We have to order the real thing."

"I know. I've never been there, but I know how it works," she gushed.

As we stood, kissed, and held each other in the middle of the restaurant, the sample wedding invitation fell from Diane's hand. I took her response as a "Yes."

Several days later, after the dust had settled and I was finally back at my desk finishing the paperwork on the last burglary case to be sent to the District Attorney's Office, Fraser appeared at my desk. As I braced myself for some smart-aleck remark, he gave me an uncharacteristically sheepish look and simply said, "Great work on solving those burglaries! The chief called from the office of the county commission chairman. Both are very happy with the results of your investigation. I told them how hard you'd worked to get them closed. For what it's worth, I think you did a great job, too, considering all the heat you've had on you." He leaned toward me slightly and lowered his voice as he continued, "Sorry if I pushed too hard. This job is still new to me. I'm still learning, okay?" He extended his hand.

As we shook hands, I was so shocked by Jay's comments and his demeanor, I almost didn't know what to say in response. "Thanks, Jay. I worked hard on the cases, but, in the end, it was just a lucky break that closed them out. The words 'Cleared By Arrest' never looked so good."

"Well," he said with a knowing smile, "like I always say, 'I'd rather be lucky.'"

I laughed at a fact we both, as police officers, knew to be true. "You're so right."

He turned and started back toward his office.

As I watched Jay walk away, I recalled the last line in one of our favorite movies. This may not be, as Rick told Louis at the end of *Casablanca*, "the beginning of a beautiful friendship," but it certainly was a very good start.

LOOSE ENDS

M. Steven Prescott moved his eyes slowly around the room as he absorbed every detail of his office. Meticulous. Detail was his specialty, and he expected his office to reflect that image at all times. In fact, everything about him—his law practice, his clothes, his car, his way of life, *even* his office—revealed his affinity for minutia. And his love of the bygone styles. "Old school" is the term he understood people applied nowadays to his thought process. Some offices here in the old building had been reduced from their original ten-foot ceiling heights to more current dimensions with suspended ceiling panels, but not in his space. The old five-bladed ceiling fan still swooped overhead below the plasterwork ceiling. From the fan, a milk glass bowl light was suspended. Adjacent arched windows were bordered on either side by large bookcases with aging law books. The office met Steven's approval: a place for everything and everything in its place.

"I loathe loose ends," Steven had often said. And he truly meant it. His attention to detail, he firmly believed, was what had made him an extremely successful trial lawyer at a relatively early period in his career. That approach to his craft had kept him at the top of his profession all these years. Convinced that he practiced law the way it had been done in former years and the way it should be practiced today, he took pride in the fact that he never overlooked or took for granted any aspect of any case. At cocktail parties, Steven often related how once he had traveled all the way to Hong Kong to take the deposition of a witness he never expected to call at trial. "Professional form" was the way he characterized his approach to practicing law when he spoke to younger attorneys.

His detractors had another, less dignified term for his nit-picking ways. "Persnickety Prescott" they called him, but never to his face. His kinder colleagues at the bar considered him a compulsive neurotic and simply smiled about his pursuit of tying up "loose ends." Even so, he knew the ridicule to which others held him. He'd actually overheard some of the disparaging remarks on occasion. He dismissed these snide comments as the sour grapes of those he frequently and soundly thrashed in court or of those who envied his reputation for success. Steven was certain that, if more of his fellow attorneys were like him in their attitudes, there would be less criticism of the legal profession. Some had said he was merely crazy. Others maintained that he was simply peculiar. After all, the difference between an eccentric and a madman is money. And he had money.

So, as he prepared to leave his office at the end of another very long day, Steven found himself looking at the late-night city lights from the windows of his sixty-third floor office atop the old Belvedere Building. He smiled. Even the location of his law practice in the older building mirrored his concern for detail, he mused. A number of years ago, when he and his partner, Kenneth Mosley, had opened their law practice together, the rent there had been perfect for two young, struggling attorneys. As the years passed and success found the pair, Ken had suggested that they move to office spaces in one of the newer glass-encased edifices like so many of their successful colleagues had done. Steven considered the structures nothing more than man's gaunt symbols of a mundane society. During the day, they glistened in the sun, hiding the moral decay within. At the night, their lights shown like those of a Christmas tree, though lacking the underlying "goodwill toward men" subtlety.

Steven had strongly opposed the idea of a move. He had pointed out the inviting elements in the architecture and workmanship of the older building, which made people feel more comfortable during the normally stressful visits to a lawyer's office. Such was just not the case in the cold, sterile environment of the mausoleum-like buildings then and now being erected. Because of Steven's persuasive powers and the strength of their partnership, Ken had acquiesced. All these years later, Steven and Ken were in the same offices, though not as close in their relationship as they had once been. He smiled again, but not as deeply as before, and this time with a tinge of sadness. Time changes people, even those you think you can count on.

Steven removed the coat of his superbly tailored suit from its hanger on the antique hat rack and slid into it. Cashmere overcoat and ostrich-skin briefcase in hand, Steven walked to his office door, running his hand along the shoulder-high tongue-and-groove wainscoting he loved so much and glancing at the Regulator clock on the wall opposite his desk, a large hand-rubbed mahogany thing. He made one last scan of the room before turning off the light and closing the door behind him, making certain it was locked. Checking the outer office as he went, he made his way across the large, deep-red Oriental rug to the door leading from the office spaces to the public hallway. At this point, he repeated his procedure with the lights and the door. The janitorial employees had been through his floor several hours earlier, and he wanted to ensure that everything was secured properly.

As he walked the corridor to the elevator, his footfalls echoing on the ancient marble, he noticed that no lights shone through the translucent door windows or the tilted transoms above the doors of the other offices. A cynical smirk crossed his face. *There's probably not another soul in this building at this late hour*, he thought. *No one wants to take the additional time, to go that extra mile to be sure they do the job correctly these days.*

At the elevator, he pushed the call button and settled in to the tedious wait that was his one objection to the older building: the elevator took what seemed an interminable amount of time to travel to and from the top floor. Finally, the elevator doors opened with an off-key "ding-dong" that Steven felt only added to the charm of the aging structure. On entering, he pressed the street-level button indicating the lobby, stepped back, and leaned wearily against the rear wall of the car for the long ride down.

After a faltering start, the elevator began to shimmy and shake its way downward, and then started to slow for a stop at the sixty-second floor. Steven was somewhat surprised that anyone else would be working at this late hour. He stood away from the wall he'd been leaning against, anticipating the entry of a fellow late-nighter. The doors slowly opened to the accompaniment of the warbled tone, framing a man standing in the dimly lighted hall, facing the elevator. He was tall and well dressed, wearing a cashmere overcoat, similar to Steven's, and expensive, highly polished shoes. Although he also wore a fedora low over his eyes, the man's chiseled features were not completely hidden from view. Steven did not recognize him.

In a deep, detached voice, the man asked, "Steven Prescott?"

"Yes?" Steven answered, swaying forward slightly.

No response. Puzzled, Steven started to step forward to speak to this unfamiliar person who seemed to know him. Before Steven could say or do anything, the stranger reached inside his overcoat, retrieved a semiautomatic handgun, pointed it at Steven and fired twice. The weapon's discharge created a deafening blast in the confined space of the elevator, drowning the clatter of the brass shell casings striking the elevator walls and floor. The force of the two bullets slamming into his chest threw Steven back against the wall.

The combination of the thunderous blast and the severe pain turned Steven's world surreal. Nothing seemed solid. He controlled nothing. The force of the bullets' impact had wrenched his briefcase and overcoat from his hands, and his arms hung limply at his sides. For an instant, he remained upright against the elevator wall. Then, he began a slow, involuntary slide downward as his shoes began to slip forward on the elevator's tile floor. Everything was happening in slow motion. As he slid down the wall, Steven's eyes and mind focused on the small scarlet stains on his shirt. Something was obviously wrong, but his mind could not fully comprehend exactly what it was. The small room swirled. Tears formed in his eyes, but he was convinced they were not his tears.

Suddenly, the searing pain in his chest, like nothing he had ever known, hit him, brought him back to reality. By this time, Steven had come to rest on the floor in a sitting position with his legs stretched out in front of him. He became aware that his attacker still stood in the doorway. Calmly, the stranger held the doors open as he stepped into the elevator, bending over Steven to check his wounds. Despite all his exertions, Steven could not move. Certain he would be dead in the next instant, he wanted to ask "Why?" When he tried to speak, the word died in his throat. He could only manage a plaintive, questioning gaze into the man's emotionless face.

After a moment, the shooter gathered his shell casings, stood upright, raised his weapon slowly, passing the end of the barrel close to Steven's face, and returned it to his coat. Some measure of relief swept over Steven. Then he watched as his assailant turned to leave the elevator. Again, Steven tried to speak. Again, nothing. The man paused at the door and ran his fingers down the two vertical columns of floor-level buttons like a pianist stroking the length of a keyboard in one movement. Now all the buttons were lighted, showing a stop at each floor below. Glancing quickly over his shoulder, Steven's attacker then pressed the "Close Door" button, released the doors, and, with a hint of a smile, disappeared as they closed behind him.

Alone in the elevator, Steven tried to stand. He could move neither his arms nor his legs. Nothing worked. His struggles only increased the severe pain and burning in his chest. At one point, he felt he was going to pass out from the agony. Only when he half-spoke, half-shouted at himself to maintain his consciousness did he realize his voice had returned. Suddenly, he again became conscious that the scarlet stain was blood and was now saturating his shirt. Perspiration, trickling from his forehead, began to burn his eyes and blur his vision. He could only squeeze his eyes tightly shut and try to shake his head to clear his sight.

The elevator made its inevitable long pause before jolting to a shuddering start on its descent. Now, it slowed for its first stop on the way down to the lobby. Steven's focus turned to trying to summon help.

Floor sixty-one was announced with the same warbled, off-key chimes, as the elevator sighed to a stop. When the doors opened, Steven screamed as loudly as he could, "Help! Anyone, please help me in the elevator! Shot! I've been shot! Please … !"

He was still shouting when the doors closed, and the elevator resumed its jerky descent. Notwithstanding his best efforts to attract attention, the results were the same on the next four floors. His spirits sank momentarily as his previous thoughts of an empty building returned to him. For some unknown reason, Steven noted the signs of age and neglect in the elevator's interior: the tarnished brass on the gilded back and side walls and the well-worn tile covering the floor. The slight impatience he'd always felt at the length of time it required for the doors to slide open and shut was now shifting to anger.

The descent was agonizingly slow. Between floors fifty-six and fifty, Steven continued his plaintive calls for help and, despite his extreme pain, began to question what had happened to him. He was perplexed. Who was the man who had shot him? Why had he shot him? Steven's memory for faces was remarkably good, and he had never seen the man before. Of that, he was certain. Mistaken identity was unquestionably not the answer. The man clearly had said Steven's name before he shot him. But then who and why?

Floor forty-nine. The elevator clanked to a halt and the doors opened, Steven's calls for help rang out, but no response came back. Another attempt to rise from the elevator floor simply brought more intense pain and further spreading of the scarlet stain below his drooping chin.

As the doors closed, Steven's mind ran amok with questions about the attack on him. If the stranger was working for someone else, then who? Steven had no true enemies that he knew of. Certainly there were those whom he had exasperated a great deal over the years. Why, he had infuriated even his loving wife, Katherine, on many occasions. More frequently, it seemed, more recently.

Katherine … his dear wife, Katherine. Trying to push the pain from his mind, Steven forced himself to wander momentarily back over the years to his life with her. He had first met the lovely Katherine during his law-school tenure.

"You're a Three L, aren't you?" Steven looked up from his law book into the eager face of an exquisite girl standing behind the chair opposite. Her voice was light and slightly high-pitched. She had dark hair and intense eyes, but you had to get past her snobbish profile to see the loveliness. Even standing across from him, she exuded an electric energy and sexiness. Steven was a very serious student, but he was not so book-bound that he couldn't sense the obvious. The girl was referring to the fact that Steven was in his final year of law school. While enchanted by the lovely female form before him, he was, nonetheless, annoyed at being bothered. This off-campus coffee shop was his last refuge of solitude in which to study. Some of his housemates were reveling in the idea that end of the law-school ordeal was within their grasp, totally ignoring the looming bar examination. Quiet study time was at a premium, except in this caffeine haven.

Steven hoped a terse answer might bring this conversation to a swift conclusion. "Yes. Yes, I am," he replied, returning to his tome on Constitutional law.

Unaffected by his words, the girl worked her way around the chair without letting go of the back, lowered herself to the seat, and continued, "I've seen you around campus. One of my 'sisters' is dating one of your housemates. I'm a senior in business admin. My name's Katherine, with a 'K.'"

"Business administration is a worthy endeavor, I'm certain, Katherine with a 'K.' But, as you might recognize from this *chance* encounter, I'm a nose-to-the-grindstone law student, and I currently have no time for socializing."

She reached out, covered his hand resting on the table, and smiled sweetly, closely, knowingly. Her voice became sultry as she looked deep into his eyes. "You will, Steven. You will." Steven read her face and realized he was blushing. Katherine with a "K" then slid gracefully from her chair and disappeared out the door. As he pondered the encounter, Steven did not return to his Constitutional law book right away. That look, that way of saying what she'd said stayed with Steven long afterward.

From that first meeting, he, nonetheless, had perceived Katherine and her frivolous girlfriends as spoiled, sorority girls, whose single reason for attending college was to please "Mater and Pater." Some of his more cynical classmates claimed the purpose was to obtain their "MRS. Degrees." Katherine later confessed that she initially had seen Steven as a typical stick-in-the-mud "law nerd." After that "chance" meeting, his initial annoyance with Katherine had evolved into an attraction as she seemed to materialize at his every location with frequent regularity, not in an in-your-face sort of way, but on the fringes. She was right. Steven did find time to spend with her as the frantic merry-go-round of the bar exam preparation and his overcooked angst eased. And, as time passed, the pair came to know one another better. A strong friendship emerged and grew to a deep and, he felt, abiding love. They married a short time after he had established himself as a young "rising star" in the legal profession.

In the intervening years, he felt their marriage had been a happy one, as he provided Katherine with, as they say, a lifestyle to which she was accustomed. In return, she gave him the nurturing and the social support to further his career and his standing in the bar. She never failed to enthrall every man in the room as she entered and always seemed the center of attention at every gathering. For his part, Steven stood back and watched approvingly. He truly loved Katherine and felt she loved him. They were comfortable with each other. Yes, that was a good word for it: comfortable.

Katherine ... , he reflected. But, lately, he *had* noticed a change in Katherine's behavior. He had the notion that maybe she'd lost interest in their marriage, that they weren't as close. Steven recognized that his commitment to the law practice had somewhat damaged their relationship. He also knew that his near obsession with minute details, in both his work and his everyday life, had often frustrated and angered Katherine. That irritation had increased steadily in recent months. Katherine was more fun-loving than he and could not be bothered with the details of everyday life or of a career. But, then, as long as Steven *did* care about specifics and was successful at looking after them, she could afford to be less concerned.

However, his ability to keep Katherine "entertained" had suffered significantly. It would not have surprised him if she had looked elsewhere for diversion. But, surely, Katherine was incapable of having anyone murdered, especially the man who kept her in her present way of life. Steven did have a substantial amount of life insurance, though—enough to provide a motive for murder for anyone other than his dear Katherine. He concluded that, despite their differences, she loved him ... in her way.

Ding-dong. The bone-jarring bump of the elevator's stopping suddenly brought Steven back to his current circumstances with mind-numbing pain. He looked up. The doors were opening to floor forty-three.

"Damn!" he cried aloud. "How the hell could I let that happen? Help! For God's sake, someone help me, please!"

When the doors closed with no reply, Steven was, nevertheless, angry with himself for getting so absorbed in his thoughts about his wife that he'd let almost a half-dozen floors slip right past him. He had always prided himself on not leaving loose ends, no stones unturned, even while thinking under pressure.

The next dozen or so floors passed at a glacial pace. After all these years in the building, not until this moment did Steven notice the obnoxious sound of the elevator cables rattling and the creaking and groaning of the old car as it descended, stopped and started again. The scraping and clacking noises penetrating the solid cage walls seemed to cause the lighted floor numbers to pause briefly. He also painfully realized how each stop and start jostled the elevator and brought new intensity to his suffering. Suddenly, the idiosyncrasies of the building's old elevators didn't hold quite the charm for Steven as they once had. Despite the pain, Steven concentrated on attracting the attention of anyone within earshot who might be working late. At the thirtieth floor, his cries for help brought about a coughing fit, a rolling convulsion that started with a small explosion and finished shaking his entire body. When it ended, he believed he tasted the sickening, metallic taste of blood. Spitting on the elevator's white tiled floor confirmed his fears. He was definitely coughing up blood.

Floor twenty-seven. Voices engaged in a conversation somewhere on the floor gave Steven's weakened cries for help renewed vigor. Amid his pleas for help, he screamed curses at the doors to remain open long enough for the owners of the voices to rescue him. Just before the doors began to close, Steven became very still to see whether his appeals were bringing an answer. His heart was racing madly. In that instant, as the doors shut off the world beyond, he realized what he had heard were the sounds of a talk-show program on some distant, apparently unattended radio.

No answer came to his calls for help at the next several floors. Panic was beginning to creep into his spirit. Tears filled his eyes. Another coughing fit. He was now feeling fatigued for the first time since being shot, and he recognized it as a sign of waning mortality. Steven would not accept this proposition. His contemplations were becoming groggy as if in a drunken stupor. He believed that this was another indication of his weakened condition. All his thoughts were becoming harder to formulate and seemed more disjointed now. Another glance at his blood-soaked shirt raised his apprehension level. A frantic attempt to move merely brought him more intense pain. Steven tried to calm himself, focusing on his thoughts. One concept kept returning to his mind. He could not eliminate from his mind the idea of Katherine having him killed. No, not Katherine. Not dear Katherine.

But, as Ken had recently said with a sly smile, "Love often comes with murderous intent."

Something made Steven stop short. Ken … murder … . Now, Ken might be a different story, he reflected. Even though they had known and worked closely with each other for a number of years, considerable disagreements had arisen lately. If, indeed, familiarity does breed contempt, Ken had long since found Steven's penchant for detail extremely maddening. What had once been a reason for Ken's admiration was now a source of serious conflict. In earlier days, the dissension took the form of a conflict between Ken's concern for the firm's bottom line and Steven's apparent endless conquest of unresolved problems. More recently, the strife resulted from Ken putting his desire to enjoy the fruits of a long, successful law practice ahead of committing every waking moment to that practice. On one occasion, Ken had been so blunt as to remark to Steven about the latter's need to satisfy the desires of the beautiful woman he very often left alone at night.

During their years together, before Ken's marriage, Steven had watched beautiful women pass through Ken's life like so many salmon making their way upstream to spawn. Steven showed a faint smile at that comparison. Now, Steven strongly suspected that Ken, still with boyish good looks, had found a romantic interest outside his marriage. The apparent liaison was causing Ken to become sloppy on his end of the partnership's work. The affair, if there was one, bothered Steven, but he never said anything directly to Ken about it. For his part, Ken seemed aware of Steven's suspicions and appeared to resent him for his perception. Steven had assumed Ken's extreme anxiety was the result of trying to juggle too many things at once.

But, certainly, none of this was enough to compel Ken to resort to hiring someone to kill anyone, much less his law partner, Steven reasoned. He recalled that Ken so abhorred violence he wouldn't handle any of the firm's criminal cases. Meanwhile, Steven had made a very handsome living representing some of the city's more well-to-do criminal types, from drug kingpins to white-collar thieves. A nasty bit of business, but exceptionally lucrative, indeed, although Steven never ceased to be amazed at how utterly ruthless even white-collar types could be to protect themselves from exposure. But they were nothing compared with the drug dealers and organized crime people. And over the years, Steven's experience in and out of court definitely had taught Ken vicariously that conspiracies to commit murder rarely go unsolved or unpunished. Some loose end always seemed to unravel the culprits. No, despite the discord that had come between them, he refused to entertain for long his lingering doubts about Ken. Steven dismissed the idea out of hand.

Steven was again trying to concentrate his reflections on his circumstances when the doors opened at floor twenty-one. More unanswered shouts for help. He kept telling himself that, if only he could continue to exercise his intellect and maintain his consciousness, he could survive this brush with death. Inexplicably, the cage grew quiet. The elevator didn't budge—no clanks, no squeaks. A new fear enveloped Steven: the elevator was stuck. Then suddenly, the car shuddered back to life and crawled downward. Oddly, Steven felt a measure of relief.

Another possibility drifted fleetingly across his mind. What if the person behind this attack is a former criminal client? In his time, Steven had represented some very despicable characters. Maybe one was uncomfortable with Steven's knowledge of his criminal activities or the like. Perhaps trying to kill him was their way of resolving their loose ends. For a second, understanding and respect for that kind of reasoning almost came over him. However, the reality of his predicament kept admiration from gaining a foothold. But wait, he stopped himself, he hadn't done any serious criminal work for nearly a year. Maybe it was more than a year. He couldn't recall.

His thoughts were becoming more and more incoherent. Possibly someone other than a criminal client was unhappy with his legal services and simply didn't feel compelled to lodge a complaint through normal channels with the bar association. More than one domestic case had resulted in violence directed at a lawyer. Maybe the shooting was the retaliation of some unhappy family law client or an opposing party or some attorney who had taken one-too-many courtroom pummelings from Steven. Too far-fetched? He couldn't decide in his current state of mind. Steven could feel his strength ebbing.

Floor fourteen. The cage seemed to be proceeding even slower now than it had before. Steven was finding it nearly impossible to think straight. He was beginning to feel sleepy despite the pain of his wounds, and the elevator was getting colder. Steven's anxiety was rising sharply notwithstanding his stuporous state of mind. Tenth floor. In response to this fear, he made another effort to rise from his sitting position on the elevator's floor. He struggled as much as he could in his weakened condition. Floor seven. The building held no signs of life. Instead of being able to stand, he found himself sliding slowly sideways downward from his sitting position. Steven's head hit the floor hard. When he opened his eyes after the impact, his brain registered, for the first time, the pool of blood in which he'd been sitting. His languid eyes widened slightly in panic. Movement of his body or his extremities was still impossible. Fourth floor. No lights were visible through the opened elevator doors.

From his position lying on his side in the elevator, Steven's cries for help became weaker and more plaintive as each floor came and went. Second floor. His lethargic mind continued to pore over the idea of his being shot. Who could have done this and why? Katherine? But why? Or maybe Ken? Or a client? Another attorney? And for what possible reason?

The elevator slowed as it approached the ground floor. God, how I hate loose ends, Steven Prescott thought.

It was his last.

[Author's Note: For those individuals wanting a resolution to this story, please look for a sequel in my next book. Until then, the answer will have to remain a Loose End.]

GAS PAINS

"This court is now in recess until tomorrow morning at nine o'clock sharp! Did everyone hear me? Attorneys? Defendants? Witnesses? Show some respect for this court and be here on time!" And with that, his honor Joseph G. Bunch, Richland County Superior Court Judge, brusquely left the bench.

As I stood at the prosecutor's table packing my files into a box, defense attorney Lee Gasque sauntered from the defense table. "What the hell was that all about? Does his honor always pontificate that much about inane, irrelevant things during the court sessions? And maybe it's just me, but the judge seems a tad on the self-centered side. Steve, please tell me we're not going to endure that all week."

I smiled. Lee, a couple decades my senior, and I had been friends since my early days as a prosecutor in another part of the state. In fact, my first murder trial had been with him on the defense side. The trial had been a great learning experience, thanks, in part, to Lee. Because he'd "opened the door to the subject," as lawyers like to say, I quietly told him, "You're right, Lee. Since you don't normally practice in this part of the state, let me just say, 'Welcome to Judge Joseph Bunch's world.' Yes," I sighed, "this is typical for one of Bunch's court sessions. In the normal course of criminal business, we get to hear all about his life, his family, his vacations, his most recent election results, his long history on the bench, so on and so on, *ad infinitum* and *ad nauseam*. And I *do* mean *nauseam*. It's become something of a game among the attorneys in the courtroom to try to guess which of his self-absorbed, recurring anecdotes the judge will repeat on any given day. As someone once said about an unknown personage, 'He's a self-made man, and he worships his creator.' " I lowered my voice further. "By the way, the 'G' stands for 'Gaseous,' as you will soon learn, my friend."

"Great! Just great," Lee said with a wince. "I'm only here now as a favor to a family friend with a stupid son. I'll be here forever and with no cash flow to show for it. Meanwhile, paying clients are sitting and cooling their heels in my office. I'm hemorrhaging cash, I tell you!" He paused, sighing deeply. "Well, live and learn, die and burn. The next time I have a case before Bunch, I'll know to hike up the fee accordingly. See you tomorrow, Steve."

"See you then. And, Lee, be here on time. Try to show some respect for this court."

He took my comment with the humor intended. He leaned back in toward me and whispered, "Oh, right. And this from a judge who takes the bench for his nine a.m. calendar thirty-seven minutes late."

"Maybe we'll have a jury by Thursday afternoon."

"That would be funny *if* this wasn't a simple methamphetamine possession case, *if* this wasn't only Monday afternoon, and, given the judge's verbosity, *if* it wasn't a strong possibility. I'll talk to my client tonight and see whether he really wants a trial. Can you give any more on the plea recommendation?"

I stopped putting case files in the box and turned in his direction. "Lee, you know it's his second offense in the last eight months. The statute doesn't give me a lot of wiggle room. I've come down on the plea recommendation as much as I can and still be able to go back to my office with my head held up. You need to remind your client that, for all of his boring ways, this judge is very tough at sentencing after a trial. Call me if anything comes up."

With my file boxes loaded on my handcart, I made my way back across the street to the district attorney's office. As the elevator opened on the seventh floor, a coworker was waiting to leave for the day. "The boss was looking for you. Somebody told him you were still in court. I think he's still in his office."

No doubt he is, I thought. District Attorney Vincent Strom, a no-nonsense, rigid type all the way, prided himself on being in the office before dawn and leaving after sundown. The problem was he couldn't understand why his assistant district attorneys didn't want to do the same. That pesky social life, to which my younger associates clung, was the problem. Darkness had barely fallen outside, so I was certain Vincent was still in his office. I dropped my case files in my office, pulled off my overcoat, and made my way to the boss' corner of the building. From his door, I could see his reflection in the darkened windows. He was sitting on his corner sectional sofa, talking to someone in hushed tones. I made the obligatory knock and stuck my head around the door to receive his permission to enter. Did I say rigid? Maybe frigid is more apt.

"Come in, Steve. Close the door behind you." Not that Vincent was ever "Mr. Personality," but his tenor was even more severe than normal. He was sitting with our chief assistant district attorney, Cliff Gossett, and one of the better detectives among the various law-enforcement agencies in the county, Marion Flanders. Marion, for obvious reasons, was known to one and all as "Bud." When I saw the solemn gathering, my first notion was that some case had been dealt with in a manner less than satisfactory to the local gendarme or had otherwise gone astray. Unfortunately, one seldom heard good news from our boss, so any optimism about the reason for being summoned to his office was a wasted thought process. After a long day of the loquacious Judge Bunch and with my seemingly overwhelming trial calendar pending, I wasn't really up for a critique of some long forgotten case. Maybe Bud was here to discuss some evildoer's most recent enterprise. Walking across the room, I knew I would just have to deal with whatever had brought about this meeting. Before long, I was wishing even the former conjecture was the reason for it.

As I approached the sofa, I reached out to shake hands with Bud and said hello. He seemed almost reluctant to respond with a handshake. I shrugged it off. People often became less gregarious around Vincent as his inflexible demeanor puts them in a more reserved frame of mind. Nonetheless, I was a little uneasy as I joined the three men, who had about them all the gaiety of a gathering of the bereaved.

"Have a seat, Steve," Vincent said. "Detective Flanders has been talking to Cliff and me about a very serious situation that has arisen in the last several days. He needs to speak to you about it. Detective Flanders."

With that ominous introduction, I turned my attention to Bud, who was perched on the edge of the sectional. Early in my tenure in this office, Bud had been transferred from a uniform patrol officer to a detective's position in the Crimes Against Persons Division, investigating violent felonies. He was the size of a sofa with a disarmingly benevolent manner, the combination of which he exploited to his distinct advantage at opportune times in dealing with people. Despite his menacing size, Bud could exude a charm that caused people to trust him, to relax, and to start talking about anything. As a result, he had proved himself a natural investigator and experienced great success. Two years ago he had been assigned to work strictly on murder cases within the same unit. He and I had tried a number of fairly serious cases together over the years, so we had come to know each other pretty well. A murder, a home invasion, or an armed robbery investigation and the ensuing trial, like nothing else I can think of, serve to give you a good idea of a person's work ethic. This is true from the standpoint of both a detective watching a prosecutor try his or her case and of a prosecutor trying a case a detective has put together. Bud and I had shared alcohol-soaked laughter in victory celebrations and, unfortunately, the harsh despair of a jury's acquittal. Through it all, we had formed an easy, friendly relationship born of mutual respect for the other's hard work and tireless efforts to see justice done. I considered us friends, or as close to friends as I ever was with anyone with whom I worked. Now, as somewhat punch-drunk as I was after a long day in court, I tried to reflect the apparent seriousness Vincent gave this occasion.

"Steve, you have a defendant by the name of Leonard McCrory," Bud said, more a statement of fact than a question.

"Yeah, Lennie McCrory. He was a no-show at the trial calendar call this morning. I asked for, and the judge granted a bench warrant for his arrest. Is this about that cocaine freak? He's probably on a bender somewhere before he goes off to prison on these charges. He has a bad record. McCrory'll turn up, and he—"

"He's dead, Steve," Bud said grimly.

"Really? Some folks'll do anything to get out of going to jail," I laughed as I glanced at the other three men. My prosecutor's sense of humor, something we tend to develop to refrain from crying at or getting depressed by the sadness, stupidity, and inhumanity the world constantly threw at us, fell on deaf ears. I laughed alone. That feeling of isolation was reinforced as I looked into the dour faces around me. That uneasiness I had felt earlier on entering the room was looming even larger now.

Before I could ask exactly what was going on, Vincent spoke again. "Steve, you have to go with Detective Flanders. He has some questions."

This had an all too familiar ring to it. A sharp ache flickered behind my eyes, and the skin on the back of my neck prickled. My defense mechanism kicked in with a stunned fury. "Wait a minute!

This is starting to sound like an arrest! Somebody tell me what the hell is going on here!"

"Steve—"

I slid to the front of the sofa and bowed up. " 'Steve,' hell! Protocol be damned. Now I demand to know what this is all about!" I glanced at Cliff, who remained absolutely still. Cliff was always the voice of reason and calm in Vincent's ear. He constantly tried to run interference between the courtroom assistant district attorneys and the boss' knee-jerk reactions and decisions. Simultaneously, Cliff was too afraid that one of those same unthinking conclusions might rain down upon him to buck Vincent openly.

The detective in Bud rose to the occasion and took control. "Steve, McCrory was murdered the other night. Your name has come up in the investigation as a suspect, and we need to clear up some questions."

"Suspect! My name? How? Why?" I stopped for a second to try to take in what was happening. I was so filled with disbelief at the absurdity of the idea that I inappropriately laughed aloud, saying, "Look I believe in punishing the guilty, but a drug charge for possession of coke doesn't carry the death penalty in this state."

Again, my response was received with sepulchral silence. Bud's face darkened suddenly, and the muscles in his jaw stood out like steel beams. In the next instant, I resigned myself to working to clear up what had to be the mother of all weird, coincidental misunderstandings. "This is ridiculous, and you know it." When none of the others expressed agreement with my statement, I turned to the detective and continued, "All right, Bud, where do we go from here?"

"Let's go down to headquarters where we can talk," he said as he rose from the sofa. As an apparent afterthought, he added, "That is unless you want to invoke your rights."

I stood in anger. "Hell no! The sooner we talk, the sooner I can get back to focusing on my job and the real criminal element in this county."

Cliff suddenly came to life and stood also. "That's something we need to face right now, Steve." He looked very uncomfortable, glancing sideways at the boss, who never made a move from his seat. I knew what was coming and didn't like it. I also knew that Vincent had put Cliff in the position of being the "bad guy" and delivering unwelcome news to me. "Until this matter is straightened out, you'll be on administrative leave. But with pay."

"For how long?"

When Cliff moved a shoulder, giving the slightest hint of a shrug, Vincent stepped in again. "Until the detective tells me everything is okay for you to return." The corners of his mouth turned down harshly.

Angrier still, I started to say something my prosecutorial career would probably regret in the morning. Cliff anticipated it and cut me off by adding, "Look, Steve, we're sure this is all a huge mistake. But think about it. How much credibility would you have in a courtroom, meanwhile, with this hanging over your head?"

"Just how many people know about this 'mistake,' for God's sake?" I asked, as the enormity of the accusation set in on me.

"Just the four of us."

"And the rest of the law-enforcement community? And then this office. And then—" I couldn't complete the thought. Already I felt overwhelmed. "You know how things like this get around."

"Let's go talk, Steve."

Holding my hands out, I tried to show my irritation through sarcasm as I said, "Handcuffs? Aren't you going to use the cuffs? You know departmental procedure, Bud."

Using his large frame, Bud placed an open hand against my back and just gave me a gentle nudge toward the door. The movement had enough pressure to indicate that I had no choice but to move as directed. As he did, he sighed, "Please don't make this any more uncomfortable than it already is." Pausing at the door, he turned back toward Vincent. "I'll be in touch."

The response was curt. "Just let me know if you need anything." Vincent's face looked as if he'd sniffed a milk bottle long past its sell-by date.

As we left the building, emotions were racing, chaotically, through my head. Although I believed that Bud knew me better than to think I'd be mixed up in a murder, my own logic came back to haunt me. In many a closing argument in a trial consisting of a parade of character witnesses for the defense, I had asked a jury to consider just how well anyone really knows any other person. I liked to suggest to the jury that what others think of a person is only his reputation. His "character" is who he *really* is when the lights are out, when he thinks no one is watching.

Later, as we settled into an interview room at the police department, Bud spun a chair around, slid it up to the table, and straddled it backwards to face me. He sat down, leaning forward and crossing his arms on the table. I'd never seen this approach to a suspect by him before. "Look," he said sliding the requisite, all-too-familiar Miranda Rights form across the table toward me, "we know each other too well for there to be any bull between us. But, at the same time, you know me well enough to know that I'm playing this straight by the book."

I nodded my understanding as I fidgeted slightly in a chair not designed for comfort.

He started reciting the rights to me as he was required to do. As he did, I saw the harsh irony of me, a senior assistant district attorney, as a murder suspect, sitting in this room with the video camera recording our every movement and word. I couldn't recall the number of times I'd watched footage of an interrogation or played one from this very room for a jury. Certainly, this question could be resolved easily enough. Suddenly, my thought process was interrupted.

"Do you, Steve?"

"Sorry, Bud. What?"

"Do you understand your rights and do you want to speak to me without an attorney present?"

"Yeah. Sure. I'll speak with you," I said, signing the form. "Let's talk."

Bud got down to his business. "For the record, how do you know Leonard aka Lennie McCrory?"

I tried to recall the circumstance of his particular case. "I don't know him in any sense outside the criminal justice process. His case file came across my desk some time back for the preparation of a grand jury indictment on his charges. At some point in the past, he had been a rather successful CPA, but apparently became hooked on cocaine as he enjoyed the 'fruits' of his affluent lifestyle. From reading his criminal history, it seemed McCrory's addiction caused him to sink lower and lower, resulting in a number of arrests and several drug convictions. Now, he's just a punk. Covered in tattoos and piercings from asshole to appetite, if I recall correctly. He's just been living on what he could earn from time to time." Bud glanced at some document he held, probably one of McCrory's book-in sheets, to see whether he had tattoos. "In his most recent arrest," I continued, "the drugs were found on him when the cops responded to a domestic violence complaint. It was not the first time the police had been dispatched to his residence on a domestic dispute call. He called himself Lennie, because he didn't like his *real* first name." I smiled nervously at Bud, my implication clear.

Bud didn't return my smile and made some notes as I spoke. "When and where did you first meet him?" He didn't look up from the notepad.

"I first saw him in court at his arraignment on these charges. I don't remember the date. It'll be on the file jacket."

"Are you sure?"

I was starting to get agitated. "Yes, I'm sure! Do you have something that says otherwise?"

Bud ignored my question and went on with one of his own. "How do you know Margaret McCrory?"

"Who is Margaret McCrory? And your question implies I know her at all!"

"Look, Steve, don't 'lawyer' with me! Just answer my questions!" The annoyance in his voice subsided as he took a deep breath and pressed on, "Margaret is Leonard's, uh, Lennie's wife." With that, he slid the photograph of a slender, very attractive brunette across the table at me. Hers was a face you'd remember after even a brief encounter. "That's Margaret McCrory, Steve. She's the victim in the domestic abuse part of your drug case. Her name has to be in your file's police reports, and yet you say you've never heard of her?"

"Well, the police reports referred to Lennie's wife as Peggy. So I didn't get the connection. My mind is not together right now. I don't recall ever seeing this woman before."

"C'mon, Steve. She tells me she's been in court with Lennie every time he's appeared on these charges, and she says you two made what she calls 'eye contact' the very first time. You had to have seen her in court."

"First of all, crime is a very popular occupation hereabouts. The courtroom is always packed with people, as I'm sure you've noticed when you've been subpoenaed for a motions calendar or for trial. I've never seen this woman before, and, seeing her photo now, I believe I'd remember it if I had."

"Exactly! We both know what a hound you've been since your divorce!"

"I've never seen her before, Bud!"

"Well, she says you have. And not just in court."

I didn't like the insinuation that statement carried. "What? Wait just a damned minute! Sure, I rarely miss a delicate female form that crosses my radar! And while I admit to being attracted to the opposite sex, I've never acted on it to the detriment of my job! And I've never crossed paths with this woman or McCrory outside of a courtroom."

"No, Steve, you wait just a damned minute! I've got a lot of questions about the circumstances of this case that don't add up! And they put you right in the middle of this mess!" Thankfully, Bud caught himself and paused to let the heat of the moment recede. He knew I had something of a temper. He stood and walked around to the side of the table, hiking a hip up onto the edge and leaning his two-hundred-plus athletic-looking pounds forward on his hands, closer to me. From this vantage point, I could really see for the first time the effectiveness of his presence on a suspect. "Now let's take this one step at a time. Do you want to talk to someone, an attorney maybe?"

"No! I *am* an attorney!" As soon as I said it, I wondered whether I was doing the right thing. As the old saying goes, "A lawyer who represents himself has a fool for a client." I settled back down.

"Have you ever been to the McCrory's home?"

"No. I have no idea where they live."

Bud grunted. "As a matter of fact, they don't live that far from you."

My frustration level rose. "It's a heavily populated county, Bud. Many people live near my place. That doesn't mean I know them, know where they live, or have ever visited their homes!"

Bud glanced askew at me with a look with which a teacher might reprove a naughty child and continued, "Where were you at about nine-thirty last Saturday night?" Bud liked to shift directions when interrogations became heated. It kept the perps off balance. I'd seen him do it dozens of times on video recordings.

I was getting increasingly annoyed with all these pointed questions, so I counted to ten and took a deep breath to try to calm down. The storm passed. "This past Saturday night? Well, you know how it is sometimes just before trials start. Everything we've planned to go to trial on gets continued unexpectedly or falls apart or pleads guilty or whatever, so we go into the 'scramble mode' the weekend before. When that happens, my investigator and I are usually out and about trying to chase down and interview victims or witnesses one last time. Or we're trying to serve subpoenas on them. That's what I was doing Saturday night."

"So, you and your investigator, Rick—it is Rick, right?" I nodded. "So you and Rick were out together Saturday night trying to find people?"

"Yes, we were out, but we weren't together. There were too many MIAs, so we split the work between us."

"Okay. Where did *you* go during that time? Who did you speak with?"

"Well, about eight-thirty I was over on Belvedere Highway at a Mexican restaurant looking for the victim in an armed robbery case. His trial subpoena was returned by the post office, but a trace of him kept coming back to the same address. According to an anonymous phone call I'd received late Friday, he was supposed to be working at one of the places over there as a waiter or something."

"Which Mexican restaurant, Steve? Belvedere Highway is like little Tijuana."

"Well, I went to several of them over there but was batting zero. So I switched gears, went to his last known address in the apartment complex, Dunedin Court, and waited to see if he showed there."

"How long were you there?"

"Until about eleven-thirty or so. Maybe midnight."

"Did you speak to anyone while you were there? Did anyone see you there?"

"No. I just sat in my car and waited. Any other time, at least according to the cases I see, one of your patrol units would have come through that 'high crime area' and rousted anyone sitting in a car in the parking lot. But that didn't happen to me. So no, I didn't speak to anyone"

"Funny you should say that, Steve. Rick told me you said that you'd gone there and staked out that victim's apartment. So I checked with uniform division. They did, in fact, drive through the complex a couple of times that night. Nobody saw you sitting in a car. And you're right. Because of the amount of criminal activity there, they would have noticed and would have stopped to talk with anyone sitting in a car."

Bud just looked at me, waiting. I was stunned at all the work he'd put into checking on me and my whereabouts on Saturday night.

"Well, I did get out of the car several times and knock on the guy's door to see if anyone was home or if I'd missed him coming in. Maybe the uniforms just missed seeing me."

"Why didn't you tell me about getting out of the car before? Did anyone see you when you went to the door?"

"No. No one saw me that I know of. At least I didn't see anybody. And no one answered the door when I knocked. As far as not mentioning it, I didn't think it was important."

As Bud started to speak, I realized what he was getting ready to say something I'd heard him tell a dozen suspects before. "Everything is important," we said in unison.

Any other time, we would have laughed. No laughter this time. Perhaps the Good Book was right: that there is a time under the Heaven for weeping. Maybe *this* was that moment for me. I sat and waited as he looked over his notes.

Finally, Bud looked up at me, concern in his eyes. "So, Steve, let me get this right. You've never met Margaret McCrory, in or out of court. You've never been to the McCrory home. And you were out Saturday night by yourself with no one to vouch for your whereabouts at about nine-thirty."

"Right, so far. What happened at nine-thirty?" At this point I was speaking with caution, not from fear. But, when spoken aloud, the words sounded like the same thing.

"That's when Lennie McCrory was burned to death on his couch. That's when Margaret, who claims you were her lover, says you poured gasoline over him as he slept in a drug-induced stupor and lit a match." As he spoke, Bud watched for my reaction, which was a nanosecond in coming.

"What? That's bullshit, Bud, and you know it! I'm nobody's 'lover'! Certainly not hers! I've never been near their place! And why would I want to kill this guy?"

He gauged my reaction before responding. "To begin with, how can you say you've never even been near their place when you say you don't know where they live?"

"I haven't *knowingly* been near their home!"

"And you claim that you haven't been in their home?"

"Sure as hell not!"

"And, if you aren't Margaret McCrory's lover, why on earth would she say that? What does she have to gain?"

"Damned if I know! But it's not true! Have you talked to anyone who has ever seen us together? You know me—"

Bud held up his hand to stop what he evidently thought would be a play on our friendship.

"No, you wait, Bud! You *do* know me well enough to know that I would *never, ever* risk my reputation, my career as a prosecutor for the sake of a little 'slap and tickle' time with some honey! That's just not going to happen! Why in hell would you take the word of some ex-con's wife that I had? Now I do feel like talking to a lawyer!" I started to get up from the table.

"Fine, Steve. That's your decision to make. But as a friend, before you go, let me just give you one more piece of evidence you'll have to deal with. The arson investigators I've been working with say that gasoline was used as an accelerant."

"Yeah, so?"

"The fire department arrived at the McCrory house in time to contain the fire to the living room, but, unfortunately, not soon enough to save Lennie. In the course of our investigation, we recovered a gasoline can from the garage of the home. According to Margaret's statement and the preliminary lab test results, it's the can the accelerant was poured from before the fire was started."

"Yeah, so?"

"Your fingerprints are on that gas can."

In that instant, my entire world crashed around me. There was no way in hell that my fingerprints could be, should be on the gas can used to commit this crime. But, according to Bud, there they were. I'd handled too many cases involving forensic evidence to doubt what Bud was saying. To say that I sat in stunned silence would be a gross understatement. I couldn't delude myself. This was very bad.

Finally, Bud spoke. "Do you have anything you want to tell me, Steve?"

"Wait," I fought back. "She told you she *saw* me pour the gasoline over her husband and light him on fire?"

"Margaret says that Lennie was using drugs Saturday night, and they got into an argument about his drug use. She's never been involved with that crap, and she hated it. He beat her. After he passed out on the sofa, she called you, her lover, for help. She did so even though she knows you get angrier at Lennie each time the abuse happens. When you arrived at their place, you became almost uncontrollably furious at the sight of her injuries. Margaret was beaten pretty severely, Steve. She stopped you from attacking Lennie at that moment and, to distract your rage, begged you to take her away to safety. When she figured she'd calmed you down enough, Margaret went to the bedroom to pack a bag. As she was packing, she suddenly smelled gasoline. By the time she ran back into the living room, you'd already emptied most of the contents of the can, which you'd retrieved from the garage, over Lennie and had struck a match. You threw the match before she could stop you, and then it was too late. She screamed. You tried to get her to leave with you, but she refused. By this time, she was more terrified of you than of her husband. She was calling 9-1-1 as you were leaving. At first, we believed she killed Lennie as retribution for the beating. Only later did she tell us what'd happened and about your involvement. Your prints on the can confirmed her story for us."

I felt like an animal trapped without hope. "I know it looks bad, but not one word of it is true, Bud." I was totally perplexed and dejected, completely at a loss for words. My face must have revealed my anguish.

"What do you want to do, Steve?"

"I need time to think, to figure out how the hell this could be happening to me." My confidence had drained away like low tide in the Bay of Fundy. I needed to start at square one and work my way through it. Then an idea returned to me. "Bud, I asked you if anyone had ever seen Margaret McCrory and me together."

"Well, the problem is that she says it was a torrid, but clandestine relationship. By their nature, such things are secret. So, no, to my knowledge, no one has seen the two of you together. Besides, it could be argued that, owing to the circumstances, it would be in your best interest to do everything in your power to keep anyone from knowing anything about the two of you being together. Your reputation, your job. All that was at risk if you two were ever found out."

"I can't prove a negative, Bud. And now my very freedom is on the line. That, by the way, is not an admission that anything she's told you is true." Again, the enormity of my predicament struck me, and a horrible thought occurred to me. "Oh, God, Bud. Am I under arrest for murder?"

Bud's initial response was terse and all business. "Yes, you are." After a moment he added, "But it's possible that you'll get a bond under the circumstances, even on a murder charge. It's happened before. Remember the Carrie Coppage trial? She was given a bond on a murder charge."

Bud was right. To my utter shock, I was able to get a bond, even though the charge was murder. I'd worked closely with several of the bonding companies over the years, approving extraditions when they found their bail jumpers, letting them know about missed court dates, and so on. So finding someone to post my bond wasn't as difficult as I'd thought it might be. The bond conditions required, among other things, an electronic ankle monitoring device to be in place while I was out. That didn't matter to me. Just because I was on leave from my job didn't mean I was going anywhere.

By the time I arrived home after making bail, it was still very early in the morning, but I was too wide awake to sleep. Instead, I sat and tried to sort through what had happened to me in the last eight hours. Nothing made any sense. Of course, the idea of Margaret McCrory and me being lovers was absurd. And I swear I'd never seen or recalled seeing the woman in or out of court. As I saw it, as far as any witnesses went, the case boiled down to her word against mine. I could deal with that. But the inescapable fact was that my fingerprints were on the "murder weapon." That could *not* be possible. How the hell could I explain that? More important, how the hell did they get there? In my experience, nothing was more rewarding to either a cop or a prosecutor than to have a suspect deny emphatically ever having been in a certain location only to have their fingerprints or DNA show up there. However, in this case, the prints were on a *movable* object. This was a slightly different circumstance than prints on a windowsill, in a car, or on a kitchen counter, for example. But still, my prints were somewhere I couldn't account for. I had lived in an apartment since my divorce some ten years earlier. During that time, I had not even *owned* a gas can. So it wasn't a matter of my gas can showing up somewhere else. I just could not see any way this had happened. I could wait to prove my innocence at trial, but I knew from my years as a prosecutor that a criminal trial can be a very blunt instrument for ferreting out the truth.

Several days passed as I waited to see what would happen next. I didn't contact a defense attorney right away, because I kept thinking either I'd wake up from this bad dream or Bud would call to tell me that it'd all been a terrible mistake, and it was over. Mine was a lonely existence during that time, locked away in my apartment. Not meaning to sound too maudlin about it, but I was drowning in my solitude. Ironically, the one phone call I did received was from Lee Gasque. He'd heard about my plight and wanted to know whether there was anything he could do. He was truly concerned. The call was more from a friend than a colleague. I assured Lee that it was all some gross misunderstanding and that I would call him if I needed anything. Although his contacting me helped lift my spirits somewhat, it was short-lived. No other calls, no visitors, nothing. Although I certainly couldn't blame anyone for staying away under these circumstances, it still hurt.

Over the next several days, the weather turned even colder than it had been all winter. The accompanying dark-gray sky only added to my gloom. Much of my time was spent thinking about what was to become of me. I was perplexed. Even if I were found innocent the charges, there seemed no way I could continue my career as a prosecutor. No matter how optimistically Cliff had put it that night in the boss' office, I didn't see how I would be welcomed back. Vincent was not one to bestow sympathy on anyone, least of all those accused of crimes. A career prosecutor himself, he firmly, yet myopically believed such a person was guilty until proved innocent. Officious little prick. My mind raced with the uncertainty of the situation. I'd never been a quitter, and I wasn't giving up now, but I saw no way around my dilemma at this point.

So, after I cleaned out my refrigerator, which took all of about fifteen minutes, I started passing my time watching an old movie channel. The showings were only a temporary diversion at best. My plight was never far from my immediate thoughts. Even so, the movies were something to do. However, when one particular offering I'd seen before, *The Wrong Man*, came on, I suddenly felt the burning need to leave, to get out. The movie, starring Henry Fonda, is the story of a man wrongly accused and convicted of a crime he didn't commit. To many people, it's probably the most harrowing of Alfred Hitchcock's movies simply because it's based on a true story. Anyway, that was my sign that I needed to escape from the apartment for any reason at all, anything.

I called the people monitoring my ankle device and received permission to go to the supermarket. Although it was the same place I always shopped and I knew several people there and they knew me, it just wasn't the same experience now. By this time, the story of my arrest for the murder had hit the local papers, and there was a decided difference in people's manner when they saw me. Even the cute little pharmacist there, with whom I always flirted, gave me a stern, disapproving look. I was glad to grab my groceries and get out of the place.

I stopped to fill my car with gas on the way back home. Since I wasn't going anywhere much, I'm not sure why I decided to fill the tank. The idea of going back to the apartment just didn't appeal to me very much, so, subconsciously, this was probably my way of delaying the inevitable. The day was metallic cold. As I stood there pumping gas, my breath making gray clouds in protest to the freezing temperature, and watching the comings and goings of people bundled against the cold, it hit me. In my excitement, I stopped pumping gas before my tank was even half full and almost forgot to replace my gas cap. I had to get home as quickly as possible!

As soon as I went through my front door, I threw the bags of groceries on the kitchen counter and reached for the phone. I was too upset, too excited to think straight at that moment. So I thanked God that I'd programmed Bud's office number into my phone's speed dial several years earlier. As luck would have it, Bud wasn't at his desk. I didn't want to leave a message on his voice mail, so I hung up and called his cell-phone number. He answered on the third ring.

"Detective Flanders."

"Bud. It's Steve Wood. I need to talk to you right away!"

"Are you sure?"

"I think I have some answers, but I need your help checking on them."

"I don't think I should be doing the work of your defense attorney."

"I don't have one. And, if I'm right about something, I won't need one. But I really need your help confirming a simple fact. This is something I cannot do myself. Can you come by my place to talk?"

The air stirred at the other end of the phone line. "If you insist on talking, you'd better come to our office."

Yeah, right. Get it all on video. "Okay. Let me call the monitoring people and get permission. When's a good time for you? I don't have anything else to do and the sooner the better for me."

"I'm out working on something right now. How about three o'clock this afternoon?"

"I'll see you then."

Four hours from now, I thought as I hung up the phone: an eternity. I relaxed, though only a little. As I was standing at my kitchen sink, drinking water from an old glass decorated with a cartoon character and trying to be optimistic, I realized that there was something critical I had to do before our meeting. When it struck me, I nearly choked on the water! What was I thinking? I spent the next hour rummaging through old credit-card receipts. When I located what I hoped would be my salvation from this misery, I calmed down a little more. Some of my appetite returned. After some scrambled eggs and toast, I sat and watched the clock for the next two hours. In my anticipation, I almost forgot to call the monitoring people and get permission to go to police headquarters. The guy I spoke with seemed a little uncertain about why I would want to go there under my circumstances, but he gave me leave to do so.

At two forty-five, I was sitting in the police department lobby. I'd been there many times before as a prosecutor and had never given it a second thought, feeling a part of it all. Conversely, it felt unfriendly and forbidding to me now, even with the newfound optimism to which I clung. Several officers I'd worked with in the past walked through the lobby as I sat there. I was invisible now. This feeling I was experiencing hurt very deeply. I'd always taken a great deal of pride in my chosen career, believing that I was on the side of right in the criminal justice system. Many people think that the term "justice" simply means justice only for the accused, but, to a prosecutor, it also means justice for the victims and their families. Almost everyone recalls that "Lady Justice" is depicted as blindfolded and holding the balance scales. Most people seem to forget that she also holds a sword, not only to mete out punishment to the guilty but to protect the innocent, especially victims. As I sat there, I wondered whether her sword would protect me or fall on me.

At three o'clock exactly, Bud stuck his head out of the door leading to the detectives' area and beckoned me with a jerk of his head. Again, as we walked through the Crimes Against Persons Division, the hurt I'd felt at the coolness I'd encountered in the lobby swept over me as I received sideways glances from the detectives there. Although I'd worked with each of them at one time or another, no one acknowledged my presence. Not even nods of recognition. Once inside an interview room with Bud, we sat at the table.

"Is the tape rolling?"

"Listen, Steve, I don't have time for grief. I'm doing my job and meeting with you only because you asked for a get-together. Your rights still apply. What do you want?"

I recognized his exasperation with the circumstances. My smart-assed comment hadn't helped any. "I'm sorry, Bud. I want to give you copies of these gas receipts."

"What the hell! Are you confessing now?"

With the certainty of innocence, I continued, "Bud, please listen. To begin with, I have nothing to confess to. Second, if you look at the receipts, you'll see that the amount of gas purchased each time was in excess of twelve gallons. Although you didn't say what size gas can was used in the murder, I'm willing to bet it was not a twelve-gallon can. Owing to that being more than sixty pounds of gasoline, if I remember my weights correctly, it would be a more than a little awkward to carry around."

He pushed back from the table and folded his arms across his chest. "So you pumped part of the gas into a car and part into the gas can. If *you* pumped it at all! That's not the answer. Next story." Bud's face was solemn, disbelieving.

Having a temper of my own, I was starting to get agitated again. I silently counted to ten and pressed on. "Look, even if someone put part of the gas in a car and put in the can, it wasn't me. Bud, about a month ago, I was stopped for gas where I always do, being the creature of habit that I am. The day was as cold as a well digger's toes in Minnesota, and I was bundled up like crazy and in a hurry. It's one of those stations that has pumps on opposite sides of each other at the same island. As I stood there at the pumps hopping from one foot to the other trying to stay warm, a car pulled up to the pumps on the opposite side. I didn't pay much attention. Anyway, a woman got out of the car and came around her car to the pumps. After a short time, she stuck her head around to my side of the island and asked if I could get the top off her gas can. I took the can, messed around with it, and, after some effort, was able to get the cap off. I handed it back to her and finished filling my car.

"When I'd finished pumping the gas, I paid, as always, with my credit card, jumped in my car, and drove away. I never thought anymore about it until this morning when I was filling up with gas again. Then I remembered what had happened. I didn't get a good look at the woman at the time, but she was definitely a brunette. Some of her hair was sticking out from beneath a toboggan hat. And she didn't have any make-up on. I remember thinking that it was too bad about the make-up, because, fixed up, she was probably fairly hot. I think that's why I didn't recognize her from the photo you showed me in here that night. I believe the woman was Margaret McCrory. She was about five feet seven inches tall, although, at the time it was hard to tell. She was kind of slumped over with the gas can. Relatively slender build, too. I could tell that even with all the clothing she was wearing."

Bud was eyeing me with what I would best describe as a cynical look. After a couple of seconds, he asked, "Okay, if you were all bundled up against the cold, I assume you had on gloves. I've seen you wear them before. How'd your prints get on the can?"

"Yeah, I was bundled up, but I don't wear my gloves when I pump gas. I always take them off in the car beforehand. My gloves are leather and, if they get gasoline on them, the odor will never come out. I wasn't wearing gloves at the time."

"This is all so far-fetched. What are the odds? How do you prove something like that?"

"That's why I brought the credit-card receipts." I tapped the receipts lying on the table between us as I spoke. "They have the date, time, and station number on them. If she used a credit card to buy gas at the same time, that shows what I'm saying is true. She was there. And with a gas can. I brought these three receipts, because I cannot remember which date it happened."

"And if she paid by cash?"

"Well, maybe the clerk will remember her. Or maybe she'll be on a security video from the station even if she paid at the pump."

Bud responded with considerable asperity. "Yeah, maybe. Steve, you know full well that, half the time, we can't find witnesses who can remember what a perp looks like an hour after a crime. And almost a month later you expect the clerk at a busy gas station to remember some bundled-up woman. And that's *if* she paid inside!"

"I'm willing to take the chance if it proves my innocence."

"But I have to do the work."

"Yeah, to see that justice is done, Bud. Deuteronomy 16:20. Remember, Bud?" That verse had become my mantra during my time as a prosecutor, and I liked best the version from the Torah.

"Okay, Steve," he sighed. "I'll see what I can find out. But don't get your hopes up, even if you're innocent. This is a long shot, and you know it. If, and I mean *if*, anything turns up, I'll call you. By the way, Steve, almost all the gas stations are designed with the pumps on both sides of the same island now. Try a different one sometime and you'll see."

I wanted to smile at his parting shot, but it seemed too early to be happy about anything just yet. I simply said, "Thanks, Bud."

Try as I might, it was difficult to be optimistic about Bud getting anywhere with my information. I knew he was right about it being a long shot, a very long shot. But it was all I had to hope for. So I sat and waited.

Four days later, my telephone rang. "Steve." Bud's voice revealed nothing. My heart was pounding so hard I swear I could hear it.

"Yes?"

"Well, you need to go buy some lottery tickets, ol' buddy." His voice was subdued, regardless of his message.

"Are you serious, Bud?" His implication was clear enough to me and, and I was relieved to the point of tears!

"Yeah. Just like you said, I ran Margaret's credit-card purchases. She was stupid enough to use a credit card in her effort to frame you for her husband's murder. She was at the gas station on the nineteenth of the month at the same time you were. Better than that, she was on the security video, like you'd hoped, handing you the gas can. Fortunately for you, that station *had* security video and the station's manager had not recycled the recordings yet. We had to get the video enhanced to get a decent picture of her and of her car's license plate, but it's her all right. When I brought her in to question her and confronted her with the evidence, she caved. She's not a very good criminal, because her conscience had been killing her. You're a very lucky man, Steve. If we hadn't come up with this lead and the evidence, you'd still be looking pretty good for this murder."

"Bud, I still don't understand how or why she did it."

"Well, the 'why' is simple. You were going to put her husband's worthless, drug-using, wife-abusing ass in prison where he belonged. As a result, she'd have no money coming in. And then she'd have to drag her very pretty butt out into the workplace, struggling and scraping to earn a living for the lifestyle, as they say, to which she had become accustomed. The alternative was to kill him, blaming someone else, and collect the sizeable insurance policy he's had since he was a more productive citizen before the cocaine took hold. As far as who to blame and how, it was either you or his drug dealer. The drug dealer was way too cautious to be set up. And you, my friend, were way too easy, being the self-described 'creature of habit' that you are. Simply put, she was very desperate to do something to salvage her situation. Having seen you in court without you realizing it, she merely watched your routine for a couple of weeks and followed you, trying to 'get something' on you, to use her phrase. The rest was easy. She just set it up and acted when the opportunity presented itself. Luck was with her when you didn't have an alibi. In her mind, it was poetic justice that two of the three men who had made her life a living hell would be 'punished' by one act."

"My, God, but she gave this a lot of thought, a lot of planning. She must have really hated me, Bud."

"Apparently so. But she also had a lot of luck on her side, too."

I sat in silence for a moment, thinking of how the events of the last two weeks had altered my life forever.

"Steve, are you there?"

"Yeah, I'm here, Bud. But where am I now ... really?"

Bud's voice seemed quietly sad when he answered, "Yeah, Steve. I know." He paused for a couple of seconds. "Listen, I've have to go."

"Okay. Thanks for the call, Bud. And, as always, thanks for your hard work."

We hung up. As I replaced the receiver, I was simultaneously thankful and depressed. I didn't know where I'd go, what I'd do from here. I was just very grateful that Margaret had a conscience and folded when Bud confronted her. Then something occurred to me that brought a smile. For all his verbosity, Judge Bunch was right about one thing. During sentencing, he often told defendants that, if they wanted to have a successful career as a criminal, they couldn't have a conscience. At least, he was right about that.

MOUNTAIN OF REGRET

It seemed a lifetime since I had been in the North Georgia mountains, and I'd never really thought about going back either. But, when the phone call came to my home in rural Maryland telling me that my daddy was dying and was asking to see me, there was no hesitation before I was on my way. Although we had not spoken and had barely communicated in decades, he was still my daddy and I was his only child, his only living relative. My husband, David, a software engineer for the Federal government, encouraged me to go despite my concerns about opening old wounds. He was right, of course. I had to go. David sympathized with my situation and offered to come along. However, because he'd never even met my daddy, knew no one in my hometown, and wouldn't have anything to do there, we agreed that he'd stay home and take care of our two granddaughters, who were living with us while our son and his wife were on a temporary assignment overseas. I'd go alone and do my familial duty.

The flight to Atlanta was filled with uncertainty about what lie ahead. As harsh as it may sound, and notwithstanding my "duty" as a daughter, the question kept arising: was this, in fact, the right thing to do? Why, after all this time, did he want to see me again? I really didn't know Daddy, and he didn't know me. I'd grown up and away from him, the area, and the life I'd known as a child and young adult. "Relative strangers" was the way I'd often described our relationship to David. It wasn't that my daddy had been a *bad* Father. We were just never very close. My mother died giving birth to me. As the years passed, I grew to feel that Daddy blamed me for losing "the love of his life." He always seemed angry. His anger never took the form of any type of physical or overt mental abuse. Daddy just always seemed on the verge of an explosion. And growing up years ago in the rustic mountains had not helped me cope with the circumstances. Although a natural tranquility was to be found there among the tall evergreens and hardwood trees, there was also a code of behavior to which one adhered when I was young. Parents were to be obeyed. They were not the "buddies" that today's parents try to be to their children. The hardscrabble life for poor mountain people did not allow such niceties.

After collecting my bags from the carousel and renting a car, I drove north, away from the Atlanta airport. I had only been in Atlanta once, years ago, and that was merely to take a bus away from all I'd grown to dread and dislike about my life. As I drove through the city on the interstate highway, nothing looked familiar. I wondered whether my daddy had changed as much as what I could remember of Atlanta. I knew *I* had. Yet, there was something comforting in going to see those mountains again. Maybe that's why, when David and I were deciding where to live within commuting distance to his job in Washington, D. C., I had more or less insisted on living in the mountains of western Maryland.

The trip north from Atlanta led from one interstate highway to another as I climbed toward the mountains of my youth. Much had changed. Only the natural landscape felt familiar, somehow comforting. It wasn't until the limited-access highway became a divided, four-lane, scenic parkway that I realized I was traversing what had once been the two-lane road I'd used years ago to leave. As the elevation climbed, the azaleas and dogwoods, planted by landscapers, gave way to the natural beauty of bluets, mountain laurel, and yellow poplars. The season had passed for blossoms of the bright-yellow tulip-like flowers for which the towering poplars were also named, but they joined the dense thickets of Catawba rhododendrons to give the mountainsides a lush green blanket. Frequently, rock formations protruded along the roadside, sustaining a resolute form of plant life jutting from sheer stone, adding to the rugged splendor. The determination of those plants to survive among the boulders mirrored the persistence of the mountain folk there.

Despite the natural loveliness of the region, my apprehension about the near future returned as I drove through or near small towns whose names were all too familiar, but whose appearances were now foreign to me. I couldn't get Daddy off my mind. For all else that lay in the past, he was my *daddy* and my *only* living blood relative from my early life, too. Seeing him would be difficult, but somehow losing him was going to be far more heartbreaking. I didn't know what I would say to him or how to say it. How do you fill the void and distance created by years of silence and separation? Now was not the time for shouts of retribution or recrimination, at least not from me. I just prayed I wouldn't be too late.

As I entered the town in which I'd grown up, very little seemed familiar. Where once had been woods and cow pastures, a large shopping complex had sprung up, including a large discount department store and a major home improvement warehouse, separated by a cluster of smaller retail shops. Nearby, a line of ubiquitous fast-food restaurants stood sentry next to the four-lane artery. A small hotel had been built on a nearby hilltop, no doubt to house the multitude of leaf peepers and apple festival attendees who flocked to these once-bucolic hills every fall. Apple orchards were still in abundance. I noticed that even the chicken processing plant had been expanded significantly since my departure.

I stopped for gas and a bottle of water at a station that doubled as a convenience store. After paying for my purchases, I asked the clerk, who was, as they say in these parts, "not from around here," for directions to the nursing home where my daddy now resided. He was "bery unable" to help me. It occurred to me that the problem was either his difficulty with the language or the fact that he, like so much else I'd seen, was new to the area. Outside I saw an older man in bib overalls and short sleeves, chaw-in-cheek, filling his truck with gas. I asked for his help in finding my way. After squinting at me briefly with a glint of recognition, he gave me the information I needed. Frankly, he looked vaguely familiar to me, too, but I said nothing. I drove away with the man watching me, still seeking that morsel of identification buried somewhere in his memory.

As I followed the directions I'd been given, I came to the old, familiar roundabout in the center of town. A flood of warm memories washed over me like so many ocean waves I'd bounced in at Maryland's Eastern Shore. Recollections of Fourth of July parades and Christmas pageants I'd watched from the sidewalks, of Memorial Day services in which I'd stood with the other schoolchildren at the veterans monument in the center of the traffic circle, and of so many other reminiscences brought tears to my eyes even after all these years. The buildings on the circle, which had once held a family-owned hardware store, a barber shop, a mom-and-pop café, and various other sundry stores, now housed real-estate offices and antiques shops to cater to the horde of tourists and newcomers to the region. On a road running out the other side of town stood a low, sprawling, white building with a sign out front identifying it as the Belvedere Assisted Living Home I sought. It appeared to be of much more recent vintage than the nearby buildings. Somehow that was a comfort.

On entering the building, I approached the front desk. A short, matronly woman, with a florid complexion and wearing a colorful, flowery smock, asked if she could help me. The brightness of her attire failed to bring me the cheerfulness it was no doubt intended to convey.

I swallowed hard, fearful of arriving too late. "Is … is Mr. Howard Gilbert still here? I'd like to see him if he is. Would you tell me what room he's in?"

"Are you a friend or a member of the family?"

The tone of her question gave me a measure of relief: Daddy was still alive. "I'm his daughter."

"Oh, I didn't know. I'm sorry. He's had several visitors, but they've all been old friends." Looking at some sort of list, she continued, "I didn't know for certain he had any living relatives."

Feeling some inexplicable need to explain, I said, "I moved away a long time ago. I haven't seen Daddy for a number of years. The owner of this home, whose family apparently has known Daddy for some time, tracked me down and called to say I needed to come home immediately. How is he?" It struck me how odd the word "home," used regarding this town, sounded coming from me after all this time.

"Oh, I see. Well, he was doing well for a man his age, but recently, he's steadily declined. Right now, he's not doing very well," she said, managing to look suitably sympathetic. After a momentary pause, she realized my anxiety and continued, "I *am* sorry. He's in room 151. He should have had his lunch by now. I'll take you to him."

As we walked down the corridor, the various nursing home smells and the click-beep-click of electronic monitors coming from everywhere only added to the gloom I was experiencing. My guide continued to chatter as we walked. "I knew you had to be from around here somewhere. Only a southern girl calls her father 'Daddy' no matter how old she gets to be," she smiled, proud of her observation. "There's been such a migration to this area over the last ten years. It's hard to find a native nowadays." She stopped, turning to me with an open-palm gesture extended toward a door, and said, "This is your daddy's room."

I stopped short and saw the room number and Daddy's name handwritten on a card on the doorjamb. As I braced myself, I smiled and thanked her for her kindness. She just stood there in the hallway facing me for a moment. I gently assured her that I was fine and needed no more help. This was not a scene to which I wanted any outsider as a witness, regardless of the emotions to be spent. She smiled awkwardly, nodded, and left me. I pushed the partly opened door and eased in. The bed closest to the door was unoccupied. Daddy's bed was next to the window. The initial shock of what I saw made me cry aloud: Daddy's severely emaciated frame was lying in a pair of pajamas on a bed, an oxygen tube running to his nostrils; his hair was light and thinning with alleys of liverish skin showing through; he was receiving some fluid intravenously; a monitor of some sort stood nearby observing something, maybe his heartbeat; his breathing was shallow and labored. Daddy had always been a proud, tall, powerfully built, robust, God-fearing man, made hard and strong by the rough mountain life he'd known. Not now. The loose pajamas he wore clung to his body as if struggling to keep from falling to the floor. To say that the man I saw before me was a mere shell of the man I'd known was an understatement of enormous proportion. I could not stop the tears. At that moment, he knew he wasn't alone. He slowly opened his eyes at my sobbing.

"Who's there?" he whispered, as he tried to focus.

I fought desperately to hide any emotion except joy as I quickly wiped away my tears. "It's me, Daddy."

"Kitty?" he asked, as his voice seemed to gather renewed strength, yet was very raspy. "Oh, Kitty."

I laughed and cried at the same time. "Yes, Daddy, I'm here." My given name is Katherine. Only my daddy had ever called me Kitty. I'd not heard the name in years.

I stepped to the bedside and tenderly grasped his hand as he made a feeble effort to reach out for me. Leaning over, I kissed his forehead and lingered there with sadness and happiness tearing at my heart. I moved a tray of untouched food, pulled a chair to the bed, and sat down. He weakly turned his head so that his eyes met mine for the first time in decades. The love in his eyes filled the void I'd been so concerned about earlier. Tears trickled down the sides of his face. "Kitty, I'm so sorry."

"Me, too, Daddy," I cried, as I squeezed his hand gently. "But it's all right now. I'm here. We're together again. It's all right." Trying to regain some semblance of composure, I continued, "So how are you feeling? Is there anything I can get you?"

He tried to look around at the medical apparatus that surrounded him but closed his eyes in apparent pain. When he spoke at last, Daddy's words came slowly and with difficulty, "They got me hangin' on waitin' an' hopin' for you. As far as what you can git me, I'd love some of that down-home cookin' you use to fix for me. Ever'thin' here tastes like cardboard. I think the cook is a Yankee. I ain't had a decent meal since you left." He looked into my eyes and smiled weakly. "You're still the spittin' image of your Momma."

I started to cry again, resigning myself to the fact that there was just no way I was going to hide my emotions from him. Through the tears, I was able to tease him gently. "You get up out of that bed, and I'll take you home and fix you whatever you want."

His body shuddered as he started crying. "I got no home no more, Kitty. This is it." This once-proud man looked away pathetically as if in shame. Before I could say anything, he looked back at me and spoke, "Kitty, that's partly why I wanted to see you before I die. The old home an' land are all gone. They had to sell 'em so's to git the money for me to stay here."

"Well, Daddy—"

"No, Kitty, I ain't askin' to be taken in by you an' your family. That ain't what I'm sayin'." He paused for a long moment, and then said, "You got to tell me about you an' your family. Please tell me about 'em an' what you've been doin' all these years."

We went through a lengthy reintroduction, talking of my life since leaving, and a brief biography of my family, including the obligatory photographs of David, our children, and grandchildren. Daddy seemed genuinely pleased with the way my life had turned out. As he gazed at my family's pictures he held in his frail, trembling hands, my heart ached wishing he could meet them just once before he died. When the conversation waned, Daddy became very quiet and still. I thought he was tiring, that maybe I should leave and come back when he'd had time to rest, but he slowly turned to me, saying, "Before I die, an' I mean to die right here in my home county, my home state, I need to tell you about somethin' I done years ago before you was born."

I was taken aback by the gravity in Daddy's voice. He was obviously desperate to tell me something. I didn't know what to say, so I nodded and listened as he composed himself and went on with the story.

"Several years before you was born, before your Momma an' me got married, I was best friends with a boy named Silas Harper. Silas an' me went ever'where an' did ever'thin' together. Some folks, who didn't know no better, thought we was brothers, 'stead of best friends. There'd been three of us that was best buddies like that back then, but then there was a real bad fallin' out between Silas an' the third boy, named Artis Knight. It was on account of some girl. 'Cause Silas an' me was closer an' for a longer time, when Silas an' Artis parted ways, I just naturally stepped back from Artis, too. Then, out of cussedness, Artis started doin' stuff to raise Silas' dander up. Well, he raised mine up at the same time."

Here, Daddy paused, obviously trying to catch his breath to continue. I smiled at him but the gesture went unanswered. He seemed troubled about his feelings and uncertain in the way to tell me the story. After he collected his thoughts, he continued, "Anyways, ever'one hereabouts knowed of the bad blood between Silas an' Artis. Well, one night, there was a fight an' Silas was stabbed an' killed up on Rabbit Hill. A bunch of folks had gone up there after a dance at the grange hall, 'cause a moonshiner named Buck Scruggs had a still up there an' put out a pretty fair product." A hint of a smile crossed Daddy's gaunt lips as if some distant, pleasant memory had returned momentarily. He gathered his strength and continued. "That fight … . Though the fight was off in the distance a ways, several people seen it in the moonlight. All of 'em swore they seen Artis beat an' stab Silas. When the High Sheriff investigated the killin', he put the time at about 2:00 a.m. Problem was no one knowed the time for sure 'cause nary a soul hereabouts ever owned a watch in those days. You could always tell a railroad worker or a lawyer or a doctor, 'cause they'd have a pocket watch. They's the only ones could afford such then or even really needed 'em. Anyways, the sheriff arrested Artis for the murder of Silas Harper."

Again, Daddy paused and rested for a minute. I gave him drink of water. But he didn't wait long before he continued. As he spoke, he had a faraway look as if reliving the entire experience.

" 'Course Artis swore he knowed nothin' about it an' was somewheres else when it happened. Trouble with that was he couldn't prove it. No witnesses. He said he'd gotten one of Scruggs' jugs—

that's what we called Scruggs' Mason jars of shine—an' wandered off to drink hisself into a fog. Be that as it was, the witnesses was firm in their testimony. Some argued that Artis had raised the ire of more than one person in the county. He was given a trial in short order, an' it finished one day at the end of the workday. The judge told the jury to come back the next mornin' to start their deliberations. Practically the whole county'd been attendin' the trial, and there was no doubt in anybody's mind what the outcome would be. Some was aggravated that the judge just didn't let the jury go ahead an' take the ten minutes they needed to convict Artis right then an' there. Artis was gonna be hanged sure." Once more, a tear rolled down Daddy's cheek. His eyes moved to mine with a mournful look about them.

"Daddy," I interrupted, "maybe you should rest for a while. You can finish the story later. I'm not going anywhere."

"No, please, Kitty," he protested as strongly as his condition would allow. "I need to tell you this before it's too late." He swallowed hard. "I don't know how much time I got."

I couldn't ignore his strong desire to continue. I simply nodded. He seemed relieved at my acquiescence.

"The night before the jury started deliberatin', Artis escaped from the county jail an' disappeared. Some figured he run away an' was killed later in the war. Some claimed he just run like the coward he was and started fresh somewheres far away from here. Well ... Kitty ... I need to tell you somethin' I done. I busted Artis out of that jail. I never admitted that to no one, 'cept here, and now, to you." As he stopped talking and looked away, I tried to read Daddy's face. After years of separation, I couldn't tell if I saw shame or uncertainty in his expression.

I was still trying to sort it all out when he turned his head back to me and said, "Only one deputy was gonna be guardin' Artis the night he escaped, an' I knowed it. Heck, the whole county knowed it. They was all convinced that he was guilty of Silas' murder. Nobody was worried that he might git found not guilty after his trial. Ever'one knowed he was goin' to be convicted an' hanged. An', like I said, Artis had done aggravated most ever'body in the county with his wild an' crazy ways. So not much concern was paid to anythin' like extra guards or jail security. Besides, no one'd ever busted out of that jail. You probably don't recall, but back then the jail wasn't much compared to nowadays. It was just a small buildin' with two cells abuttin' the old courthouse just off the square."

As I smiled to myself recalling that everyone referred to the downtown roundabout as "the square" despite the obvious difference in shape, Daddy continued. "The jail had what they called a front door that led into the courthouse proper an' a back door that led to the alley where both the sheriff's office cars was parked when they wasn't out on business. The sheriff always drove his car home at night, an', thankfully, he was gone when I got there that night. I doused the back door's outside light an' banged on the door. When the deputy opened the door, I popped him good with my fist an' he went down for the count. He never knowed what or who hit him. I went inside to Artis' cell. He thought I was there to kill him 'cause of him killin' Silas. He was a mule-headed son of a buck. It took all I could do to convince him I was there to get him out an' away safe. Finally, we made our way right quick to my mule an' wagon, tied nearby, an' left town as fast as could be. I *broke* Artis out of that jail. I just couldn't let 'em hang him." With this, Daddy seemed to sink further into his bed and relax. An idea occurred to me, but I didn't say anything.

Daddy's voice had grown steadily weaker as the telling of this narrative had taken its toll. He'd been struggling to keep his eyes open. Finally, thankfully, as he imparted his last piece of the story, he closed his eyes in sleep. I was shocked by this confession! But what was I supposed to do with the information? He obviously felt he had to get this off his chest before he met his Maker. As I sat there pondering what he'd told me, I had a question I wanted desperately to ask him, but it would wait until he'd rested some. I glanced at my watch and was shocked to see how late it was. Afternoon visiting hours surely had to be over by now. I quietly left the room. Making my way to the front desk, I found the same woman who'd been sitting there when I'd come in. She looked up and smiled.

"Well, did you have a good visit?"

"Yes, thank you. Daddy drifted off to sleep. He seems very tired and weak, so I'm going to leave and come back in the morning. What time are your visiting hours in the morning?"

The woman smiled broadly, and then became slightly more serious as she stood and leaned closer to me. "Don't you worry about the hours, Honey," she whispered. "You just come on back when you can. I'll be here. Just see me, okay?"

I nodded gratefully.

"Did you just get into town? Do you have a place to stay?"

"Well, yes and no. I guess I'll go back to that hotel out on the highway."

Before I could say another word, she threw her hands up and said, "Look, Honey, I don't know what your purse allows, but there's a bed and breakfast back toward town that's really nice. And very clean. It's a little more expensive than that hotel, but it feels just like home. A friend of mine owns it. Just tell her Gertie sent you and tell her I said to give you the 'hometown' rate. She's got a big back porch looking out over the woods toward Walnut Mountain. Get a cup of tea and go out on the porch. You'll love it! And, if you need a place for supper, try the Taylor House Restaurant just off the square on Main Street."

It sounded great to me! I was ready for the feeling of a home versus an over sanitized, at least theoretically sanitized, hotel room. Gertie assured me she was going right down to Daddy's room to see that he had his medications and was set for the night. After thanking Gertie for her kindness, I made my way to the car and started back toward town. On the way, I found and checked in to the bed and breakfast Gertie had recommended. The owner was a truly charming lady who made one feel like she'd been expected all along after an extended, arduous trip. The room was very spacious and comfortable. I was glad for the recommendation. Dinner at the Taylor House was equally nice. I thought the name sounded familiar when Gertie mentioned it. As it turned out, it had been a family-owned restaurant back when I called the area home. The same family still owned and operated it.

After a pleasant meal, I took the opportunity to walk around "the square." Most of the real-estate offices had listings posted in their front windows. Looking at some of the offerings made me gasp. The huge sums being asked for and, in fact, received for land and homes in the area were astonishing! I just shook my head in amazement.

Later, I walked out into the bronze late-afternoon light and sat on the back porch of the bed and breakfast with a glass of wine. The setting was as glorious as Gertie had promised. As I listened to the chorus of cicadas fill the evening air, I considered the things Daddy had told me earlier. What *was* I supposed to do with his confession? I couldn't condone what Daddy had done, but, whatever his actions back then, they seemed to me to have lost their significance over the decades since. I gathered that his previous friendship with Artis had simply overcome his grief in the loss of Silas. He probably thought that, since hanging Artis wouldn't bring Silas back, he couldn't let it happen. Rather than lose two friends, he just took matters into his own hands. Seemingly, this Artis Knight had either been killed in the war, as some had speculated, or had gone on in life "to sin no more" since no one seemed to have heard of him again. No, I certainly wasn't going to the authorities with what Daddy had told me. His shame at telling me the story was evident enough without making matters worse by exposing it to the public. Besides, what would be gained by it at this late date?

But something else now weighed on my mind: the question I'd wanted to ask Daddy earlier. When I was growing up, I remembered an "uncle" named Arthur who would come to our house for short visits, but he never had any suitcase or bag with him. He was friendly enough, but always seemed a little restrained about things. We would never go anywhere when he was there, and no one else was ever invited over during his visits. I recalled that Daddy often told me in very strong terms that I was never to mention Uncle Arthur or his presence to anyone, because he was something of a hermit and a little "pixilated," as Daddy had put it. Ever the obedient daughter, I never mentioned Arthur to anyone. Because I left home as soon as I could after high school, I never heard what'd become of him. Now it seemed very likely to me that "Uncle Arthur" was, in fact, Artis Knight. And now I believed that Artis had lived somewhere up in the thick forest and undergrowth of our mountain.

Artis' presence up on the mountain could also explain another thing about which Daddy periodically cautioned me. More than once, he warned me about going up the mountain. He told me that a family of black bears lived there, and the mamma bear was one nasty critter, very protective of her cubs. His warnings more than chilled any desire I might have had in my younger tomboy days to try to sneak a peek at the cubs or to explore our land up the mountain. Later, as I grew older, I was less concerned about bears or wandering the property than about getting through school and leaving. Consequently, roaming the mountaintop never entered my mind. This evening, the questions and possibilities kept spinning around in my head. So I called it a night, telephoned David and the girls, and went to bed. Sleep was elusive and fitful at best.

The next morning, after a wonderful breakfast, I returned to the nursing home. As promised, Gertie was at the front desk. Before I could speak, she made her report.

"Honey, your daddy had a rough night, but he's all right. Apparently, he woke up late last night expecting to find you still there. When you weren't, he became very upset, and they could barely get him calmed down. The nurses had to sedate him to get him to sleep. Right now, he's still under sedation and probably won't come out of it for another hour or so." Gertie's voice reflected genuine sympathy and concern.

Trying to hide my distress at the situation, I simply said, "Maybe you should have called me."

"The problem is, Honey, in his weakened condition, he needed rest. The staff was afraid he wouldn't rest if you were here. They felt sedation was the best thing for him. Anyway, do you want to go do something, look around the town and see the changes for the next hour or so? By that time, he should be awake and ready for a nice visit."

With an hour to kill and resting on Gertie's assurances that Daddy was all right, I decided I would take a ride. "Yes, maybe I will. But I won't be far away if you need to reach me." Taking a piece of paper from the counter, I wrote my cell-phone number down, as I went on, "Here's my cell number. I used it last night so I know I get good service here. Please call me if *anything* happens. I'll be here in a matter of minutes. I should have given you the number last night, but I walked out of here in a slight state of shock."

"Yes, seeing them like this can be very disturbing," she agreed.

I smiled politely. Gertie was only partly right about the reason for my distress, but I let her think what she wanted. As I started to leave, I called back to her, "Oh, by the way, thanks for the bed and breakfast recommendation! It was wonderful!" She smiled and waved me a "you're welcome" as I departed.

I decided to take a drive to see if I could find the old homestead. Not certain whether I could locate it or even get to it, what with all the changes around here, I wanted to at least try. When I was young, we'd been what some might have called "the landed poor." We'd owned a sizeable parcel of land, extending to the top of one of the local mountains. However, before the area had been discovered by the Floridians escaping the unbearable heat of their summers and the Atlantans escaping whatever they felt the need to leave, land permeated with rock and not much else wasn't worth very much. Unlike today, when people will pay a million dollars for a mountain-top tract of land on which to put a two-million dollar home, back then, if it couldn't be farmed or wouldn't sustain cows or didn't have old-growth timber for harvesting, it wasn't worth much. Owning it meant very little. That was why the prices I'd seen in the real estate office windows were such a shock.

Collecting my memories about the best way to proceed, I drove north out of town. After a time of traveling the winding, two-lane roads, I reached what had been the dirt track that led to our little house. I almost didn't recognize it. The way was blocked by a chain between two posts. Nearby was a sign announcing the future site of "Black Bear Estates: Homesites from the low $300,000s, Homes from the low $800,000s." I sat there in the car in stunned silence as the immensity of life's changes swept over me. Although this land was my special world as I grew up, I never would have imagined the value it now held. Returning to reality, I saw that I could go no farther in trying to reach what might be left of the old house, so I headed back to town. As I drove, I recalled Daddy saying that the land had been sold to pay for his nursing care. A developer must have jumped all over the opportunity to grab a beautiful mountaintop parcel like we'd had. What's more, he probably paid next to nothing compared to what he was about to make on it.

Back at the nursing home, Daddy was awake and eager to talk some more, though still very weak. He had himself propped up as much as he could be so we could visit better.

"Kitty, I'm sorry 'bout yesterday. I didn't mean to drift off like that. I don't have the strength I used to. If you have time, there's somethin' more I need to tell you."

"We have all the time in the world, Daddy. I'm just so glad to see you." When I tried to steer the conversation to other things, Daddy seemed more concerned about taking up where he'd left off the day before. I assured him that he didn't need to explain anything to me. I told him that I loved him and understood why his friendship with Artis led him to do what he'd done. He tried valiantly to shake his head emphatically to my comments.

"You don't understand, Kitty. There's more to the story than I told you yesterday. Lots more."

Concerned about him getting upset, I tried to reassure him that my guess was that "Uncle Arthur" might well have been Artis Knight. He seemed relieved that I'd guessed correctly about that much of his tale. Daddy confirmed that, yes, Arthur had been Artis. He also told me that they'd agreed to use the name "Arthur" in case I, as a child, slipped up and said something about him elsewhere. But Daddy was determined to return to the story where he'd left it.

"Let me start back," he began weakly, "to after I broke Artis out of jail. I tried my best to git Artis to leave town. I even offered him what few dollars I could scrape together to start him out. But, like I said, he was the most cantankerous, stubbornest man I ever knowed. Artis just flat refused to leave. He told me that this town was his home an' he intended to die here." Daddy hesitated and swallowed hard, a tear sliding down his cheek in his understanding of what his friend had felt. "I put Artis up in that old logger's shack at the top of our property. He come from dirt-poor stock, even poorer than my people, so that shack weren't that much of a change for him. Nobody ever went up there anyways, so's he was out of sight. I'd take him food ever' now an' then. And Artis grew some vegetables. Not much, though. He'd trap for some meat, too, up on the mountain. He was pretty good at it. Plenty of squirrels, wild turkey, an' such for him to catch. He even snagged a deer a time or two. So he made out. He just wouldn't see the wisdom of movin' on. My biggest fear was that the revenuers would come snoopin' around an' find him, but it never happened. An', of course, on a signal from me when it was clear, he'd come down to our place ever' so often, playin' your Uncle Arthur. Nary a soul ever knew. Couldn't do it today, what with all the developers an' surveyors roamin' around."

Daddy stopped his story and asked for a drink of water. I was beginning to be very worried about the exertion of his talking. He seemed so frail, but insisted on continuing. As I helped him drink the water, I told him that Artis was not the only mule-headed person in the county. He showed me another faint smile.

"Artis lived up on that mountain all those years an' nary a soul knew. Several years ago, I went up one night to take him some food an' check on him. He'd been feelin' poorly of late an' I was worried sick 'bout him. I found Artis dead in the shack that night. He'd just finally give out. I buried him that night near the shack he called home all those years. Over the years, we'd become fast friends again. He sorta took the place of Silas. He really became my best friend, Kitty." Daddy clasped my hand as tightly as his weakened condition would allow. He sobbed softly for a minute, and then said, "Kitty,

I'm afraid that they'll find his remains now that they're gonna develop the land. They'll be diggin' ever'where. When they do, I know they'll call the sheriff, who'll call somebody, who'll use their fancy science to figure out who he was. Ever'body'll know I busted Artis out an' hid him." Daddy paused again. "When God took your Momma from me, He was punishin' me for what I done."

"Daddy, after all these years, I don't think anyone will care. You helped a friend. And I don't think God took Momma to punish you for helping Artis."

Daddy closed his eyes. He shook his head and whispered, "But it don't stop there, Kitty. You don't understand yet. There's more I got to say. When the sheriff figured the time Silas was killed, I was helpin' my paw calf a cow. We knowed the time 'cause ol' Doctor Johnson passed our way comin' back from deliverin' a breech baby at the Murray place. Doc stopped an' visited with Paw a spell, seein' if we needed any help with the calf. Like I said, Doc owned a pocket watch an' mentioned the lateness of the hour. An' Artis couldn't prove where he was when Silas was killed."

"I don't understand, Daddy. What does—"

He raised his hand slightly to stop me. Choking back tears, he said softly, "It was such a mess, Kitty. You see, Silas, like Artis, got drunk the night he was killed. In his drunkenness, he found my girl, my intended, your momma, comin' home from the dance an' messed with her. When I found her a little later, she was hysterical. I made her tell me what happened. Kitty, your momma was the most precious thin' I ever knowed up 'til then." With this, he squeezed my hand gently and tried to smile, but the painful memories he was reliving kept the promise of a smile from being fulfilled. He cried. I cried. I didn't know what to say.

Sobbing, Daddy went on, "I went crazy. I tracked Silas up to Rabbit Hill an' found him some distance from the gatherin' of folks there at the Scruggs' place. He was drunk as a skunk. When I confronted him with the god-awful truth of what he'd done with your momma, he pulled a knife on me. He was my best friend, Kitty ... . My best friend. I always knowed that, when Silas'd drink, he'd git tetchy. The liquor must have made him crazy or he wouldn't have done your momma wrong like that an' he wouldn't have pulled a knife on me. Sometimes, later, I reckoned that, in his drunkenness, maybe his mind had confused me an' Artis, since we was both 'bout the same size an' colorin', it bein' dark an' all. I reckon that the other fellars at Scruggs' place that night figured I was Artis, too, in the moonlight in the distance, what with Silas bein' killed an' there bein' bad blood between the two of them. Anyway, we fought over the knife an' I stabbed him. I killed him. I killed my best friend, Kitty ... ."

Daddy wept quietly for a short time before continuing, "When it was over, I ran home. You see, Kitty, the sheriff didn't reckon the time of the killin' right. It was me, not Artis. I killed my best friend. That's what they'll learn when they dig our land. When I heard some developer bought our land, I *had* to tell you before they learned it. I had to tell you, Darlin', that, all those years, I wasn't angry at you 'cause your momma died givin' birth. You thought I blamed you, an' I knowed it, but I didn't know how to tell you otherwise without tellin' you the whole truth. I was angry at myself 'cause of what I saw as God's punishment of me bein' took out on your momma. Kitty, I was so ashamed an' so scared. I've always loved you with all my heart. Always. I was just so afraid God would take you, too. An' when you left like that, I reckoned it was God's way. I was just always *so* grateful He spared you. I love you, Kitty. Always have."

I cried with Daddy. I held him as we cried. So many years wasted, so much misunderstood. I stood and went to the room's tiny bathroom to rinse my face and get a damp washcloth for Daddy.

When I returned to his bedside, Daddy was gone forever. I held him close as I cried again, longer, deeper than before. My guess was that Daddy felt he'd lived long enough to set the record straight. More important, we'd renewed the love between us that had always really been there, buried beneath a mountain of regret. I will always love my daddy and the mountains in which he lived and died.

THE GOOD DOCTOR

The fat woman was dead all right. As dead as anyone could make her anyway. And *someone* had made her dead. Very dead.

Dr. Barney Ostrowski rose slowly from beside the body with a groan earned through years of odd-hour, preliminary examinations of premature, violent deaths. He looked at the nearby senior detective. "She's been dead only a couple of hours at most. Strangled. That seems apparent at this point, Chet." The doctor looked back at the deceased as if studying something, waiting for an answer. After brief pause, he turned and continued, walking around the body as he spoke. "But not a certainty. The autopsy will tell me more." His voice was hollow and without energy.

"Yeah, Doc. Even in this light, you can see the ligature marks," Detective Chet Wadford agreed. He watched the medical examiner rub his overworked eyes. Ostrowski's nose-heavy and chin-shy face reflected the sum total of years of hard work and the unshakeable knowledge that had earned him the respect of law enforcement and prosecutors alike, as well as the reverence, yet dread of defense attorneys trying to poke holes in the state's case. Dr. Ostrowski cared about the truth a deceased's body could speak to him after their demise. If those facts pointed to their cause of death and their killer, so be it. On the other hand, if they did not, then that was simply the way it happened to be. While reasonable minds could disagree on the meaning or interpretation of a finding, he didn't truck with anyone trying to distort the truth of a matter for unwarranted gain, no matter their position in the issue. He'd become something of an instant legend in some circles when dealing with a particularly nasty, arrogant, and argumentative defense attorney in a trial much earlier in his career. During his cross-examination of Dr. Ostrowski, the attorney was trying to undermine the medical examiner's experience and asked him how many autopsies he had performed on dead people. Ostrowski responded by telling him that all the autopsies had been on dead people. The courtroom had erupted in laughter at the obvious answer to an ineptly put question. The medical examiner was held in a measure of awe by law enforcement. *We're going to miss him when he's gone,* Wadford thought. *One of a kind.*

The doctor looked around to the young detective, Jim Carter, standing on the other side of the woman's body and making notes in a small, flip notebook. His speech suddenly drew new life. "You're looking for a guy about six feet tall, with dirty blond hair, and driving an old Chevy Nova."

"No shit, doctor?" The rookie detective, wide-eyed, was writing furiously. Carter's face was like an impatient sponge waiting to glean any tidbit tossed out by the more learned. Wadford smiled as he flipped his notebook closed and looked from Carter back to the medical examiner.

After an appropriate pause to allow Carter time to finish writing, Ostrowski continued. "And he ate a large spaghetti dinner just before he killed her."

The rookie stopped writing and stared at Ostrowski. "Are you sure about that, doctor?"

"Nah. It's just that Sherlock Holmes and all those TV and paperback cops and medical examiners seem to make such massive leaps of logic and detection, I thought I'd inject some conjecture of my own into your investigation." His fatigued face broke into a broad grin.

Wadford laughed quietly as Carter tore the page out of his notepad. For his part, Carter wasn't sure whether he should show his disgust, this being only his third day in the homicide unit and his first murder case. So he merely stuffed the paper into his coat pocket in silence and smiled sheepishly.

The good doctor is unique, all right, Wadford thought. Ostrowski had slowed since he'd started his treatments for the cancer ravaging his body, but his sense of humor was as keen as ever. He was a tough old bird who just wouldn't or couldn't give up his daily routine. Having lost his wife a decade or so ago, the job seemed to keep Ostrowski going, despite his catastrophic setback. Wadford believed he was like some old workhorse, ready for the harness, eager for the bell, even when it suffered from a painful leg injury.

Carter made an effort to regain some of his lost dignity by bringing the investigation back to ground. "Her name was Esther Williams, according to the identification found in the purse next to the body."

Ostrowski gingerly eased up next to Wadford. "Esther Williams? Really? Well, that explains the tan lines," the doctor trumpeted. His voice reflected a renewed enthusiasm for the moment.

Carter's expression was uncomprehending. The name meant nothing to him. He glanced at the fully clothed victim. "What 'tan lines,' doctor?" Carter was more cautious now.

Ostrowski shook his head and released most of the air in his lungs. " 'Pearls before swine,'" he muttered to the detective by his side.

"More likely the 'youth and inexperience' of your 'opponent.' And imagine you quoting from the New Testament, Doc." Wadford kept his voice at a conspiratorial level.

The medical examiner smiled and looked askew at his companion. "Probably more surprising than you paraphrasing your favorite President, Chet."

Wadford smiled as an early-morning drizzle started falling, a small course of water running from the brim of his fedora, that identified him as one of the "Hat Squad," as the Homicide Division was unofficially known. "You finished with your examination, Doc?"

"Yeah, Chet. You guys can finish up. And then they can go ahead and take her to the medical examiner's office. I'll get more 'into' the examination later this morning." The weariness had returned to his voice as he paused, inclined his head, and looked at the body once more as if still seeking a response to a query bouncing around in his head. The doctor then turned to walk to his car. As he turned, Wadford patted his shoulder. The pat was the kind that one man gave another, simultaneously indicating respect for the man and his knowledge as well as admiration for a lifetime's job well done. That feeling was heartfelt for Chet's part. He was only one of a few people in the county's law-enforcement community who knew about Ostrowski' condition. Having known and worked closely with Dr. Ostrowski for a long time, it was tough to watch him fade.

In their early days together, before the ME's Office had the luxury of having investigators assigned, the medical examiner would always come to the murder scene. Nowadays, the ME's investigator would normally show up on scene and make the appropriate account of the scene to be included in the medical examiner's postmortem report. But Ostrowski usually chose to appear, even in his weakened condition. He always said he'd write a book someday about all these experiences and didn't want to miss a good story by not coming to the site.

"Doc, any idea what time you'll do the autopsy? I'll need to be there as usual."

"Let's say 10:00 this morning, Chet," Ostrowski called over his shoulder in the direction of the detective. As he shuffled up the slight incline toward his car, gravel crunching beneath his feet, the doctor questioned his continued devotion to going to these crime scenes. His responding to murder scenes was a matter of habit by now, but the exertion was certainly wearing on him physically. While the simultaneous fragility and resilience of the human body he saw during a postmortem examine continued to fascinate him after all these years, the crime scene was always the most interesting aspect of his occupation. Ostrowski chuckled to himself as he recognized the irony of his application of the term "simultaneous fragility and resilience" to the bodies of those departed while ignoring it in his own circumstances. Maybe this *would* be his last trek to the place where some poor soul had been suddenly and violently ripped from among the living. Ostrowski sighed. *Homo homini lupus.*

Ostrowski realized that, without the concern of a murder victim and the accompanying crime scene to occupy his mind, the severe pain that racked his body was bearing down on him again. He leaned inside his car and retrieved one of the pain medications prescribed for people in his advanced stage of cancer. As he stood beside the car, he lifted his face to the sky and tried to take in a mouthful of the light rain to wash the pill down. The effort had little effect. The pill felt stuck in his throat. Great, he thought, a lot of good it'll do me there. He sighed again, this time more deeply, as he got in his car and drove away.

At ten minutes before ten o'clock, Detective Wadford appeared in the Medical Examiner's Office, sweeping off his fedora as he entered. Dr. Ostrowski was with another "patient," he was told. ME Office's humor. After a few minutes, Wadford was directed to go to the "examining room." Dr. Ostrowski was still washing his hands and lower arms after the previous procedure when the detective opened the door. Ostrowski looked even more haggard than he had some hours earlier at the scene where Mrs. Williams' body had been found. His countenance stunned Wadford even though he knew of the doctor's condition.

Ostrowski stood at a sink in an ill-fitting scrub smock, scouring as if going into open-heart surgery. "Give me a second, detective. Don't want to spread any infections between 'patients.'" More morgue humor. The doctor never stopped. "Our next contestant will be right with us. I believe she's just down the hall in the 'green room.'" As if on cue, the doors from the cold storage room burst open and the late Mrs. Williams was wheeled in by a morgue assistant. When the deceased was in position on the autopsy slab and Dr. Ostrowski was sufficiently sanitized, he stood by the table and adjusted the overhead recording microphone. As the doors were closing behind the attendant on his way out, the medical examiner declared a loud "thank you," referring to him as "Igor."

While he checked some instruments and read over a document on a clipboard, he cleared his throat and spoke. "Now, madam, would you please tell our viewing audience your full name, what you did for a living, and, finally, if you know, who did this to you?" Despite his fragile appearance, Ostrowski was in rare form today. Wadford assumed that he had taken some type of medication to bolster himself. After a brief pause, Ostrowski continued, still addressing his bone-tired voice to the dearly departed, "I have it on good authority that your name was Mrs. Esther Williams. Uh, probably still *is*, I suppose. Since you seem to be a bit shy about talking, we'll just dig into the matter and try to determine the answer to that last question, if within the realm of medical science."

With this, Dr. Ostrowski turned on the recorder and began his legitimate examination. As usual, he began with his external observations about the dead woman, including her weight, height and any identifying marks, such as scars (one from an appendectomy and an old one of unknown origin on her left leg) and tattoos (a small rose on the back of her left shoulder). Again he noted for his report the ligature marks around the neck and the corresponding petechial hemorrhaging in and around Mrs. Williams' eyes.

After some other preliminary matters of the external examination, Ostrowski began his internal exam, observing the weight and general condition of the various organs. The doctor examined the deceased's brain and pronounced it to be "unremarkable," indicating there were no abnormalities about it. Wadford smiled at the irony of this procedure. Absent some medical anomaly, even Einstein's brain would have been declared as such.

As he proceeded with the internal exam, Ostrowski muttered to himself about his observations. The detective often wondered how anyone transcribing the proceedings was ever able to make sense of the autopsy recordings. After completing the rest of the internal exam, Ostrowski returned to the woman's dissected stomach. He pointed with an instrument and called it to Wadford's attention. The detective saw the trace of a thick, green, mortar-like material in the stomach. Despite the years of attending these procedures, Wadford often, as now, saw the thing being indicated but didn't know exactly what he was seeing. Ostrowski wiped perspiration from his forehead with the sleeve of his scrub gown and looked to Wadford. "Did you notice the disruption of the soil around the body, Chet?"

"Yeah. I did, Doc. I assumed it was the result of the struggle between Mrs. Williams here and her attacker during the strangulation." When no response was forthcoming, Wadford prodded. "Right?" Ostrowski appeared distracted, as the detective stared at his face, seeking confirmation. "Do you have something else in mind?"

"Well, I don't know to an absolute certainty, detective. The ligature marks threw me off initially. But finding this stuff in her stomach gives me pause to wonder. I could be wrong, but a lab analysis should tell us for certain. I'll send off the stomach contents, along with bile, liver, blood and kidney samples to be tested." Ostrowski seemed to be thinking aloud as he continued, "The lab tests will tell me whether I'm correct. That'll tell us for sure. Those specimens will show the highest concentrations, if it's present." The doctor paused, sighing heavily, wearily. "Between the scrapes on the ground, the marked postmortem rigidity despite the relatively short postmortem interval, which I attribute to violent muscle contractions, and now this green matter in her stomach contents, I suspect that someone poisoned the dear lady with strychnine, and then, having second thoughts, strangled her to throw us off the trail. He or she may have hoped that, if we saw the ligature marks, we'd jump to the easiest conclusion and not look further for any other attack on her person or another possible cause of death. A cause of death, I might add, that might easily lead us to his or her door. Some people can be very sneaky about their method of doing away with another, and then hope it gets past a postmortem exam." Ostrowski gave Wadford a knowing smile and added, "It happens on occasion, you know."

Chet Wadford returned the smile. Yes, he *did* know.

Like the Sperry case. Several years earlier, Ostrowski completed an autopsy on an unfortunate soul named Sperry, who the attending physician was certain had died of complications from an irregular heartbeat due to clogged arteries. Nevertheless, the resolute Dr. Ostrowski noticed calcium oxalate crystals in the man's kidneys during the postmortem procedure. Curious about their presence, he sent several urine and blood samples to the state crime laboratory for analysis. The test results from the crime lab toxicologist indicated nothing was amiss. Still not satisfied, Ostrowski sent additional samples to a nationally renowned, independent laboratory in Pennsylvania.

In due course, that lab reported to Dr. Ostrowski the presence of high levels of a toxin, ethylene glycol, in the man's blood and tissues. Ethylene glycol is the principal component of antifreeze, and a substance not naturally found in humans. The good doctor surmised that the man in question either had to have been exposed to large doses of the substance or had somehow ingested it. Whatever the source, Ostrowski listed the cause of death as antifreeze poisoning. Based on his findings and his report, local law-enforcement authorities launched an immediate investigation. The lead investigator was Chet Wadford, who learned from the man's family and friends that he had been suffering from nausea and dizziness a day or so before he died. Sperry had also complained of headaches and shortness of breath. Most of the people interviewed had just assumed he was suffering from a severe bout with the flu. They did, that is, until he died. Some suspected foul play at the hands of the winsome widow Sperry. But none had the nerve to voice their suspicions openly, despite the obvious friction recently seen in the Sperry household, until approached by the police. Later, the state crime lab toxicologist in the Sperry case admitted that his failure to find the toxin was the consequence of misreading test results.

Significantly, Wadford's investigation also revealed that Mrs. Sperry's first husband, with whom she'd lived in another state, had died suddenly several years before her marriage to the unfortunate Mr. Sperry. Spouse number one's death followed an affliction with a very similar set of symptoms as those encountered by Mr. Sperry. The attending medical examiner in that case was satisfied that the man had died of some complication related to an enlarged heart, a natural cause, and listed as much in his report. When the law-enforcement authorities in the two jurisdictions started communicating with each other, the previous medical examiner adamantly stood by his initial findings, despite the remarkable similarities in the two cases. Only after pressure was brought to bear by the deceased's family, did the very defensive medical examiner reluctantly order the body exhumed. On further testing, the very embarrassed doctor changed the first victim's cause of death to antifreeze poisoning. The common element in both cases was Mrs. Sperry. A spark of avarice that inflamed Mrs. Sperry was the apparent motive.

Wadford attended Mrs. Sperry's trial for the murder of her first husband. During the proceedings, an expert chemist from the company that supplied the embalming fluids to the funeral home, which had interred the first husband, testified. He swore without hesitation that their company did not use any substances containing ethylene glycol, thus deflecting the defense's theory that the toxin found was the result of the embalming process. The funeral director also appeared and caused quite a titter in the courtroom when he meekly testified that, in his devoutly religious part of the world, his grieving families would consider it an affront to even hint that their dearly departed would require protection from any "heat," as the use of a coolant would imply. Finally, Dr. Ostrowski testified, explaining that his experiments with antifreeze demonstrated it easily could be put in Jell-O or some other food without changing the texture or color of the food, thereby being ingested by an unsuspecting victim. Ostrowski's tenacity had solved not one, but two murders, and the lovely and talented widow Sperry was sent away to prison for the remainder of her somewhat unnatural life. Dr. Ostrowski was something special, all right.

Ostrowski's voice dragged Wadford back from his reverie. "Detective, I'd be looking for someone with a motive *and* who is involved in pest control or farming or some line of work with access to rat poisons. And I'm not just 'injecting some conjecture of my own into your investigation.' I'll bank on that."

103

Wadford was simultaneously stunned and grateful. "I'd say you can, Doc. *Mr.* Williams works for a pest control company. We've already made contact with him about the death. We located him on his job. I'm meeting with him later this afternoon. If you're sending the samples to the lab right away, you won't complete your report until the results are back, right?. I think I'll play this one close to the vest for now and see what he has to say. I can always spring what we know on him later when we get the test results. I'll wait. That is, I'll hold off if he doesn't act like he'll bush bond on us."

Ostrowski nodded. "Chet, if you have the time, let me wash up, and then join me in my office for a short while. I'd like to talk." He sounded ominous.

"Sure, Doc!" Wadford liked Ostrowski a great deal. Besides, how could he say no to someone who had just seemingly handed him the solution to a murder case? Dr. Ostrowski was already in the process of scrubbing.

Later, when the pair was comfortably situated in his office, Dr. Ostrowski told Detective Wadford that this would be his last case. The detective was flooded was sorrow. Not only was he going to miss working with the old reprobate, but this sounded like a final, fatal farewell. Ostrowski was a dear friend and a knowledgeable colleague. Wadford swallowed hard.

Ostrowski, never one for maudlin scenes, quickly pulled open a desk drawer and produced a bottle of Belvedere Vodka and two glasses. "Have a drink with me, Chet?"

The detective started to remind the good doctor that he was on duty, but, instead, pulled his cell phone from his belt and dialed. "Darla. This is Wadford. Put me down for personal leave the rest of the day. Yeah, something's come up that I really need … no, I *want* to attend to. Thanks." As he spoke, he watched Ostrowski set fire to a comforting cigar. "Oh, and Darla? Have Carter call Mr. Henry Williams and reschedule our meeting for first thing tomorrow morning. Carter'll know who he is. Just tell him as soon as you can, okay? If there's a problem, you can reach me on my cell. Thanks, kiddo."

Dr. Ostrowski was smiling through his weariness. "Thanks, Chet." He poured two drinks and shifted one across the desk to the detective. Raising his glass, he proposed, "Na zdrowie!"

Wadford, uncertain of the meaning but nonetheless optimistic about the message, likewise raised his glass in tribute to his friend. "Right back at ya, big guy!"

As the men nursed their drinks, Wadford reached over and picked up the bottle, looking at the label. "Polish vodka. I've not tried it before, Doc. Smooth stuff. Any significance to the building?" he asked, indicating the structure on the label.

"That's the Polish presidential palace. It's named Belweder, spelled B-e-l-w-e-d-e-r, but pronounced like the name on the bottle, Belvedere. We visited it a number of years ago, before Stella passed." Ostrowski grew momentarily somber as he mentioned his wife's name. Wadford could not remember the last time he'd heard him say it. Her death had really hit the doctor hard. After a moment, he continued, "Our people were originally from Poland. In fact, my folks came from a little village near Zyrardow, a little southwest of Warsaw, where that vodka is produced. Her people were from a town farther north. Lovely country, that. You need to go for a visit sometime, Chet." He took another sip of his drink. "Think of me when you do."

Dr. Ostrowski was correct on two counts. For one thing, his assessment of Mrs. Williams' death was spot on. The lab analysis showed she'd been given a fair amount of strychnine, enough to kill her but not right away. It didn't take Wadford long to get the story from the "bereaved widower" once he'd been confronted with the evidence. Mr. Williams admitted that, in his frenzied thought process, he had tried to "doctor" the scene with strangulation after poisoning his wife. And, second, as Dr. Ostrowski had said, the Williams case was his last. He retired, but came back one last time to testify at Williams' trial. In the end, Mr. Williams went the way of the widow Sperry. That trial was the last time Wadford saw the doctor outside of a hospice.

Shortly thereafter, Dr. Ostrowski died of cancer. His memorial service that preceded the Levayah was mobbed with mourners, crowded with law enforcement, medical professionals, and lawyers, both prosecutors and defense attorneys. One of the men who Wadford saw and spoke to at the service was the attorney who'd asked the question of Dr. Ostrowski that had produced the laughter in the courtroom those many years ago. Despite the embarrassment Ostrowski had put on him, the lawyer admitted to Chet he'd secretly remained in awe of the doctor and his abilities over the years.

Doctor Ostrowski was one of a kind, all right.

A QUICK STUDY

All I wanted to do was to publish a short story in a magazine. Sounds easy enough, right? Wrong. For several years I'd tried to write a mystery that would really grab an editor, but, after each submission, the same sort of form letter came back. "Thank you very much for the opportunity to read your manuscript. Unfortunately … ."

A normal person would have given up a long time ago, but I *had* to publish a story. Not because it's my chosen vocation. It's just my passion. I love mystery books, magazines, and movies. And I love to write. Not that I'm necessarily any good at it, but it's an escape from my real life as a government attorney working in contract law. *BORING!* So, I kept trying, although the editors were beginning to wear me down. Many people in this world suffer pangs of hopelessness, but, when it comes down to one's true passions, ambition can become a desperate motivator. That's how it began.

On a particular night, a thing called writer's block hit me while I was working on my latest "masterpiece." That it was a little after 2:00 a.m. and I couldn't sleep may have had something to do with my lapse, but, every time I tried to doze off, story ideas ricocheted through my brain making slumber impossible. So, I stood up, stretched, and walked out onto the small balcony of the second-floor apartment where I'd lived for several years. Leaning against the rail in the dark and trying to glean inspiration from the dimly lighted parking lot, I watched a car slowly approach a parking space near the building across the way from mine. For lack of anything better to do, I continued to watch. At first, there was no movement from inside the parked car. Then the driver's door opened slowly and the lone occupant emerged, looking around the area as he did so. The car was either a dark blue or a black compact. I knew most people living around the complex, even if only by sight, but I couldn't recognize the driver due to the low lighting. He appeared relatively young, tall and slender.

Quietly closing the car door, he moved across the grassy area to the entrance of a nearby apartment building, constantly casting furtive glances about as he walked. He disappeared into the building. I was about to go back inside and give sleep another chance, when, suddenly, a balcony light came on across the way and the same figure I'd been watching came outside. He moved to the storage closet each apartment had on their balconies. The young man unlocked the closet and quickly, but silently returned to his car. After opening the passenger side door, he leaned in. His dark clothing made it impossible for me to see exactly what he was doing, but he immediately emerged, holding what appeared to be a box containing a rather large television. After depositing the container in the closet, the young man returned to the car and hauled out another sizeable box. As well as I could tell, this appeared to be a stereo unit or some other type of electronic device. Likewise, he placed this box in the same closet. I continued to watch in rapt silence as he returned yet a third time, leaned inside the car, and retrieved another box of undeterminable contents. The fact that the small car could hold this number and size of boxes was astonishing in itself.

Owing to the presence of nearby twenty-four-hour discount department stores and the odd hours some people must work and shop, I gave the episode no more thought. Not, that is, until, during similar bouts of insomnia, I witnessed nearly the identical event with the same individual two other times in the early-morning hours within the next month. Each time, the contents of the car appeared to be new, still-in-the-original-box electronics equipment. Loving a good mystery, my curiosity was naturally aroused. However, my efforts to find and observe this mysterious stranger during normal waking hours proved futile.

A couple of days after the last episode, I was at a loss for story inspiration and decided that a change of scenery might help overcome my stagnation. So I went to our swimming pool, which was across the parking lot from my apartment building. As I lay beside the pool or drifted in the water, my mind kept wandering to my failure to write a good mystery. Maybe my eleventh-grade English teacher had been right. Mrs. Todd had often admonished us to write about subjects with which we were familiar. Admittedly, I truly knew nothing of crime or of the criminal himself except through Hollywood or the news. My reflections also kept going back to those early-morning events with the puzzling man that I'd watched. The sudden shout of my name interrupted my thoughts as some guys I knew from the complex called to me to play a game of pool volleyball. For lack of anything better with which to pass time, I joined them. As I moved toward their location, I was stunned to see the person I believed to be the young man I'd observed during those late-night episodes emerging from the dark-blue compact in the parking lot. I paused to watch him and make as certain as possible that it was the same person. As he walked toward and entered the same building as before, there was no doubt in my mind. His cocksure stroll left no uncertainty.

A short time later, he arrived at the pool. I casually asked some of my companions about him, on the pretext of thinking he worked in the same building I did. The others laughed when I mention him and work in the same sentence. They told me that his name was Jimmy, and he was a high school dropout who lived with and sponged off his older sister, who lived there in the apartment complex. The consensus was that he was one of those types who maintained no apparent ambition and was in no hurry to change his prospects. "Lowlife," "punk," and "petty criminal" were the terms that were mentioned most often regarding him. From his appearance and the descriptors used, he sounded like the kind of guy you wouldn't necessarily notice on the street, but, if he showed up at a party you were throwing, you'd call the cops.

Although I returned to my routine, dull-as-ditchwater life after that Sunday, my failure as a writer continued to occupy my mind constantly. Moreover, my failure to write continued. At the same time, my thoughts were intertwined with my buddies labeling Jimmy a "petty criminal" and the admonition to write about things with which I was acquainted. It occurred to me that, if Jimmy were mixed up in illegal activity, and what I had observed appeared to bear that out, maybe he would let me "interview" him to get insight into the criminal mind and his way of life. And so it went until a couple of weeks later.

During another of my nightlong bouts of sleeplessness, I happened to hear a car entering the parking lot. I eased out onto my balcony. Sure enough, there was Jimmy unloading a box from his car. Instantly, I decided to act. After Jimmy disappeared into his apartment building, I slipped out of my apartment and quickly moved across the parking area to the driver's side of his car. I crouched and waited for his return. Very soon, Jimmy was back at the passenger's door, softly grunting and groaning as he removed another box from the car's back seat. I slowly stood up as he emerged with his plunder in his hands.

"Good morning," I said quietly.

Even in the dim lighting of the parking lot, I could see the startled look on his face. He froze. "Mornin'."

I simply stood there smiling at him and saying nothing. Then, his expression turned to one of suppressed anger. "Whadda ya want?" he demanded.

"Just thought I'd say 'Hello' and see if I could help you move your boxes inside."

He sat the box he'd just recovered on the front passenger seat and looked around. "No, thanks. I'm good to go. Just a little late-night shoppin'."

I tried for a knowing, yet friendly smile. "It seems that you do a lot of 'late-night shopping'."

He retrieved the box. "I dunno what ya mean."

"Nothing really, it's just that this is the fourth time I've watched you come home in the middle of the night with your car packed with boxes of electronic equipment."

Gradually, he seemed to sense that I wasn't simply going to walk away and that I knew too much about his coming and going for his comfort level. With that, his demeanor changed to a more menacing presence. He set the box down and walked around the car toward me. Now, he was no ominous hulk, more inclined to sinew than muscle, but, at this distance, I realized that he was what some might call "wiry," capable of doing some damage when cornered. His fists were clenched. However, I knew that, if I wanted to accomplish my goal, I'd have to take a chance and stand my ground, though street fighting had never been my forte.

Trying to reduce the tension of the moment and to stop his movement, I put up a hand. "Hold it right there. I'm not here for trouble. I only have a favor to ask. Besides, if anything happens to me, my girlfriend will have it recorded on my camcorder. That's the same camcorder, by the way, I've been recording you on every time I've watched you," I lied. "She'll take the recordings to the police, complete with dates and times of your activities right there on the recordings. How hard will that be for the cops to match that information with the what, the burglaries or thefts of these items?" I hoped my words sounded bolder than I felt.

Jimmy stopped dead in his tracks and glared at me. He glanced around the area, obviously trying to catch sight of someone recording us. During this glimpse at our surroundings, he momentarily looked at a nearby streetlight. Jimmy seemed to come to a sudden enlightenment of his own. "Your girlfriend is recordin' in this low light? Bullshit! I don't believe you!"

"Really, Jimmy? I would've thought you might've learned something about the things you've been stealing. Or don't you have a market for camcorders? They're pretty remarkable pieces of equipment nowadays and very capable of recording in all levels of lighting. Haven't you ever seen videos on television of undercover cop operations or military missions? Fairly low light and yet very distinct pictures. All the recordings of you I've made so far have turned out just fine."

His surprise that I knew his name was evident. After contemplating his situation for a minute, Jimmy scrunched up his rodent-like face and asked through clenched teeth, "So, whadda ya want, jerk? A new TV, a sound system? What?"

"No, nothing like that. I want you to teach me about committing crimes. About what you do."

"What? Get the hell away from me, ya freak!" His voice was low, yet threatening. After a second or so of considering his next move, he recovered the box and turned to leave.

"No, Jimmy, I'm very serious." As he turned back toward me, I went on, "I'm a writer, and I want to write a crime story. But I don't know anything about committing a crime: what it feels like, what goes through your mind, how you feel afterward. You can teach me."

He paused to mull over my suggestion. "So what're ya gonna do? Videotape it so ya can hold it over my head? No way!"

"No, no video. Just you teaching and me learning."

"What about the video of me ya already have?"

"When we're done, they're all yours. Period," I said, continuing the lie. "Really, Jimmy, I'm not out to hurt you. I just want some background material for my story. Anonymously, of course."

Again, he considered the idea and shook his head vigorously. "No! I've got a pretty good thing going. If I take ya along, I'll get busted for sure. Nope!"

The thought of "going along" with him had never occurred to me, but suddenly the idea held great potential. New possibilities opened before me in that instant. I fully realized that, if we did get caught, my life, my career was over. That was a heavy consequence to consider, but I was hooked on using Jimmy now more than ever. And I was definitely obsessed with writing a story that would sell, maybe a book. What's more, Jimmy must have had some clue about what he was doing. He'd done it a number of times, apparently, without getting caught. I persisted, "Look, you'll be the 'boss.' Whatever you say goes. You set things up, you say when we go, and you can have whatever we steal. I'll take the blame *if* we get caught. Hey, I'm not stupid, and I'm fairly athletic. So doing whatever you tell me to do won't be a problem. I'll … I'll even pay you to let me go with you." I gave him a second or so to think, before continuing, "Besides, you can't afford to say no with the video of you I have."

He wasn't happy about the prospects. "Let me think about it."

"Fair enough."

With that understanding, we parted ways for the night. We didn't cross paths again for the next several days. When I didn't see his car either, I wondered whether he'd just taken off rather than deal with me and the consequences of my "videos."

"I gotta talk to ya," a whispery voice came to me as I lay half asleep by the pool the following Sunday. My supposition about his departure proved wrong when I opened my eyes and squinted up at Jimmy's lean, hard face.

"Sure," I responded, as I sat up and tried to hide my surprise.

"Over by your mailbox," he mumbled in his best cloak-and-dagger manner, motioning in that direction with a nod of his head.

He walked away. I put on my flip-flops, picked up my towel and followed him at a distance. Once at the small mailbox pavilion servicing my apartment building, he turned around quickly to face me.

"You're a lawyer. A government lawyer," he sneered, glancing around to be sure he wouldn't be overheard. Then, Jimmy's angry dark eyes studied me suspiciously. "Why didn't ya tell me? Are ya some sort of cop or what? Or just tryin' to earn some sort of promotion?"

I smiled at the idea that Jimmy had checked on me. "Yeah, I'm a lawyer. But, to begin with, I work in government contract law. You know, contracts dealing with how much the taxpayers will spend on copying paper or toilet seats, for example. It has nothing, absolutely nothing, to do with any type of law enforcement. And it's boring as hell. Second, my being a lawyer has nothing to do with what I'm proposing to you. My proposition only has to do with my writing fiction. That's why I write: to escape my bore-ass life."

A young couple, approaching to check their mailbox, caused us to pause in our conversation. Jimmy took the interlude to read my face as if to gain some insight into my thoughts. As he did, he wiped his hands on the paint-streaked sweatshirt he was wearing. Its sleeves had been severed at the shoulders. I wondered how anyone with Jimmy's apparent abhorrence of legitimate work could get that much paint on anything.

As the couple walked away, I continued, "I'll be glad to answer any other questions you might have, Jimmy."

He shook his head. "I don't like the idea of draggin' some nerdy asshole around on my 'jobs.' You'll just be excess baggage. I can't afford the risk."

"Think about it for a second, Jimmy. The fact that I *am* a lawyer means I have a hell of a lot more to lose than you do if anything goes wrong. Hell, I'm not asking to you take me with you on some major bank robbery. We can do whatever petty crime you can think of, as long as I can get the feel of what it's like."

Again, he studied my face, frowning thoughtfully. This time his stare was longer, deeper than before. Then he glanced around again. "Okay, but what I say goes. Ya do what I say, when and how I say it, understand? And if ya screw up, I'll kill you right there on the spot. No joke, I will. I swear it."

I was nodding enthusiastically the whole time he was delivering his conditions and the threat. I extended my hand to seal the agreement. Jimmy slapped it away, deriding me, "You're such a geek. I'll let ya know when." The low regard in which he held me was very evident as he turned quickly and walked away, shaking his head in laughter as he went.

Waiting to hear from Jimmy, I recalled the conversation by the mailboxes. Somehow I felt stupid for being in a position of needing and wanting the help of such a lowlife individual. I certainly didn't like him, and I wasn't all that crazy about me at the moment. Was what I was embarking on worth it? Writing was important to me, sure, but at what price?

A couple of days later, Jimmy approached me as I collected my mail. "I have somethin' lined up. What are ya doin' Friday night?"

"Nothing. What's up?" I hoped my words did not betray my racing heart.

"I thought we'd do a little 'shoppin'' together. At Belvedere Mall."

"A burglary?"

"No, we're gonna do somethin' sorta minor. A shopliftin', in legal terms. Can you handle it?"

"Yeah, sure. When and where?"

"Meet me at your car at 7:30 p.m. Friday. We'll take *your* car. I'll tell ya the rest then. And if I find out you've said a word to anyone, including that girlfriend of yours—"

"I swear I won't say a word," I interrupted before another threat could be thrown my way.

As he left me standing there, my heart raced suddenly at the idea of actually committing even a relatively insignificant crime. The workweek dragged by. Friday finally arrived. Any attempt I made at steeling my nerves was futile at best. At work on Friday, everything I did went awry: I couldn't think, talk, or act straight, while work kept piling up on my desk. Calling in sick had occurred to me, but that would have made for an even more tortuous day without anything to occupy my time. Although I'd never considered me "nerd" or a "geek," as Jimmy had said, maybe he was closer to the truth than I wanted to admit. On the way home, I considered meeting Jimmy and calling the thing off. His possible response to that decision was a concern to me. Besides, I truly did want to write from the experience.

At the appointed time, I was standing by my car, dressed in black jeans, a black long-sleeve shirt and black running shoes. As Jimmy approached me, he guffawed. "What the hell are ya made up for, ninja boy?" He lowered his voice and leaned toward me, saying, "I said that we were going to do a shopliftin' at the mall. We're not breakin' into CIA headquarters, ya geek! Now go back to your apartment like a good little boy and put on somethin' like ya'd go shoppin' in. 'Inconspicuous' is the key, jerkwad." In the timbre of his voice I heard the haranguing tone he'd probably once used to bully other kids on the playground, prodding them into attempting some risky venture, and then conveniently disappearing when the harm was done. As I walked away, he called after me, "And bring a ball cap and a windbreaker!"

My antagonist was still laughing as I entered my building. Changing clothes in my apartment, I wondered how Jimmy would ever know the meaning of, much less be able to use the word "inconspicuous" in a sentence. His was the type who was more comfortable lazing on the sofa in a wifebeater, drinking beer, watching television, and occasionally slapping the "old lady" around. The word "geek" kept echoing in my brain. My intense dislike of Jimmy was growing in proportion to my embarrassment at being so naive. After I'd changed into something more "suitable," I returned to my car. Jimmy was still grinning in amused contempt at my foolishness. I tried not to show either my anger at his ridicule or my nervousness. Even so, I accidentally squealed my car's tires as we pulled away from the parking space.

"Easy there, Clyde Barrow. Are ya sure you're up for this 'great adventure'?" Jimmy asked, the derision in his voice clear.

I smiled back at him, embarrassed by my clumsy driving and somewhat shocked that this dimwit even knew who or what Clyde Barrow was. Apparently, the time he'd spent flaked out in front of his sister's television instead of working had not been a total waste. When we reached the mall, my "partner" directed me to park near the outside of, but not too close to the entrance of a particular department store.

"All right, here's what's gonna happen." Jimmy had turned in his seat to face me after I'd parked, his demeanor all business. "We'll go into the store and—do ya know what ya want to take? Shirts, socks, underwear?" I just stared at him, my mind racing. I'd never considered *what* things I might want to steal. Without waiting for an answer, he continued, oozing sarcasm, "Never mind. Let's just say dress shirts. A *sharp* lawyer like you can always use more dress shirts. First, I'll size up the salespeople. Then I'll get their attention some way. When I think the time is right, I'll take my hat off. When I do that, ya stuff whatever shirts ya want into this bag. Take this and use it to put your stuff in." He handed me a folded shopping bag with handles and with the store's name emblazoned across both sides. He'd been holding it earlier when we met at the car. "After ya put the shirts in it, casually walk to that outside door and leave. When ya get outside, come back to the car as fast as possible, but *do not run*. That way, if mall security happens to be nearby in the parking lot, ya won't arouse their curiosity. Get in the car. I'll be right behind ya. Got it?"

"Yeah, I understand. But this store has those antitheft tabs on their clothes items and the sensors at the doors. The alarms will sound, and I'll get caught," I pleaded.

Jimmy reached for the bag and opened it. "Look, stupid. The bag is lined with aluminum foil. It blocks the sensors from pickin' up the security tabs. Okay? Now slide it inside your jacket in back, out of sight. And *don't* pull it out until you're ready to use it!" He picked up the ball cap sitting in my lap and shoved it hard into my chest, adding, "And here. Wear this pulled down low over your eyes to keep your full face out of the security cameras."

I'd completely forgotten the presence of the store's security cameras! Suddenly, this didn't seem like the great idea I'd envisioned. But Jimmy didn't give me any time to think about it. In short order, he was out of the car, had walked around to my side, and was tapping on my window, chiding me, "Ya comin', geek?"

Once more, I had to suppress my anger. Not that any schooling guaranteed a comparable level of common sense or intelligence, but I had nearly twenty years of formal education and here was this high school dropout calling me stupid and deriding me because I was ignorant of the ways of society's underbelly. Seething would have to come later. Now I had to focus on the matters at hand. My knees nearly gave out as we walked into the store. Surprisingly yet fortunately, customers were rather sparse at the moment we entered. Only two sales associates were working in the men's clothing area where dress shirts were located. We loitered briefly while Jimmy cased the situation. After a minute, one of the two employees called out to the other that he was going to the stockroom for some reason. The second salesperson acknowledged him as she approached us. When she asked if she could help us, Jimmy gently guided her toward another section of the department. I watched for any signal from Jimmy or for any trouble as I pretended to look at shirts. The saleswoman kept glancing in my direction, but Jimmy kept her attention pretty well occupied the whole time. He was smooth. You'd have to give him that much.

Casually, he directed her attention to some item and, as she turned her back to me, he removed his hat with a certain flair and apparently said something funny. She laughed sweetly as I removed the shopping bag from my jacket and starting filling it with shirts. When, in my extremely nervous state, I dropped two of the shirts, I ignored them and kept packing the bag. After what seemed an eternity, I turned and made my way toward the exit we'd come in. Moving across the store, out of the corner of my eye, I could see the sales associate with Jimmy look at me. All my willpower came into play to keep me from running to the door. I approached the sensors at the exit, swallowing hard. Would this gizmo Jimmy had given me really work or was he setting my geeky butt up for a fall and a good laugh? Oh, well, nothing ventured! I passed the sensors without a peep from the alarm and left the store. Once outside I decided that mall security be damned: I was terrified! I walked at a near run to my car. Dropping my keys twice at my car, I finally unlocked the door and got in. Jimmy was right behind me.

As I fumbled to start the car, he looked around the area as he said, "Easy, dude! We're good! That babe didn't suspect anything'! Just leave easy! No burnin' rubber this time, okay?"

As my car cranked, a short-bed pickup truck, marked as mall security, pulled up behind us. The small, flashing amber light atop the truck's cab felt like a giant spotlight aimed directly at me, showing the world a desperate criminal snared in the act of his heinous transgression. I was frozen in place by absolute terror. Jimmy and I looked at each other, he calmer than I. The look on my face must have revealed my panic to him, because he broke into a wide grin. Jimmy was enjoying my horror with every fiber of his being. As the uniformed officer emerged from his truck, all I could see in my rearview mirror was his badge. A civilian joined him beside the truck. Was this some unseen security person from the store? My companion eased out of the car and strolled to the officer.

After a brief conversation, during which Jimmy pointed toward me sitting in the car, the officer looked at me, and then my car. His back to the light placed his features in shadow so I couldn't tell what he was saying. But that bastard Jimmy had given me up! Of that, I was certain! What should I do? What could I do? My car was blocked in! I tried to swallow but realized my mouth was absolutely dry. Before I could act, the officer walked to my side of the car and tapped on the window. As I rolled the window down and looked up into his stern, jowled face, he told me that I had mud on my rear license plate, obscuring it. That, he muttered, was against the law and could get me stopped by the police if they couldn't read the plate. With that, he returned to his truck and moved the vehicle several parking places down the row. As I held back tears of relief, Jimmy slid back onto the seat beside me.

"Take it easy, sport. Some good citizen just now had their car broken into. The mall 'rent-a-cop' was just goin' to make a report on it and noticed your plate. That's all. We're good to go, *unless* ya do somethin' stupid. By the way, what'd he say to you?"

"Something about mud on my license plate. I don't understand how—"

"Oh, yeah," he smiled, "I took the liberty of dirtyin' up your license plate just in case some nosy good citizen or security clown followed us outside and tried to read it as we were leavin'. Just a precaution." He was really enjoying my anxiety.

Still shaking slightly, I eased out of the parking lot. Never had my heart beat so fast! The drive back to the apartment complex was a total blank, except Jimmy babbling all the way about various things. I didn't hear much of what he said except when he "welcomed" me to the ranks of felony offenders as he tallied the prices on the shirts I'd taken. Apparently, their dollar value totaled above the difference between a misdemeanor and a felony charge for theft.

Back at the apartments, we separated after I "thanked" him for his help and promised to return the "special" shopping bag to him when the shirts had been safely deposited at my place. Back in my apartment, I made a drink to try to relax but, nevertheless, paced the floor like a man waiting for the warden to escort him to the death chamber. I couldn't sit. My heart was racing as I pondered what had happened, what I had done. And this was *only* a shoplifting. Writing about a crime, a criminal, and his emotions *had* to be so much easier now. But not tonight. I was too restless in my excitement to write or to succumb to sleep's undertow that night!

Although I saw Jimmy in passing, we didn't speak for a week or so. His concern about my "video" seemed to have waned once I entered his criminal world. The playing field had leveled somewhat. Meanwhile, I sat at my computer and tried to pound out a story. But something was wrong. The words didn't flow like I'd thought they would. The high I'd felt after our Friday night escapade had faded. Committing a shoplifting wasn't much of a basis for a story plot. The emotions and exhilaration I'd felt seemed lacking now, and frustration in my writing attempts resurfaced. Furthermore, I was bored, more lethargic than before. Eventually, the realization that I had to go to the next level of criminal endeavor struck me. While the experience was primarily for my writing's sake, I faced another truth now. I wanted more of that rush I'd experienced! My mind was made up. When I returned the shopping bag, I was going to pressure Jimmy for another "job," as Jimmy had put it.

I spent the following Saturday at the pool, watching for Jimmy. His "special" shopping bag was with me in a gym tote. Late in the afternoon, Jimmy sauntered into the pool area with that arrogant, "I've got the world by the tail" bearing he always reflected. He meandered right past me, not speaking but giving me a knowing smile. He must have looked upon me something like a puppy eager for attention or recognition, neither of which came my way at that moment. Suddenly, I had the same sickening feeling that prey must experience in the wild when they realized they've been singled out for destruction by a predator. But I knew I wanted to go on another job. And I also recognized that I had to be leery of Jimmy and the underlying threat he posed to me. My distrust of him was rising in proportion to his increasing trust in me. It suddenly occurred to me that there was the very strong possibility that Jimmy's actions that night in getting out of the car, talking to the security guard, and pointing at me as I sat in the car were calculated to bring about the very fear I'd felt. He was, in fact, playing with me. There's probably a term for people who enjoy the fear they see in or impose on others. Besides "psychopath," I mean. But the word, whatever it was, escaped me. I'd read about people who get their kicks creating uncomfortable or dangerous situations for others, and then watching them wallow through them. Maybe this was part of Jimmy's psyche.

Lying there, I kept waiting for him to give me some sort of signal so we could talk. Later, Jimmy again walked past my chaise lounge. I pretended to be unaware of his presence. This time he deliberately bumped my seat and moved on. I watched as he left the pool area and walked toward the same mailbox pavilion. Like that small puppy I must have seemed, I dutifully got up and followed him. No one else was in the area when I arrived at the mailboxes where Jimmy waited.

He greeted me with the same sarcasm and contempt. "Well, *Mr. Badass*, did ya sleep much that Friday night?"

"Like a rock, all night long."

"Yeah, right. So you're a wimp *and* a liar." He paused to watch my reaction. I let it drift. When I merely stared at him, he went on, "Ya got my bag, jerkwad?"

"Yeah, it's right in here," I said, indicating my tote. "But, before we get to that, there's something I want to say. I—"

He bowed up at me. "Look, if ya don't like my attitude, go cryin' to your mamma. I don't like some college boy doin' this on a whim. I do this to eat. You're doin' it for kicks. I don't like ya! And I don't care if ya like me! So don't whine to me!"

Enough was enough. "I'm calling 'bullshit!' on your claim of doing it to eat! You're perfectly capable of getting any number of jobs! So don't hand me that crap about needing to steal to eat." I stopped short of telling him I believed he was just too lazy and "no account," as my grandma would say, to get productive work. My anger spent to some extent, I continued, "Look. I don't want to argue with you. What you do is your business if you'll just help me."

"What was that Friday night, jerk?"

"Yeah, but I want to do more."

"Another shopliftin'? Whadda ya need some pants or *lawyer* ties to go with your new shirts?"

"No, not another shoplifting. You obviously have that down to an art form. What else have you done? I mean, I want to step it up a notch. No offense, but shoplifting won't make for very exciting reading in my story."

"You're kiddin', right? 'Step it up a notch' ya say? Ya almost had a heart attack tryin' to pull off a crappy theft," he declared dismissively. "Ya couldn't handle anything tougher!"

"I know you don't like me, Jimmy, but don't sell me short. If you can plan it, I can pull it off."

"Yeah, right!"

"Just try me, *sport*!" I threw his sarcasm back at him, determined to make this happen.

"Okay, *sport*, whadda ya have in mind?"

"What's next up the ladder on your 'résumé'?"

Jimmy studied me for a minute or so, and then looked past me as if lost in thought. Of course he was "lost" in thought, I mused, it was new territory for him. When he broke into one of his wide grins, I didn't know whether to jump with excitement or tremble with fear. "What?" I asked.

"Are ya game for something like a burglary, geek?"

A burglary? Summoning all the bravado I could muster, I leaned toward my "partner in crime" and asserted, "Like I said, Jimmy, if you can plan it, I can pull it off."

"I'll look around a bit. Just hang loose," he said, as he grabbed his bag from me and walked away unexpectedly.

Out of the corner of my eye, I saw what must have caused Jimmy to leave so abruptly. A girl was approaching to check her mail. So I pretended to check my mailbox, and then left.

As I walked back to my apartment, I wondered whether a burglary wasn't more than a *little* over my head. Well, what the hell: two weeks ago, I would have believed the same thing about a shoplifting. Besides, burglaries had to make for much more interesting writing material. Just now, my bigger concern was staying on guard against Jimmy's shenanigans. Aside from distrusting Jimmy, I was growing to hate him increasingly, not simply because of what he was, but because of the level to which I was so willing to sink to get his help. My anger and mounting loathing of Jimmy had not overcome my fear of him, however. And they had not risen above my desire to gain the experience to write a story. To anyone else, going through all this anguish just for the sake of creating a story probably sounded insane, but that's how much I wanted to create a publishable tale.

Several days later, Jimmy signaled to me as I crossed the parking lot outside my apartment. When I walked to where he stood, he told me he'd set up a "job," a burglary, for the coming weekend. Apparently, a buddy of his had reliable information about the comings and goings of a well-to-do family across town. The family kept a fairly large sum of cash in a jewelry box in the master bedroom. Jimmy said it was "there for the taking." Their home security system was in the process of being updated while they were out of town and would be disconnected for a short period of time. I assumed that this security work was probably the source of his inside knowledge. Jimmy made disparaging remarks about the stupidity of the home's owners. After receiving "orders" to wear clothes like the ones I'd initially worn for the shoplifting caper and to buy a pair of dark-colored knit work gloves at a local hardware store, I was sent on my way until late Saturday night.

"Ya know, in all this time, I've never seen ya with a woman. That first night ya said ya had a girlfriend who was tapin' us. Where's she been?" I was driving Jimmy in *my* car toward an upscale neighborhood just before midnight on Saturday. We were using my car again just in case "things went wrong," as Jimmy had explained. As we rode, Jimmy started questioning me.

In for a penny, in for a pound. "She's married," I lied. "It doesn't behoove her or me for us to be too obvious in our movements together. Her husband is somewhat important." I paused and gave him a knowing smile, "She's around."

Again, Jimmy seemed to be studying my face, trying to read my thoughts, my motives. Going through life thinking everyone else is just as conniving and dishonest as you must be tough on one's nerves. Finally, he spoke. "Huh. Who'd a thunk it. A nerd like ya messing around with some important guy's wife. She must be either as dull as dishwater or as ugly as hell or bored out of her skull." He didn't speak for a minute, shaking his head and laughing to himself. His mood hardened, his tone tougher, as he returned to type. "Ya haven't talked to anybody about any of this, have ya?"

I passed on telling Jimmy that the original simile was actually "as dull as ditchwater." That would have amounted to wasted effort. So I merely responded to his question. "No. Why would I talk to anyone? I told you that I have more to lose than you. Besides, I don't even know where the hell we're going." He furtively glanced through the car's back window. "And if you think we're being followed, you can take the wheel anytime!"

That seemed to satisfy him as he relaxed into the seat for the rest of the drive. I grunted, grateful for the reprieve. Later, we parked at a shopping center on a main road and walked some distance through a wooded area behind the stores, which, as it turned out, also abutted the backyard of the target home. Obviously, Jimmy had done his homework.

The surrounding privacy fence was easily scaled, and, as we landed on the other side, I could see Jimmy in the dim moonlight signaling me to be quiet. I wondered what the hell he thought I was going to do! My heart was racing, my mouth was dry as sawdust, and I was too damned frightened to murmur a peep! He then gestured for me to put on my gloves. As I did, Jimmy appeared to be counting windows across the back of the house. When he finished, he nodded at me, and we scurried across the yard to the back of the house. He pointed to a ground-floor window next to us and motioned to me to open it. As I raised my hands to the window, my distrust of Jimmy again came to the forefront. Was his story about the security system being disarmed true? Was the family really out of town? Or was this all a setup? As small a consolation as it might seem, the only solace in the situation was that Jimmy was standing next to me and would also be subject to any harm or retribution I might get in the next few minutes. So I raised the unlocked window slowly. No *audible* alarm anyway. So far, so good.

Jimmy boosted me into the shoulder-high opening. Pushing the drapes aside, I found that the room I was climbing into was pitch black. I reached out to feel the area in which I would be landing and realized that there were no obstacles present and the bottom of the window was only about a foot above the floor. I crawled inside and pulled Jimmy in behind me. He produced a small LED light. In the light, we could see that we were in a large bedroom, possibly a master suite, with no apparent signs of life.

Jimmy grabbed my shoulder, pulled me toward him, leaned into me, and whispered, "Go over to the door and keep a lookout in the hallway, just in case."

"Here it comes," I thought. The double-cross. But, in the dim light of the LED, I could see nothing in Jimmy's face that gave me greater concern. He seemed focused only on getting what we'd come for. As I crossed the room, he moved to a jewelry box on a nearby dresser.

I stood in the hallway just outside the bedroom door, trying to make sense of what I supposed I could see in the darkness. Then I heard them! The unmistakable sounds of claws moving cautiously, stealthily on a hardwood floor! Now my heart was about to burst out of my chest! Suddenly, I heard the claws scuttling faster across the floor as their owner seemed to realize he was not alone. When I turned to go back into the bedroom, the door was slowly closing behind me! I fell against the door as I looked back down the long hallway. My eyes had adjusted to the dim light. Gradually, I could make out the form of a large, snarling dog coming my way. Then the canine began to charge as I pushed hard against the nearly unyielding door and forced my way back into the bedroom! The dog hit the door just I managed to close it! As the animal on the other side of the door raised holy hell, growling, barking, and clawing, I realized that Jimmy was beside me, leaning his back against the door, laughing. "This is funny, you son of a bitch? Were you closing the door on me, asshole?" I demanded in the loudest whisper I dared.

"Cool it, jerkwad. We've gotta get out of here!"

We both moved for the opened window, clambered out, and ran like hell.

"What were you trying to do back there? Get me killed?" We had reached the parking lot safely, and my anger overcame my sense of urgency about leaving.

"No, I—"

I stopped running and screamed at him, "Look, asshole, that door didn't close by itself!"

"Of course not!" Jimmy yelled back, moving on to the car. "When I heard the dog, I tried to move over to the door to get ya outta there! I accidentally hit the door, and it started to close about the time ya were tryin' to come back in the room! My laughin' was just what ya might call a nervous reaction! That's all, geek!" Still angry and not satisfied with his inane excuses, I followed him to the car. Once back inside the car, I maintained such calm as I could muster. He, too, quieted, continuing, "Now shut up and drive us out of here! And don't burn no rubber!"

As my shaking hand started the car, I couldn't decide if Jimmy was calm because he was telling me the truth about what had happened or because he'd just intentionally scared the hell out of me and was savoring the moment. As much as I might think the former was possible, I knew the latter to be far more likely. Jimmy truly was a pissant. As we rode through the night, I caught a sideways glimpse of Jimmy's face in the street lights. It held the faintest hint of a knowing grin. At that moment, I recognized the truth. He knew the dog would be there.

When Jimmy caught me cutting my eyes toward him, he tried to divert my focus. "Ya didn't ask if the money was there. Check this!" With that, he pulled a large wad of bills from the pocket of his hoodie. "Half of whatever's here's yours."

"I told you I'm not in this for any money. All I ever wanted was the experience."

"Okay. So you're sayin' ya don't want *any* of this?" His voice was disbelieving, yet hopeful.

I merely shook my head in disgust while I tried to slow my breathing back to normal, from the frisson that encompassed me.

Despite my concerns about Jimmy and my questions about his actions, my adrenaline was still pumping. A rush, a high like this was new to me. Learning that I'd passed my bar exam had not brought me this kind of excitement. I'd read about criminals who committed crimes just for the sheer rush of adrenaline, the exhilaration. But I'd never dreamed that it could be like this.

Before Jimmy got out of the car at the apartments, I asked about trying one last "job" to complete my "experience in crime." I knew he wouldn't be able to resist tormenting me one more time. When he asked what, if anything, I had in mind, I threw out the idea of a robbery, fighting to keep buried my disbelief in and distaste for what I was proposing. Jimmy seemed truly taken aback but smiled at the idea. He put up no argument. He said he'd think it over and get back with me.

"Well, are ya still up for a new 'adventure', Mr. Badass?" Jimmy had walked up behind me at the mailboxes several days later. He glanced around before he spoke again. He made no effort to hide his contempt for me.

I looked him hard in the eyes and reminded him that I'd held up my end so far, and that, if he could plan it, I could pull it off. Despite his disdain for me, he couldn't argue that point.

He bowed up his sinewy frame. "I'm bettin' ya didn't sleep much Saturday night. But ya get used to the feeling. I can pull anything now and come back here and sleep on a clothesline."

Despite his attitude, I smiled slightly. "No, I didn't. Not much." I decide not to lie this time. "I'm just not in your 'league', Jimmy. I—"

"And ya never will be!" he interrupted. His swagger returned with my admission of 'weakness.' "Just remember that!"

"Okay, you win," I conceded. "What's the verdict?"

He smiled wickedly. "Don't like the word 'verdict,' geek." He looked around before continuing. "But we're going after a convenience store. Are you game?"

"Yeah, I'm in."

"Okay, tonight we're meetin' somebody to buy a gun."

"A gun?" I asked louder than I meant to.

He grabbed my arm, pulled me toward him, and, through clenched teeth, seethed, "Why don't ya say that a little louder, jerkwad? I don't think all the folks at the pool heard ya."

Pulling away from his grip, I lowered my voice. "Sorry. Do we need a gun? I didn't say anything about an *armed* robbery!" He was grinning at me, knowingly. I swallowed hard as I fought to save face. "Besides, don't you already have one?"

"No. I don't normally use a gun in my 'line of work.' And, yeah, we need one. Convenience store clerks aren't likely to hand over cash if we just point our fingers at them and ask politely, dumbass. And if they pull some smart move, I want to be able to at least bluff 'em."

I hated his condescending attitude, and I wasn't crazy about where this was going, but I was in too far now. "All right. When and where?"

"Meet me at my car tonight at nine o'clock."

"*Your* car?" This was out of character for him and my wariness was aroused.

"Yeah, *my* car. These folks we're meetin' know me and my car. A strange car might blow the deal. After we get the gun, we'll come back here and get *your* car for the job. Any problem with that?"

"No." In his criminal logic, it made perfect sense. I relaxed a little. "What kind of gun are we getting?"

"Why? Ya thinking of becomin' a collector, geek?"

"Forget it, asshole! I just—"

"Okay," he relented slightly, "we'll probably just get a 'Saturday night special.'"

"That's a thirty-eight caliber, isn't it?"

"Maybe it will be and maybe it won't be, college boy. Could be a 40 caliber or a 9 or a 357. Haven't made up my mind. And it depends on what's available to buy. See ya at nine. Wear something inconspicuous. And, by the way, ya need to bring two hundred dollars for the gun."

Inconspicuous. That two-dollar word had been broadcast again from that ten-cent brain. "Two hundred dollars?"

"Yeah. You're buyin'. Besides, you're not in this for money anyway. Right?"

"Yeah, okay," I called out in a stage whisper as he sauntered away.

Nine o'clock tonight. I looked at my watch. That meant that I had seven hours to get set before we'd meet again.

At the appointed hour, we met and were on our way to make the buy. We found ourselves in a section of town with which I was unfamiliar and in which I was *very* uncomfortable. Jimmy did all the talking to a tall, black male in a vacant lot. The man's entourage was obviously familiar with Jimmy but repeatedly gave me the once-over. After we'd bought the gun, we started back to the apartments. Leaving that area of town gave me no regrets whatsoever. Back at his building, Jimmy went inside for a minute before we switched cars and drove away.

When we arrived at the store Jimmy'd chosen, he told me to me drive past it and park in a small strip shopping center around the corner. We were in a high-crime area, well known in the local media for robberies, drug deals, and prostitution. I looked around. Most of the shopping center was abandoned and boarded up, with what remained of its masonry charred and crumbling. Any segment of the shopping center that *may* have been occupied by businesses was closed for the night. The shoddy convenience store was on a corner, perpendicular to the strip shopping center and its parking lot.

He turned in his seat to face me and handed me the gun we'd bought. "I'll go check things out first. Ya stay a little behind me, around the corner of the store, and watch me. If and when it's all clear, I'll give ya a signal. Then ya put this on," he said, handing me a toboggan hat with mouth and eyeholes cut out of it, "and go in holding the gun and demand the money. Then—"

"Wait just a damned minute! I'm not pulling this off by myself while you watch!"

"We *are* doing this thing together, ya moron! Look, I don't expect to find anyone except some foreigner behind the counter. This time of night's not normally busy for this place. That's why we're here. And this place doesn't have security video. The hats are just a precaution." As he started to get out of the car, he stopped, turned back to me, and continued, "So's ya know, the gun's empty. No sense you hurting someone accidentally, including me. Now give me a ten-second head start. Then follow me to the front corner of the store."

As I watched him move away, I found that I was actually counting the seconds. I was that scared! Was I really crazy enough to go through this with a person like Jimmy who I hated and distrusted so much? This would be it! If I didn't have the experience I needed to write after tonight, too bad! In the dim light, I tinkered with the gun as the final seconds passed before getting out of the car. As I held the gun, it felt cold and totally foreign to me. Time. Moving to the front corner of the store, I saw Jimmy peering in a window. He glanced around, then looked at me and nodded. As I approached him, I pulled the toboggan hat over my head and adjusted the holes so I could see what the hell I was doing. Jimmy was doing the same. We entered the door at the same time. Just as Jimmy had said, an undersized, young man with Middle Eastern features stood alone behind the counter. No one else appeared to be in the store. Jimmy took up a position off to my right.

Holding the gun in front of me, I yelled, "This is a robbery! Give us your money!"

The clerk stood there in stunned silence, only slightly raising his hands.

More nervous than anything else, I screamed again, "Give us your money! Now!"

Jimmy moved behind the counter. He shoved the clerk to the cash register and made him open it. The young man was clearly as frightened as I was. After Jimmy got the money, he appeared to be looking for something else behind the counter. Suddenly he pushed the clerk in the shoulder, pointed to something on a lower shelf behind the counter, and yelled him, "Use it, his gun's empty! Shoot him! Do it now, damn it!" As he punched the clerk again, Jimmy looked at me and laughed.

My eyes quickly moved from Jimmy to the clerk and back again, waiting for either one's next move. I didn't have to wait long. The young man fainted and fell forward over the counter before dropping back to the floor and out of sight. I took the opportunity to run from the store and around the corner to the parking lot where my car was parked. Stopping there, I was bent over trying to catch my breath, as I removed the toboggan hat. Jimmy ran to my side, laughing his ass off. My eyes were quickly adjusting to the dim light. I could see that he'd already removed his hat.

"Man, that was hilarious! Ya should have seen your face, geek! And that kid! Was he scared or what?" Jimmy stood upright from his doubled-over position as he howled with laughter between words. "Did ya see—?"

As he spoke, I quickly put the barrel of my gun against his sternum. Without a second's hesitation, I pulled the trigger three times in quick succession. The gun discharged with momentarily deafening blasts. In Jimmy's face I saw a dying look of utter shock and disbelief. No one can imagine the sense of satisfaction I took away from his expression in that moment. As he dropped to the ground, I walked to my car, throwing the gun, the hat, the various calibers of ammunition I'd purchased earlier in the day, and, finally, my pair of work gloves on the roof of the various sections of the closed strip shopping center. I glanced back a Jimmy's body as I quietly, calmly drove away. How would the authorities see this? A drug deal gone bad? A falling-out among thieves? It mattered not to me.

Now. Now I'm ready to write.

ONE MORE STATISTIC

Irving sat in the dimly lighted breakfast room, just off the kitchen, drinking a cup of coffee. Even though he couldn't hear it clearly, he knew the wind's velocity was increasing. The cover of the stove vent fan began to clatter. It always happened the same way: the vent cover started rattling, and then the rain came. He normally found the noise unnerving. But now, it was soothing somehow. The authorities had issued an evacuation order, but he remained. Fran stayed, too, but, then, she had no choice. He'd waited three hurricane seasons for this very eventuality and nothing, no one was going to stand in the way of his plans. In due course, the banging increased in its frantic, irregular tempo. And the rain came. Came hard and stayed.

At one point, Irving stood and walked to the living-room window. Oh yeah, this storm was going to be a doozy. It had rained steadily, with a ruthless vigor, throughout the night and into the morning. Through the unrelenting rain and the faint, early-morning light, he could see that the wind was already bending the palm trees like so many blades of grass, as they danced in time with the wind and the downpour. A wooden Adirondack chair and various items of debris gamboled down the street. A faint smile crossed his lips. And the height of the storm was yet to come, he thought. We're just to the east of the hurricane's center, the more dangerous side of its path. As a result, we're bound to take the worst it has to offer, because the wind's strength is increased by the hurricane's forward motion. Irving smiled again, broader this time. He'd learned a *few* things in all these years living on the coast.

He returned to the kitchen, poured another cup of coffee, and sat back down at the breakfast table to resume his vigil. As the raindrops hit the vent cover like so many pebbles thrown by an angry sky, he thought back about what had brought him and his anger to this point.

His and Fran's marriage had been a hurried, reckless undertaking at best, he recently returning from the craziness of Vietnam and trying to catch up with the time he felt he'd lost while in the service, she trying to overtake the lives her married peers had been living without her. Soon after their nuptials they learned Fran was pregnant. But, by the time the child, a daughter, was born, Irving and Fran found themselves in a loveless union. Divorce wasn't the answer for either. Fran was willing to continue living the lie by keeping up the appearances of a normal family scene. For Irving's part, he loved his daughter too much to risk losing her, even part of the time, in a custody battle. So they settled into trying to make the best of a bad situation. From this arrangement, Irving had learned just how close the words "marriage" and "mirage" really could be in their meanings. The "stalemate" was barely tolerable as the years passed. What made it bearable for Irving was his very close bond with his daughter. Nonetheless, as time passed and the cloud over the marriage grew to a thunderhead, the girl grew more distant from the family unit, including Irving.

Eventually, their daughter went off to college, married, and moved on, obviously very happy to be out from under the dour existence that her home life had become. Irving often rebuked himself for letting the misery of the marriage keep him from being a better father. Maybe he should have tried harder while they were all together. He'd never been able to do so. Although it was a situation of his own making, he resented being "trapped" in the marriage, and it affected every aspect of his life, including the relationship with the girl. Psychologically, he'd become a wretched creature.

About the time he'd "lost" his daughter, Irving came face to face with the catastrophic illness that had struck Fran, leaving her wheelchair bound and in need of constant care and attention. At the time, he'd told himself that he was really stuck in the marriage now. Despite his feelings of anger and resentment, he could not, would not walk away and be seen as a heartless fiend who left a loving, devoted, helpless woman at a calamitous time. Not surprisingly, the many years of such duty to a woman he detested made Irving's bitterness grow exponentially. Now, that servitude was about to end.

Suddenly, the appearance of car headlights brought Irving back from his reminiscence. The evacuation had long since been called for. What was this? He moved quickly to the living-room window. As the beams raked the house, Irving stepped aside from the window and watched from the darkened room as a Belvedere Township Police Department vehicle passed slowly down the street, creating a wake from the chassis-deep water and dodging wreckage as it moved. The authorities were out and about making certain, as best they could, that the evacuation order had been followed. Irving had no cause for alarm. All their neighbors had left the area some time ago with Irving's assurances that he and Fran would be right behind them, joining the massive exodus of evacuees. His car was safely tucked away in the detached garage behind the house, and no lights were on in the house. The house looked "abandoned." But there was no need to let some sharp-eyed, young officer spy him standing in the window at this late stage. The prowl car moved away, no doubt heading for the dry safety of the police garage before the brunt of the storm skidded across the panhandle.

He turned and moved back to the breakfast room table where the radio softly hummed a storm update from the National Hurricane Center. "The category three storm is coming ashore in the area of Staysail Beach," the stern-voiced announcer warned. "The storm, which has gathered strength as it plowed across the Caribbean and carved a path of devastation, has left dozens of people dead in its wake. Local and state authorities are making every effort to eliminate, or at least minimize that statistic here. Please … ."

As the radio broadcast continued, Irving smiled to himself. Well, he thought, there's going to be at least one fatality left here in the path of this storm. At that moment, the house shuddered. He looked around. He hoped to hell that wasn't the roof trying to pull away. He'd been paying premiums to that bloodsucking insurance company all these years, but he didn't want to deal with them any more than necessary this time. The paperwork on Fran would be enough of a pain in the butt.

He poured another cup of coffee and moved toward the patio door. As he walked, the house seemed to moan in protest against the hurricane. Behind him, the radio went silent. "Power's gone," Irving said softly. "We're in for it now." At the door, he peered over his cup at the backyard. One thing in particular caught Irving's eye. Between the slats of the partially opened vertical blinds, he could see that stupid mimosa tree Fran had insisted on planting, bending helplessly against the merciless wind. It might not survive the tempest. Two birds with one storm. He smiled. Fran called it a "heavenly" tree, but he saw it as the tree from hell. That damned thing propagated everywhere. He'd long since decided to forego the backache involved in pulling the seedlings and simply mowed them down as fast as they appeared. And that "weed tree," as he called it, left mounds of pink fuzz all over his vegetable garden. The sooner it's gone, the better. He momentarily studied the translucent corrugated fiberglass panels covering the patio. They vibrated slightly in the high wind. Just so they stay in place until he needed them, he reflected, all would be fine.

Before going back to the breakfast room, he walked down the hall to check on Fran. She was slumped in her wheelchair in the bedroom where he'd left her, sleeping off the effects of the sedative he'd given her. If his calculations were correct, and they usually were, she'd be out when it happened. He was known for his meticulous planning. This time would be no exception.

Satisfied, Irving walked back to the kitchen. The automatic timer on the pot had turned the thing off. He poured another cup before the coffee cooled. As he stood there looking out the kitchen window, he picked up the telephone. Dead. Good. Again, his luck and timing held true.

He returned to the breakfast room and switched the radio from electric to battery power. The device hummed back to life, spewing forth information on the latest developments. Sitting at the table, he contemplated what the next several days would bring. In about forty-eight hours, he would be known across the country, possibly around the globe. Irving would be held up as an older, arthritic-prone hero, who, alone and with no means to obtain help, tried desperately to evacuate his invalid wife from the fury of a killer hurricane. In her terror, she fought his efforts to the point he'd had to sedate her in order to try to save her. The fact that he started the evacuation too late, in no small part due to his wife's resistance, would be forgiven and forgotten when the world learned of his valiant labors against the wrath of the storm. Unfortunately, he would be unsuccessful. Fran would die in the storm's mighty rage. And he would be "trapped" until he could get someone's attention with calls for help and be rescued. Known to only himself, it would be another "trap" of his own making. And sympathy would wash over him like the storm surge now covering the area. The story should be good enough to get him, red-eyed and suffering the anguish of loss, a spot on Fox News or CNN. Irving thought he could possibly sell his painful, yet gallant story to *Reader's Digest* or maybe one of those sappy made-for-television movies. People eat that crap up, he thought, smiling to himself.

Irving sat quietly for a while, listening to the hurricane's rage. He had no difficulty hearing it now. Only periodic, unidentifiable crashes outside interrupted his solitude. Funny, he thought, how his despair would end in a storm pouring from the heavens. He'd often joke to his few close friends that his and Fran's marriage was made in heaven—the same place that produced thunder and lightning. They never knew just how sincerely he meant those words.

Irving glanced at his watch. By his estimation, the time had arrived. He left the half-finished cup of coffee on the table. No sense making things look too neat and orderly under the dire circumstances. Back in the bedroom, he scattered some of Fran's clothing about to give the appearance of a man frantically trying to dress and move the dead weight of a heavy, invalid woman. The stage was set.

Fran still slumbered as Irving pushed the wheelchair down the hall to the room overlooking the patio. He paused there as he braced himself for the ordeal to come. This would be a test of his strength and will, through which, he'd repeatedly told himself, he could and would prevail. Irving rubbed his knobby, achy hands together, not in relish, but in determination to see his plan through. In his resolve, he refused even to look at Fran from this point on. She was a mere object which he would cast aside with no more thought than one employed in disposing of a used tissue.

A strong rush of air pushed past Irving as he opened the patio door. The sources of the crashes sounding in the rooms behind him would have to be dealt with later. Fearing excessive damage to his home, Irving hurriedly pushed Fran through the open door and, just as quickly, closed it behind them.

The rain, driving all but horizontally against him, stung his face. Fran didn't stir. The violent wind made his every effort to move her a nightmare in pain. Moving slowly against the storm, Irving placed Fran's wheelchair in the position he'd calculated would cause her the most injury when the patio cover "fell." Since the first warning that the hurricane would probably make landfall in their area, he'd worked meticulously in preparing the patio roof to be manipulated into its crash and on locating the proper point of impact. His strength was ebbing, but his greatest challenge lie ahead. Nearly blinded by the driving rain, he fought the wind to move to the point of the patio from which he could raise the cover slightly before letting it drop, crushing Fran. If, by chance, the structure didn't finish her life, he would simply use a piece of four-by-four lumber and complete the job himself before assuming his "trapped" position.

Summoning all his remaining strength, Irving used a timber to lift the corner of the cover and pushed its support away. Just before he released it, he saw movement in his peripheral vision. To his horror, he realized that the wind had blown Fran's wheelchair from the spot in which he'd placed her. He had forgotten to set the brake. As it rolled backward toward the house, Irving panicked. Fighting the strong, gusting wind and biting rain, he reached out for her. As he did, he lost control of the timber holding the roof above him. The timber he held fell away, and the patio cover dropped on him.

Although the crash stunned him and he was held down by the structure, Irving initially felt no pain aside from a few minor scratches and soreness. He was convinced he'd come through the crash otherwise unscathed. *This is only a momentary setback*, he reasoned. He could see Fran, stupid, oblivious Fran still flopped safely in her wheelchair, now protected from the chief force of the elements by the fallen cover. Suddenly, he coughed and tasted the metallic flavor of blood in his mouth. At that point, Irving became conscious of the strawberry-colored blood disgorging from his neck, covering his shirt and spreading across the patio. Apparently, the sharp edge of a corrugated panel had scraped across his neck and cut his jugular vein! Now, his reasoning turned to terror! Irving's frantic efforts to lift the structure and free himself were in vain! He'd exhausted most of his strength positioning Fran and raising the patio roof. Despite feeling himself turn to liquid below the waist, his body began to shudder involuntarily, his legs kicking senselessly. Gradually, he began to feel chilly despite the warmth of the day. As he continued to struggle, Irving grasped the hopelessness of his situation. As he lie there, he realized that his predictions would only partly come to fruition. He would be seen as a sympathetic, yet *unsuccessful* hero, *unable* to safely evacuate his wife from the killer storm. And there *would*, indeed, be at least one more death here in the wake of the hurricane.

Blood and rain almost blinded Irving. His thrashing about diminished as he grew steadily weaker. Just before his eyes closed for the final time, he looked at Fran with vision blurred by blood and rain. Her eyes were open. Had the noise of the crash awakened her? The howling wind? The stinging rain? He focused on her face. Their eyes met. Fran returned his hard gaze. And smiled.

THE NAKED BANKER

The sun rose on a cold, rainy Saturday as Jeff Hutchinson turned his somewhat dilapidated 1964 Plymouth Belvedere into the parking lot, eased down the hill, and pulled into a parking space in front of Lori's townhouse. He sat for a long time listening to the idle of the car's newly restored 426-horsepower hemi engine. If only the rest of this heap was in the same shape as the mill, he thought. He smiled with mixed emotions: a work of love in progress costing money he didn't have. Restoring a "classic" like this just takes time and money—mostly money. He sighed.

Jeff was still smiling with satisfaction at the purring of the engine when he heard Lori calling his name from her front door in her best stage whisper. Looking up through the drizzling rain, he saw Lori, standing in her bathrobe, frantically waving him into the townhouse. He said to himself, "Oh, God, what now?" Lori was always getting hyper about something: the old car he drove and into which he poured what money he could scrape together, the "sloppy" clothes he wore, the jobs he couldn't keep. Life with her was an estrogen-powered roller coaster. No wonder their relationship was what the experts might call "on-again, off-again." Lori was a real looker with a fantastic body and was great fun, but there were other things in his life that made him happy, too. Besides, this was way too early on a Saturday morning to be as keyed up as she apparently was.

Lori couldn't understand what Jeff saw in that rolling scrapheap he called a car. Now, when she desperately needed his help, he just sat there like an idiot with the engine running. Sometimes it seemed as if he cared more about that car than he did her. Jeff had a great body and was a lot of fun to be with, but, when he wasn't in jail for some petty crime or another, he was under the hood of that stupid car. No wonder her dad referred to him as "jailhouse Jeff." Truth be known, while she felt she loved Jeff, Lori often thought that the *only* reason she stayed with him was to irritate her dad, who had always tried to control every aspect of her life. Besides, she had always been attracted to the "bad boys" she'd met, even in college where she'd first met Jeff. But his lack of attention and dread of commitment had brought her to her present predicament. Now she stood with the cold drizzle blowing against her, fighting back tears of fear and frustration, and trying to get Jeff inside.

Jeff climbed out of the car and hurried through the rain to Lori. As he approached her, she stepped back inside the doorway. When he reached her, she wrapped her arms around him and held him tightly, more than her usual welcoming hug. He reciprocated, smiling widely, thinking he knew where this would lead.

"Oh, Jeff," Lori sobbed plaintively. "I really need you."

"I'm here for you, Babe," he smiled. He drew back slightly and saw the tears in her eyes. This was worse than normal, even for her. "What? What's the matter, Lori?"

She pulled him close to her again and began to cry quietly. "Jeff, I need your help and understanding. Mostly your understanding."

A sudden wave of panic swept over Jeff. His first guess was that she was pregnant. What in the hell would he do now? Jeff loved Lori in his own, unconventional way, as she must love him, but he was not ready for a kid or a marriage. He had too many things he wanted to do without those obligations, those burdens. With mixed concern, annoyance, and dread, he pressed on, "What is it, Lori? What's wrong?" When she didn't answer immediately, his frustration rose at his certainty of her answer and he continued, "Let's have it, Lori. Tell me!"

Lori pulled back slightly, looked up into Jeff's eyes, and read his thoughts.

She smiled through her tears. "Oh. No, Jeff. It's not what you think." The smile disappeared as she said, "It's really worse than that."

"What could be worse than that?" Realizing the harshness of his words, Jeff tried to soften his tone. "I mean what could be this bad, Babe?"

Lori led him to the sofa and eased him down. She sat beside him and started crying again. Jeff waited. Finally, she spoke. "Jeff, something terrible has happened. I need your help. But I need you to not be angry with me. You know I love you. And I'm counting on you loving me as much as you've told me you do."

"Okay," he said with uncertainty. "What is it?"

"Come with me."

Lori led Jeff up the stairs to the townhouse's only bedroom. As they climbed the steps, she spoke over her shoulder. "Please, Jeff … ." She squeezed his hand. He squeezed hers in return, mostly out of habit.

Her bedroom door was slightly ajar. When they reached it, Lori pushed it open slowly, turning away as she did. Jeff looked in, not knowing what to expect. There on Lori's bed was an older man, his face and shoulders pressed down into the sheet-covered mattress. His lower body rested on his knees with his naked butt sticking up in the air. The man appeared to be dead. Jeff was simultaneously dumbfounded and amused at the absurdity of the image before him. He turned to Lori, who had begun to sob again.

"What the—Who the hell is that?"

"He's … he was my boss at the bank. Mr. Baynham."

Jeff's disbelief now turned to anger. "Baynham? The 'Baynham Savings and Loan' Baynham? What the hell was going on here?"

"Jeff, please—"

" 'Please,' hell! What is this, Lori? I thought we loved each other!"

"I do love you, Jeff, but, lately, you haven't seemed the slightest bit interested in taking our relationship to the next level."

"What the hell does that mean? You know how I feel about you! And you're having an affair with some old fart behind my back?"

"It was not an *affair*, Jeff!" Lori reacted angrily.

"Really? What *were* you doing? Auditing the bank's books?"

"This was the first time he'd come over here, Jeff!"

"Really? First and last, it looks like! So where'd you get together before today?"

"No! I mean we'd never done this before last night! And nothing happened last night!"

"Last night?" Jeff exclaimed.

Lori grabbed his shoulders to calm him, and then tried to compose herself before continuing. "Before anything could happen, Mr. Baynham became 'excited' and began to curl up like he is now. I thought at first he was just being kinky. Then, when he grabbed his chest and his eyes began to bulge, I realized something was wrong." She reached out and took Jeff's hand. "Please, Jeff, I've been through a lot. When it happened, I lay there and cried hysterically for a long time. Then it took me almost an hour to get out from under him."

" 'Out from under him'? Oh great!"

"Where'd you think I was when he started getting excited, Jeff? Downstairs vacuuming? Look, he's been coming on to me for some time, and I've deflected his attentions until now. You weren't around, and, since you didn't seem to be interested in being around, I gave in. Besides, Mr. Baynham's very rich and can do a lot for me at the bank."

Jeff composed himself slightly. "Wait a minute! 'Last night'? If this happened last night, why are you just now calling me?"

Lori stamped a foot while screaming, "Oh my God, Jeff! I was scared out of my mind! After I finally got out from under him, I sat here all night crying, wondering what to do about a naked dead man in my bed! Trying to figure out who I could get help from!" Lori's voice softened as she wrapped her arms around Jeff. "Every time, I came back to you, Babe. Please … please help me. What can I do?"

Realizing that Lori really needed him and that his anger would not solve any problems facing her at that moment, Jeff inhaled deeply and relaxed a little more. "Well, first of all, let's go downstairs and get away from this lovely image. And then we'll talk." Jeff pulled the door closed and started downstairs with Lori close on his heels, as if the specter in her bedroom would come after her in retribution for her abandonment.

As they sat down on the sofa, Jeff asked Lori whether there was any beer in the place. Her shock at the early hour for drinking beer, even for Jeff, was short-lived when he reminded her of the unfamiliarity of the circumstances with which they were dealing. Sitting back a few minutes later, beer in hand, Jeff went through a series of questions trying to analyze the situation. His first thought of just having Lori call the police and telling them the truth, after giving him a substantial time to leave the area, of course, was dismissed by Lori. "He's married, Jeff. I can't deal with the shame of possibly having to face his wife with this. And it would mean my job, for sure."

"Yeah, you're right. The old girl would probably keel over herself."

Lori shook her head, "Oh, Mrs. Baynham's not old. Not nearly Mr. Baynham's age anyway. That's a joke at the bank: Mr. Baynham's money getting him a trophy wife. She's much younger than he is …

uh, was. And beautiful, too. I've seen her when she's come into Mr. Baynham's office at the main bank."

"Mmmm. A trophy wife, huh? How could that old fart manage that?"

"Well, the bank is one of the few family-owned and operated community banks left in the state. Mr. Baynham's dad started it after the depression, and it's been a huge success. He won't give in to pressure to sell out to the bigger multistate banks. He took it over when his dad got sick years ago. He's built BS&L up to an even stronger institution with six branches in this part of the state. Besides, Baynham's very rich."

"You sound like a damned commercial, Lori. Just how rich was this guy anyway? How come I've never heard of him outside of you working for him?"

Lori gave him a cynical smirked. "Jeff, when's the last time you read *any* financial page or the social page of *any* newspaper?"

"Okay, okay. So he's rich. And he has a beautiful young wife. So, no offense, but what's he doing here with you, Lori?"

For a moment, Lori just glared at Jeff. When she felt he'd finally realized the stupidity of his comment and regretted it, she responded. "The story at the bank is that she may be young and beautiful, but his wife's cold as a fish to Mr. Baynham. Janean, his private secretary at the bank, heard him talking to her on the phone one day. Janean said he sounded like a dog begging for a bone. But Mrs. Baynham obviously loves his money."

"So calling the police is out. Besides, they're going to give you hell for not calling last night when this first happened. Why don't we just leave his body on his wife's doorstep?"

"Oh, Jeff, what a horrible thing to even think about! I'm upset enough without you suggesting something like that!"

He raised his eyebrows and responded sarcastically, "I didn't realize Baynham meant so much to you."

"It's not that, and you know it! But he was a sweet old man who seemed to care a lot for me!"

"Yeah, right! One look at that carcass upstairs and I know what he cared about!"

Lori was stunned and hurt by the snide remark but stopped herself from responding. Jeff was lucky to have her and he knew it, she reassured herself. Likewise, Jeff knew immediately that he'd said the wrong thing. I'm lucky to have Lori with me, he said to himself. Thinking the better of it, he didn't say anything more, not even to apologize. The two sat in silence for a long while. The quiet was broken by an occasional heavy sigh or a whimper from Lori. Jeff kept thinking how glad he was to have Lori in a position to really need him, to have him take charge in a manly way, and to handle something this important for her.

Suddenly, Jeff was struck with an idea but was hesitant to suggest it to Lori. After waiting a time, his nature finally got the better of him. "Look, we both need money, right? I mean you don't want to be stuck in that bank the rest of your life and I'm employment-challenged at the moment. What if we call Mrs. Baynham and try to get some cash for the geezer? Like a ransom?"

Through an outburst of renewed sobs, Lori screamed, "Jeff! If I couldn't think of just leaving him on the doorstep, how could I possibly think about doing something like that?"

Jeff sat quietly, appropriately chastised for his inappropriate suggestion. Finally, he spoke. "All right, here's what we do. I'll make an anonymous call to Mrs. Baynham and tell her that her husband died of an apparent heart attack while at a meeting or something. I'll offer to leave the body somewhere for her to claim or deliver it for her to pick up or something." At Lori's harsh look, he assured her,

"No ransom demand! I won't give my name. That way, just in case something goes wrong, there'll be nothing to connect you with me or with the body."

"But, Jeff, he's dead! There'll be questions!"

"It's a natural death, Lori. No crime was committed. Like I said, we can say he was meeting with me in my car or his car when he had—oh my God, Lori, *his car*! I didn't even think of that before! Where is *his car*?"

At that question Lori started sobbing uncontrollably again. After a time, she managed an answer. "It's in a parking space about two townhouses down! It's a black Lexus! What'll we do about his car, Jeff?"

"Just calm down, Babe!" Jeff's mind raced. "Wait! Let me think!" After a minute or so, he went on, "Okay, this is the deal! Probably nobody's looking for his car yet. No reason to, I hope. We'll worry about his car after I talk to the misses. Wherever we decide to take the body, we'll get there with his car first. You can drive my car, and I'll take Baynham in his car. Still no connection to you." Jeff stood up suddenly. "I need to go to the store real quick."

"What for?"

"I'm guessing the rich all have caller ID. So I'm not using your phone or mine. And I'm not risking being seen using some pay phone somewhere. I'm going to pay cash for a disposable cell phone."

Lori's tears subsided as she was taken aback at Jeff's deliberative process. "Wow. You've thought this out!"

"Pretty much." He bent down and took her hands in his. "I'll do anything for you, to protect you, Lori. You need to know that, Babe."

She smiled warmly and leaned forward to kiss him tenderly, when he continued, "By the way, do you have $50.00 I can use to get the phone?"

Despite the affection of his earlier words, this last question brought Lori back to the reality of her circumstance. "Sure," she sighed. "I think so."

She retrieved her purse and the money. Cash in hand, Jeff turned to leave. He stopped just short of the front door and turned back to Lori. "Just stay here 'til I get back. Don't answer the phone or the door." As he went through the door, he stuck his head back in. "Lori, while I'm gone, why don't you save us some time later on and put Baynham's clothes back on him?"

"I will not! I'm sitting right here 'til you get back!"

He suddenly realized the absurdity of asking her to do something like that in her present state. "Oh, yeah. Sorry," he said as he ducked out of the door.

When Jeff returned a short time later, he found Lori still on the sofa, wrapped in a blanket. The scattering of used tissues around the living room, which had been there when he first arrived, had grown in number. He realized that she was still pretty shaken. She was crying aloud when he came in. He needed desperately to calm her for the task ahead and the best way would be by showing her he was in full control.

"Okay, I have a phone with sixty prepaid minutes on it. Use 'em up and throw it away. No problem. I'm driving somewhere else to call the widow. Do you have her number?"

"Yes, but why not call from here?"

"Just a precaution, Babe. In case something goes wrong, I don't want cell-phone tower triangulation to lead anyone here."

"How do you know about any such thing?"

"As much as I hate to bring it up at a time like this, you can't spend time in jail without learning a few things here and there."

"But I want to go with you. I don't want to stay here alone again while he's up there."

"Fine, but you need to get dressed so we can go. We can't drag this out."

Lori hesitated. "Jeff, would you please go upstairs and get me my jeans, a sweater, and some shoes?"

Jeff dutifully climbed the stairs and gathered the clothing. As he started to leave the bedroom, he glanced at the late Mr. Baynham. Something occurred to him. Jeff didn't know much about handling a dead body, but he was vaguely aware of a thing called rigor mortis and of a body stiffening up after a period of time. If we have to move this guy, he thought, it'll sure be easier if he's flat and not in this fetal position. Jeff pushed and pulled on Baynham's extremities to place him flat on his back on the bed, arms folded across his chest. Dismissing the idea of taking the time to dress him then, he returned to Lori in the living room. After she dressed, they left in his car.

Once he had driven some distance from Lori's townhouse, Jeff parked at a shopping center. As they sat in his car, he dialed the number of the Baynham residence as Lori read it from a piece of paper. A woman answered the phone after several rings.

"Hello." The voice was soft and very feminine.

For a split second, Jeff's mind wandered before he spoke. "Mrs. Baynham?"

"Yes? Who is this?" Very feminine, indeed.

"Never mind that. I'm calling about your husband."

"Oh, yeah?" Very much less soft, less feminine now. "Where is the old bastard? He never came home last night! Not that I miss his decrepit ass! Do you know where the little weasel is?"

"He's nearby. That is, I … he's—"

"Well, you can tell him to keep his sorry ass where it is, for all I care! I hope he croaks!"

"But—" Jeff gulped at this unexpected reception. A decided click at the other end of the line abruptly ended the conversation. Jeff was stunned. He held the cell phone in his hand away from his head and looked at it in disbelief.

Moving her eyes between Jeff and the phone, Lori sat with a look of puzzled expectation on her face. "Jeff, what is it? What did she say? What's wrong?"

At last, Jeff looked at Lori and managed to speak. "She doesn't care. She doesn't want the old guy back."

"What? Oh, no! You must have misunderstood her!"

Jeff swallowed hard, still stunned. "No, Lori. I think I understand the meaning when someone says 'I hope he croaks.'"

"She didn't say that!" After a pause, Lori asked in disbelief, "Did she?"

"Yes, Lori. She did. The Widow Baynham likes his money all right, but, apparently, that's where she draws the line with him."

Lori's tears started again. Hard. Jeff started the car, but then decided to give Mrs. Baynham another try. He turned off the ignition. As he picked up the phone, Lori stopped crying long enough to ask him what he was doing. When he explained, Lori insisted on listening to the conversation. Jeff redialed the Baynham home and held the phone so both of them could hear the conversation. After a few rings, the call was answered. A male voice this time. "Hello?"

Jeff asked whether Mrs. Baynham was available. Before the person at the other end could respond, a woman's voice intervened in the background. "What the hell are you doing?" she whispered, her voice seething with anger. "I told you *not* to answer the phone! Are you crazy? You're not supposed to be here!" Jeff recognized the voice of Mrs. Baynham, who, despite apparent efforts not to be heard, was coming through loud and clear even on this cheap phone. More whispered dialogue between Mrs. Baynham and the man briefly ensued. Then rustling and muffled sounds were followed by a sweet and, again, very feminine, "Hello?"

Jeff disconnected from the call. As he laid the phone down and started to turn the ignition, he looked at Lori, who sat wide-eyed, mouth agape. "What? What's the matter, Lori?"

"That man sounded like Mr. Cook, the bank's attorney. I've only spoken to him at the bank a half dozen or so times, but I would swear that it was him. I wonder why he's at the Baynhams' home."

"Well, maybe she called him when the old guy didn't come home last night."

"Maybe. But from what she said to you, it doesn't sound like that would cause her enough concern to seek help or support. Or solace for this missing 'loved one.'" Lori paused, working through the possibilities. "Maybe she's getting comfort of a different sort."

"You mean that they might be dancing the old Serta samba together? You really think so?"

"I don't know, Jeff, but he's young and pretty good looking. And he's very well-to-do in his own right. Not up to the Baynham level, but up there in the socioeconomic stratosphere. Just the type that somebody like Mrs. Baynham would find attractive." Lori was quiet for a minute or so, recalling past events. Then, she continued, "And I remember one time Mr. Cook was talking to me, flirting really, when Mrs. Baynham came into the office. She saw him before he knew she was there. When he spied her, he stopped flirting with me immediately and sort of turned white as a ghost. She gave him one of those raised-eyebrow, reproachful looks. At the time, I just believed she disapproved of his being so friendly with 'the hired help.' She could be very snotty that way. I never really thought much about it until now. I wonder … ."

"Well, the way it adds up now, I think there's a pretty good chance that the merry widow doesn't care whether she ever sees the old guy again."

"But she wouldn't have a lot to gain by his death."

"Why's that, Lori?" Jeff believed Lori was too upset and not making any sense. "If the old geezer's as loaded as you say he is, she should be fixed for the rest of her life, right?"

Lori paused, thinking about the situation for a moment. "No, not really. I'm not supposed to know this, but Janean told me something once when we'd been drinking on a girls' night out. Janean said that Mr. Baynham had *this* Mrs. Baynham sign a prenuptial agreement. He puts a certain allowance into her bank account each month, so she has access to some of his money while he's alive. But when he dies, she'll only get a hundred thousand dollars in a life-insurance policy he has. Apparently, the bulk of his money is in some sort of trust fund for his children from his previous marriage and for his grandchildren. It goes to them when he dies. Only he has … uh, had access to the trust while he was alive." Lori paused for a long moment, and then added, "Jeff, what do we do now?"

"I don't know exactly. But I *do* know that we have to get rid of Baynham and his car. And soon." Starting the car, Jeff said, "Let me think about it. And if you come up with any ideas, feel free to chime in."

As they drove back to Lori's townhouse, Jeff's mind raced. He saw that Lori was just staring out the window in total despair. Trying to lighten the moment, he laughed, "I guess it's a good thing we didn't try to ransom the old guy to his wife, huh?"

She tried to smile, but it looked more like a grimace. "Yeah, I guess. I just feel so lost, Jeff. That dead old man up there in my bed, and no one cares about him. No one wants him. Not even us."

"It's not a matter of not caring about him, Babe. It's more like we need to do something with him to get the heat off you and yet preserve his dignity as much as possible. Does that make sense?"

"That is so sweet of you to think that way, Jeff. But what do we do?"

Jeff just shook his head and sighed deeply as they drove on in silence. Back at the townhouse, Lori decided that she needed to shower and get cleaned up. "But I don't want to go up there," she whined.

"Well, that's where your bathroom is. I can go up and get clothes for you, but when it comes to a shower, that's something you have to do for yourself. Unless you want company," Jeff said half jokingly. He saw Lori's reaction in her face and immediately regretted the comment. "Okay, okay don't say it. I apologize."

As Lori disappeared up the stairs, Jeff flopped on the sofa. No sooner than his head hit the armrest, he heard Lori screaming in unmistakable terror. He bounded up the stairs three at a time and burst into the bedroom to find Lori cowering on the floor in a corner as far from the bed as possible, crying uncontrollably and screaming, "He's alive, Jeff! He's alive!"

Jeff turned from her to the late Mr. Baynham. He lay where and in the same position as Jeff last saw him. "What is it Lori? What do you mean 'he's alive'? He's dead! Look for yourself! He's dead!" He needed to shout at Lori to be heard above her shrieks.

"But he's moved, Jeff! He's moved!"

It suddenly occurred to Jeff that he hadn't told Lori that he'd changed Baynham's position earlier. He grabbed her arms to try to calm her and to get her to listen to him. Lifting her from the floor, he yelled, "He didn't move, Babe! I laid him out like that when I was up here getting your clothes before!" When Lori stopped screaming and calmed down somewhat, he went on, "That's all that happened! I moved him! He's dead, has been, and likely will be for some time!"

Jeff's overwhelming need to laugh at the situation receded as Lori's blank look turned to one of anger and she began hitting Jeff's chest with her fists, tears streaming down her cheeks. "How could you do that to me? Why didn't you tell me? You jackass! You nearly scared me to death!"

Jeff embraced her tightly, trying to calm her and abate her anger. "Okay, Lori, it's all right. I'm very sorry I scared you. I'm ... I'm ... just sorry." She went limp in his arms. After a moment, he said, "Listen. Right now we need to focus on what we are going to do from here. Stay put for a second." Jeff moved to the bed and covered Baynham's body with a blanket. He returned to Lori and held her again. "Okay, Babe. He's covered. Now get your shower, get dressed, and come downstairs. We need to talk this through." She held onto him for a short time longer as he walked her to the bathroom door, where she kissed him passionately and turned to go into the bathroom, still sobbing. Jeff, feeling closer to Lori than ever before, watched her as she disappeared through the door.

Jeff drank another beer as he waited for Lori to join him. Ideas about how to handle the situation, what to do next, ran through his mind. Also, he could not help but think about Lori and their relationship. She'd told him more than once that he needed to grow up. Maybe this was his "coming of age" time. Soon, Lori plopped on the sofa beside him. She took his beer and drank some. Jeff smiled at the easy feeling between them. "Feeling better?" he asked.

"Much better, thanks. I think the shower and clean clothes have helped my mindset a lot. I just can't help feeling sorry for that sweet old man up there. All his money never seemed to bring him any peace or happiness. His wife is a bitch and hates him. Apparently, she only *pretended* to love him for the sake of his money. It just makes me sad." They sat quietly for a few minutes before she asked, "Any ideas about what we can do, Jeff?"

"Well, first of all, we need to do something with his car. Do you have his keys?"

"They're probably in his clothes upstairs. But, please, don't ask me to look for them," she winced.

"I wouldn't think of it, Babe. I'll be right back."

Upstairs, Jeff rifled Baynham's clothes he found on the floor beside the bed. He located the old man's keys. As he looked at them, an idea crossed his mind. Maybe not much of an idea, he thought, but what the heck. He returned to Lori as she sat on the sofa finishing his beer. He jangled the keys at her.

"Found 'em. There are a lot of 'em."

"So I see."

"Lori, I have an idea, but, if you agree to it and we do it, it'll require a lot intestinal fortitude on your part. But, if Mrs. Baynham's as greedy as she seems, it should work out with a little luck. And, even more important, it might make you feel better about the old man's plight."

"God, Jeff that sounds ominous. I want to do *something* for Mr. Baynham, but I'm not agreeing to anything before I know what your plan is."

"Fair enough," Jeff smiled and held out Baynham's key ring. "I found the car key on here easily enough. But would Baynham have a key to the bank on this key ring and would you recognize it?"

"Sure, it's one of these two," she answered, pointing to two of the larger keys.

"So he has two keys to the bank?"

"Well, yes. But I'm guessing that only one of these is to the bank's front door. You see, the main bank is still in the same old building that was used when the elder Mr. Baynham started it. It actually has two entrances. One is the front entrance, the business entrance. The second is a door leading directly into Mr. Baynham's office from a parking lot out back. There used to be an alley between two buildings, but now the other building is gone and there's a parking lot there. I understand that it's about the only change since the bank began. But I don't know which key goes to which door."

"Okay, who else has a key to the main bank?"

"Well, as far as I know, only Mr. Baynham and Mr. Stillwell, the manager."

"Are you sure? The assistant manager doesn't have a key? You loan officers don't have keys either?"

"Well, I don't, and I don't think the others do either. Like I said, as far as I know, only Mr. Baynham and Mr. Stillwell have keys and that's it. It's a relatively small operation, and Mr. Baynham is, uh, was very particular about the setup and how things are run. Mr. Stillwell is the first to arrive every morning. He lets the rest of us in. They say that he's never missed a day's work in all the years he's been with the bank. And he's the last to leave every night. Why?"

"Do you know which one of these is Mr. Baynham's house key?" Jeff asked, extending the keys to Lori again.

"This looks like a house key, but I'm not sure."

"Yeah, it looked like a house key to me, too."

"Jeff, where are you going with these questions?"

"Just go along with me for another minute. What does the Widow Baynham look like?"

"Well, she has blondish hair, a little lighter in color than mine. She's a couple of inches taller than me, and we're about the same weight, I'd guess. I don't know what color her eyes are, though."

"The color of her eyes doesn't matter. Is her hair about the same length as yours?"

"Hers is longish like mine, but I'd say it's several inches shorter than mine. Why? What's this all about, Jeff? What are you thinking?"

Jeff outlined his scheme. After a number of questions and some hesitancy, Lori agreed to go along with his idea. The two waited for darkness to fall. Then, dressed in a sweater, jeans, a jacket, and a pair of tennis shoes, Lori made her way to Mr. Baynham's Lexus followed closely by Jeff. Wearing a pair of dark, cotton gloves he'd purchased at a local hardware store, Jeff unlocked the car, and Lori climbed behind the wheel. As he'd instructed her, she kept her hands in her coat pockets so as not to touch anything in the car. Jeff adjusted the seat to suit Lori's height. He then removed the gloves, handed them to her, and she put them on. After she closed the car door, Lori pulled a baseball cap from a jacket pocket and put it on, making sure that a pony tail of long, blondish hair protruded from the back of the cap. As she started the Lexus, Jeff went to his car and started the engine. The Lexus followed the Plymouth as they drove toward the airport.

While Jeff waited nearby, Lori entered the airport's long-term parking lot and eased the Lexus into a space. Before she exited the car, she removed a pair of dark sunglasses from one of her pockets and put them on. She opened the car door and removed the gloves, stuffing them into a pocket with the keys before getting out and into the view of the ubiquitous security cameras. Closing the car door with a nudge of her butt, Lori made her way out of the parking lot. At the terminal, Lori caught a city bus, which took her to a bus stop where Jeff was waiting. She entered Jeff's car, and the two drove away.

"Are you okay?" Jeff asked, squeezing her hand.

Lori caught her breath. "I'm fine. What's next?"

"Now, we wait until tomorrow morning. *Early* tomorrow morning."

Shortly after midnight, Jeff was again on the disposable cell phone, calling the Baynham home. A sleepy Mrs. Baynham answered the call. "Hello," she yawned.

"Mrs. Baynham. This is a friend."

"What? *Friends* don't call at this time of night." Jeff could hear a muffled male voice in the background. Someone tried to cover the receiver and speak where Jeff couldn't hear. The attempt was only partly successful, although Jeff could not make out the words. Mrs. Baynham returned her attention to Jeff. "Besides, this sounds like the guy who called about my husband before. What the hell do you want now? Has the old buzzard croaked yet?"

"Mrs. Baynham, I'm calling as your friend. I understand that you're locked into a prenuptial agreement at the present time." Initially, Jeff's statement met with a moment of stony silence.

"Who the hell told you that and what damned business is it of yours anyway?"

"Well, I have some info to pass on to you that may help you get out from under that prenupt in a court of law, if you care to hear me out. I tried to tell you before but you hung up on me."

Again a hand covered the receiver at Mrs. Baynham's end, followed by a muted conversation. Jeff waited while, he supposed, she obtained "legal advice." When she returned to Jeff, he had her full attention. "Tell me what you have to say, and it had better be good, mister!"

"I just wanted to let you know that your loving hubby is in a motel room out on State Route Five and locked in the clutches of a gold digger. I'm sure *you* understand what the term 'gold digger' means, Mrs. Baynham. Catching him in that scenario should be a real boost to getting that prenupt declared invalid. And that can lead to all sorts of rewards for you and yours."

After a period of silence, the widow regained her voice. "Why are you telling me this? What's in it for you?"

"To begin with, the gold digger in question is my wife. I'm sick of her being unfaithful. Second, do you think you're the only person who hates your husband's guts?" Jeff paused for effect before continuing, "But the 'lovebirds' will probably only be at the motel a couple of hours more, if you want the proof."

"How do I know you're telling me the truth?"

"Well, you don't know one way or another. But *we* know he's not with you and hasn't been, because he's been holed up with my Doris for more than a day. Also, we both know the bee hasn't been getting his honey in his own hive, now has he?"

"Who are you?" This was more a demand than a question, but Jeff remained mute. A few seconds passed. "What motel?" Mrs. Baynham demanded after the brief pause, her voice revealing an impatient anger mixed with the recognition that she would only get so much information from her caller.

"The Cardinal Motel. It's about forty-seven miles north on State Route Five. And before your try to check it, he's not registered under his name. Hell, the room may even be in a name that tramp Doris has made up! I *do* know they're using her car, so don't look for his! But the best thing you can do is just stake the place out with a camcorder, if you can get one, and wait for that slut of a wife of mine to show her face with your darling husband in tow. She'll come out of the room before long because she gets awfully hungry when she's been randy. Just look for the tall, slender woman with mousey brown hair. And I assume you'll recognize your loving husband. Good hunting!" Jeff disconnected from the call before Mrs. Baynham could ask about Doris' car. Dropping the cell phone on the car seat between Lori and him, Jeff moved his eyes from the phone to Lori.

Lori was staring at Jeff in wide-eyed amazement. "What was all that?"

"Well, when we talked yesterday, I didn't tell you all the details for two good reasons: first, it would've been too time consuming, and, second, I hadn't figured 'em all out yet."

"So what's happening now?"

"We want Mrs. Baynham out of her house for a while and unable to account for her time in any credible way. I guessed that she'd jump at the chance to get something on the old man that might get the prenuptial agreement he made her sign thrown out by a court. So I invented the story about him being shacked up with some floozy. I made the scene of the tryst far enough away to give us time to do our thing. By the way, Cook was with her when I called. At least, it sounded like Cook, from what I could hear of the guy. She'll surely take him along as a witness. In her mind, what better witness in court to her husband's dalliance than a lawyer? Anyway, if we're lucky, she'll haul it out to the Cardinal Motel looking for an unknown woman, driving an unknown car, and registered under an unknown name. Hopefully, that last part will keep her from trying to speak with the motel staff to find Baynham and his "lover" by a name. Those issues should add a fair amount of time to the roundtrip time they'll need anyway. Also, it'll sound like a contrived story, if she should ever need to tell it to the police. And I'm guessing that she will." As Lori smiled knowingly, Jeff continued, "By the time they get back, we will have visited the bank and her house. Then we sit back and wait for the fireworks."

"Where'd you get all this deep insight into people, Jeff?"

"You remember that psychology class we took together our sophomore year of college?"

"The one you flunked."

"Flunked, yeah, but I got something out of it after all," Jeff laughed. "Seriously, though, Lori, I know I've wasted a lot of time—yours and mine. It may sound weird with all this going on, but I see things differently now. I feel more committed to straightening up my act and being a better person. I never again want to make you experience what you must have felt to get in this kind of situation. I want to be the kind of man you want, you need, you deserve. No more goofing around with my life or with yours. I only hope you'll have me or, at least, give me a chance to prove my sincerity."

Tears welled in Lori's eyes. "Are you serious, Jeff?"

"Yes, if you'll have me. And if you'll promise to never let us get to this point again. Talk to me, yell at me if you have to. I'll never push you into this position ever again. I promise. You deserve a better man than I've been, Lori. I'm not preaching, but you're a better person than this, too. And I want to think I can be, too."

They embraced and kissed passionately. They held each other for a long time. As much as he hated to leave this scene, Jeff knew that there was work to do before the sun came up. "Babe?"

"Yes?" she purred against his neck.

"We need to get some things done."

"Not now, Jeff."

"They won't wait. And then we can go back to your place and spend the rest of our lives finishing this chapter. I promise."

Lori acquiesced. Later, at her place, she dressed in the same outfit she'd worn to the airport, carrying the gloves and sunglasses in her jacket pockets as before. Jeff laid Mr. Baynham's clothes on top of his corpse. He then rolled him in the freshly washed and dried blanket he'd used to cover the body earlier. Because Lori was still traumatized by the situation, Jeff carried the cadaver over one shoulder through the darkness alone to his car's trunk. Once Mr. Baynham was safely ensconced in the car, Jeff drove straight to the area of the bank and parked on a side street nearby. In the car, he went over what they had discussed earlier at Lori's townhouse. Again, Lori assured Jeff that she had access to the accounts necessary and was capable of doing exactly what needed to be done in the small window of opportunity they would have. She donned the hat, the sunglasses, and the gloves and got out of the car. As Lori calmly walked to the rear entrance of the bank, Jeff told himself that she was much stronger than she realized. He now saw it, and he was determined to help her find it in herself. He wanted to be the man in her life who did that. And he wanted to be the man who could and would be strong *for* her.

Although there were security cameras in the area, Lori knew the rear door entrance to the bank did not have any security alarm associated with it. This lack of a door alarm was a holdover from the first Mr. Baynham's reign and a closely guarded secret. Inside Mr. Baynham's office, Lori sat at his desk and worked furiously at the computer. Her pace was dictated by her desire to set things right for her former employer, compounded by her fear of police intrusion. After about ten minutes, she'd finished the task she'd set out to do. Lori left the bank, being careful to lock the door behind her. She walked casually to Jeff's car, keeping the bill of the baseball cap down, and got in. "Done," she whispered. Simple as that. Nothing more needed to be said.

Jeff and Lori then drove to a location near the Baynham home. With Lori, who had been at the residence several times, leading the way, Jeff hauled the dead man through the woods surrounding the house. Fortunately, the house sat on several acres of wooded land, preventing the eyes of nosy neighbors from getting any good look at their coming and going. From the edge of the woods, they could see the house was completely dark and apparently empty. Once at the door, Lori, using a small LED light, quickly determined which key from Baynham's key ring was the house key.

Lori stopped and turned to Jeff before she opened the door. "Jeff, these people probably have an alarm system," she whispered.

"I'm counting on it, Babe. Listen. We open the door and dump this thing in the basement or a closet or somewhere out of the way *very* quickly. Then we get the hell out of here even quicker. These systems normally have a thirty-second or so delay before the alarm sounds. In that time, we ditch this 'load' and get most of the way back through the woods. Okay?"

Lori winced at Jeff's reference to Mr. Baynham as "this thing" and "this load," but nodded her understanding. She opened the side door that led into the kitchen. A continuous, high-pitched beep sounded immediately, indicating the alarm was on and activated. In a matter of seconds, Jeff had returned Baynham's keys to his pocket and located a door just off the kitchen that led to the basement. In the same amount of time, he'd carried the corpse and its clothes to the basement, thereby returning Mr. Baynham to his rightful home. Lori was already waiting outside when Jeff reappeared, blanket in hand. They ran for the cover of the nearby trees. In short order, they were back at his car. The two could hear the Baynham alarm blaring as they drove away.

They drove the old Plymouth slowly back to Lori's townhouse and went to bed. Much later in the day, they awoke in each other's arms. As Jeff got out of bed, Lori rolled back over to try to get just a little more sleep. She could hear Jeff showering and found comfort in the sounds. Even after he finished and went downstairs, her efforts to sleep proved futile. Finally, she gave up the fight and climbed into the shower.

Later, she joined Jeff on the sofa. He sat there, clean-shaven and dressed, beer in hand, watching the end of a football game on television. She ran the back of her hand across his smooth cheek. "Very nice. And on a weekend, too."

"I told you I'm a changed man, Babe. I meant it."

She smiled and playfully thumped the beer bottle with her finger. He looked at her sideways and returned the smile. "I've changed, but don't expect miracles."

She snatched the bottle away and took a long drink from it. "Yeah, I know. And I'm very happy."

"Well, don't faint, Lori, but this week I'll be looking into a lead I've got on a pretty good job." Lori was stunned. She moved toward Jeff and embraced him tightly, moaning into his ear as tears filled her eyes.

The early news was coming on. The lead story momentarily broke the mood.

"Breaking local news!" exclaimed the talking head. "A local institution is at the center of a remarkable story tonight! The president of Baynham Savings and Loan is dead and his wife is in jail under arrest!"

Lori and Jeff quickly looked at each, returned their gazes to the television, and leaned forward slightly.

The anchorman continued, "Marcie Shupe is joining us live from the Aiken County jail. But this story doesn't evolve as one might think, right, Marcie?"

"That's right, Ken!" pert little Marcie effervesced. "The authorities are still investigating the circumstances of this story, but here's what we know so far. Mr. Curtis Baynham, president of Baynham Savings and Loan, is dead at the age of sixty-five. He died of an apparent heart attack, possibly late Friday night or in the very early hours of Saturday morning. The results of an autopsy, to be performed tomorrow morning, will confirm the cause and time of his death. However, at this time, it looks as if his thirty-two-year-old wife, Darlene, may have hidden his death from authorities for, as yet, undisclosed reasons. The body was found in the Baynham home when police arrived there, responding to an activated burglar alarm. Sources close to the investigation have told channel four news that Mr. Baynham's car was located in a long-term parking lot at the airport, thanks to an anonymous tip to police. And it appears that Mrs. Baynham can be seen on a security video leaving the car in the lot early Saturday morning. Finally, Ken, and its only speculation to this point, but sources also hint that Darlene Baynham may have used her husband's keys to get into the Baynham Bank and illegally transfer large sums of money from a trust account to her personal account. Oh, there is one last aspect to this story, Ken. The same source has told me that an as yet unnamed, local attorney is a 'person of interest' in this investigation."

"So, Marcie, exactly what charges, if any, are pending against Mrs. Baynham?" Ken inquired excitedly.

"Well, Ken, I've learned that, as of now, Darlene Baynham is charged with the misdemeanor of 'concealing a body.' Possible additional felony charges of 'fraud' and 'theft' may be handed down later. The district attorney's office will be looking at the case. That's all from here for now, Ken. Reporting live from the Aiken County jail, this is Marcie Shupe. Back to you, Ken!"

"Well, that's quite a lot, Marcie!" Ken smiled broadly. "Rest assured that channel four news will continue to follow this breaking—"

Jeff turned off the television and sighed deeply. Lori grabbed his arm. "So, is this what you had in mind all along, Jeff?"

"Pretty much. But I wasn't sure whether it would work. The cops'll see a 'Mrs. Baynham' on the security videos from the airport and at the bank. They will also find that Mr. Baynham's car is set for her driving position. You see, that model Lexus has two memory settings for two different drivers. So with you and Mrs. Baynham being about the same height and him being much taller, I simply put the seat at the one that was farthest forward when you sat in the seat and drove it. That had to be her setting. Parking the car at the airport just looks awfully suspicious and adds another element to the story that Mrs. Baynham can't explain. Plus, she was gone when the cops went to their home and found his body 'hidden.' Finally, at about the same time she was gone from her home, the money was transferred from the trust to Darlene Baynham's personal account. The story she'll try to give the cops regarding her whereabouts won't be very plausible under the circumstances. In total, it's what they call circumstantial evidence, but it sure looks bad for her. And her only alibi witness appears to be a coconspirator, Attorney Cook."

Lori was all smiles. "And you made the anonymous call about the car at the airport?"

"Yeah. Now, maybe Mr. Baynham can rest easy."

"And we can start the rest of our lives … together."

"Together," Jeff echoed.

And the sun set on a cold, windy Sunday.

WITNESS PROTECTION

All the guys in the neighborhood made fun of the man. But never to his face. But, then, truthfully, no one ever really *saw* his face. Certainly not up close, that is. Which was part of the reason we joked about him. The distance he kept, that is.

And the neighborhood isn't really much of one. We live on a slightly hilly, curving street that serves our town, in the northwest Atlanta suburbs, as a two-mile-long east-west cut-through between the two main north-south roads at either end. Large late-1960's four-sided brick, ranch-style homes on expansive lots occupy most of the plats that line either side of the road. Someone came in at about the same time and threw up what were called "contemporary-style" homes. The contemporaries are clapboard structures, comprised of awkward architectural lines and occasional odd shaped windows. These monstrosities are the subject of some amusement among the neighbors, too, but that's another story for another day. There's barely a spattering of them along the road, though, and most are located at the far end, away from our area. A sidewalk snakes its way along a single side of the road. For what it's worth, I live on the side of the road with the sidewalk.

But, such as it is, the neighborhood has changed as the original homeowners have died off and their adult children have moved in, taking advantage of nice, solid paid-for homes in a volatile housing market, or the houses were sold to younger families. The last vestige of the "old guard" is the octogenarian couple living several doors down from me, Mr. and Mrs. Catchings. Back in the day, Mr. Catchings built most of the ranches at our end of the street.

So, enough about the neighborhood—hopefully, you get the picture—and on to the man who was the subject of the harmless jokes. He and his much younger-looking wife lived across the street from me at a slight angle. Their ranch-style home, like a few of those in this hilly area, was built slightly below street level and sat at one end of the two side-by-side lots they had. A driveway entered the property at one end, sloping downward and passing an attached garage, set perpendicular to the house, then turned right and moved along the full length of the residence before turning right yet again and rising to return to the road. Except for the driveway openings, the house was mostly hidden from view by an abundance of trees, well-maintained evergreen shrubbery, and various other plants. A four-foot-wide grassy area stood between these plantings and the road and ran parallel to the road. No one had any idea what the rest of the property looked like because of the dense foliage and since no one ever set foot on it as an invited visitor that we know of, except the occasional repairman. We knew there was more to be seen of the yard, though, owing to the lawn mower, weed eater, or chain saw racket we'd hear emanating from the back of the property on a routine basis.

Nonetheless, the two constants about the neighborhood were this seemingly older man with his much younger-looking wife and Mr. and Mrs. Catchings.

The couple in question had been living there when my wife, Janet, and I moved in about three years ago. That's about the time the age of the homeowners started to change dramatically toward a more youthful look. Other young families soon followed. Understand that when I say "more youthful look," it's in comparison to the Catchings couple and even the strange guy across from our home.

The fellow, who, as I said, looked much older than his wife, was tall, possessed no neck that you could see, and was somewhat barrel-chested. A bruiser, no doubt, in his younger days. His wife, by comparison, was tall but relatively thin, with long, dark hair. She may have been one of those women, who, because of their build and long hair, seem much younger and more attractive when seen from afar than they actually are. But no one ever got close enough to settle that issue. We only saw her occasionally when he was working in the yard and she'd come out and speak to him or bring him something to drink. And, other than that, I couldn't give you a better description of the pair if you put a gun to my head.

Even in the blistering heat and humidity that can envelop our part of the world, when he mowed his lawn, what there was of it that we could see, or worked in his yard, he always dressed as if he had been a first responder to the Chernobyl disaster. A cammie fatigue hat, worn low across his brow, was topped by heavy-duty firing-range ear protection. He was also attired in industrial-strength goggles and a small canister-type respirator. These items were in addition to his long-sleeved shirt, buttoned at the collar, long work pants, heavy-duty work gloves, and massive brogans. I often watched him move back and forth across that narrow strip of grass, seemingly oblivious of the oppressive temperature, as waves of heat ribboned up from the pavement that separated us. He made me think that he, like the folks who intentionally put the fire of a cigarette or cigar to their already blazing faces, needed long-term psychological analysis. If I happened to be mowing my yard at the same time, I would intentionally slow the process, often mowing the same patch repeatedly, to try to catch his attention and get nothing more than a nod of acknowledgment, a glimmer of a "hello" from him. Never happened. Ever.

Shortly after we moved in, my wife and I started trying to salvage our front yard from the original owner's plan, which apparently was to do nothing and see what happened. As we worked in the yard, we would periodically see one or both the residents across the way turn in to their driveway and ease into the garage, with the garage door closing resolutely behind them. Never did they get out of their cars while outside or while the garage door was still open. Every so often, we would catch a glimpse of the man coming back out to his mailbox at the street. However, if we were working in the front yard, he never seemed to appear until we'd gone back inside our home or adjourned to the backyard for whatever reason. And it never seemed to be the female member of the pair. Only the male. Always. If we dawdled in the yard, hoping to catch him at the mailbox, he would wait us out. The man was blessed with the patience of Job, and, I swear, left his mail in the box overnight on occasion, rather than be approached by a neighbor. If we caught sight of this trip from wherever we were and made an effort to intercept the guy, he would canter back down the driveway with his correspondence and into his abode, tout de suite. For his large, slightly rotund fame, he could move like a gazelle. Additionally, the lack of a sidewalk on his side of the road kept anyone from just casually approaching him. So, that fact also worked to his obvious advantage.

Initially, we thought that maybe we'd done something to offend these people somehow. But that misunderstanding was set straight when we attended a "welcome to the neighborhood" cookout at the home next door about a month after we'd moved in. Bob, a prosecutor in the local district attorney's office, and his wife, Rose, were kind enough to have this little party for us. Because most people living nearby attended, the gathering gave us a chance to get to know some neighbors better and to learn more about the area. While the wives huddled at a nearby picnic table and the various children romped around the large backyard, the men congregated at Bob's rather expansive grill. Banter was going back and forth about the local sports teams and someone's latest effort to control dandelions, as our host deftly turned hot dogs and flipped burgers every so often. The inviting aroma of both filled the air.

I surveyed the gathering, hoping to catch a closer glimpse of and to meet finally my reclusive neighbors from across the street. They were nowhere to be seen. Since Bob and Rose didn't seem the types to exclude anyone from such a get-together, I asked about the absent pair. When I referred to them, apologizing for not knowing their names, most male conversations around me died down, and the group moved in closer for what was to follow. All eyes looked to Bob, who evidently was the unstated leader of the neighbors.

He laughed. "Oh, you mean 'Witness Protection.'" Most of the others joined in with snickers and chuckles.

"Are you serious?" His response surprised me so much I chortled aloud as I said it. Now, laughter exploded from the men around me. The women stopped talking and looked our way momentarily before returning to their chitchat.

Bob turned slightly in my direction, still attending his charges on the grill. "Nah. That's just what we call him, because no one has ever spoken to him. Or to her, for that matter, as far as we know. And they're such recluses. We gave up long ago trying to get them to come to social functions. You can't get near them when they're outside. If you approach, they scurry like gophers caught aboveground trying to find a hole and disappear back inside. And when you knock on the door, they never answer. Even when you've just watched them get home, and you know they're there. I'm not sure anyone even knows their names for certain."

"I think its Wood or Ward or something like that." One of the men, whose name I hadn't quite caught yet, chimed in. When we turned to him, he shrugged slightly and followed up, less certain of his proclamation. "Well, that's what I heard." He came across as a man who'd claim to know all about how radiation worked because he owned a glow-in-the-dark watch.

The group then refocused on Bob. "Bob could find out if he wanted to, what with the resources he has available to him." This contribution came from a power-tool salesman named Ken, who lived on the other side of Bob from me. Nearly all concurred with a chorus urgings for Bob to do so.

When that refrain died down, but before Bob could respond, someone else offered that he'd heard the couple in question was from somewhere in the New York City area. He, like the earlier contributor to the conversation, was not definite about that, however.

"That's your neck of the woods, isn't it, Joe?"

All eyes turned to a rather beefy guy, shorter than average, muscular but running to fat with a graying crew cut. I later learned that he had moved in somewhere nearby recently and was reported to be in the plumbing business. Joe nodded slightly. He lacked enthusiasm for being in the spotlight even in this small group, muttering, "Yeah, but don't look at me. The City's a big place. Lots o' people. *I* don't know 'em." His thick New York accent stood out in this group. His eyes sought the ground.

At this point, Bob finally took the opportunity to respond to the push for him to research the subject. "Hey, look, guys. I say live and let live. If they want their privacy, that's their call. Who am I to intrude? We tried to get to know them, but it didn't happen. They're not breaking any laws as far as we know. Let them be." He paused, grinned, and retorted, "Besides, any of you can get off your duffs, go to the county's real-estate office, and find out who they are. The property owners are listed on the tax rolls."

"They aren't the property owners!" Jeff Haywood, who lived next door to me on the opposite side from Bob and Rose, blurted this morsel of information. Immediately, his face reflected regret that he'd come forth with what he'd learned. As Bob smiled knowingly and the others turned their attention to him, Jeff sloshed the remnants in his beer bottle and went on with his confession. "Okay, okay, so I did some research on them. So sue me! I've got a right to know something about my neighbors! Like I told Joe, here, it ain't natural the way they act!" As he spoke, he swatted away at some no-see-ums that can permeate the air here during a large part of year.

"What exactly is 'natural,' Jeff?" Bob chuckled, trying to bring the conversation to ground. He handed Jeff a can of bug spray. "Like I said, let them alone if they don't want to be bothered. They're not hurting anyone."

"Except themselves, missing out on this great food!" One of the men had appeared with an open hamburger bun on a plate, ready to start the meal rolling, and was jokingly elbowing his way though the group toward Bob and the grill. Because the meat was ready for consumption anyway, that pretty much broke up the group discussion of the solitary couple.

As Bob was dishing up his wares to the band of ravenous neighbors, he leaned toward me and said, "Don't take it personally, Roy. Everyone here has encountered the same reception from the old man and his wife. It is what it is, as they say."

Later that evening, as Janet and I were preparing for bed, she asked from across the bed, "Well, did you learn anything about the couple across the street from 'The Belvedere Road Irregulars'?" When I looked up, she was smiling broadly.

"'The Belvedere Road Irregulars'? What or who the heck is that?"

She broke into laughter at some joke unknown to me. "That's what the girls on this road call their husbands who've spent so much time trying to solve the enigma of the pair across the street." When I looked at her with an evidently uncomprehending expression, she frowned playfully. "You know. From the Sherlock Holmes stories. The Baker Street Irregulars. The gang of young street urchins that Holmes used on occasion to help with his cases."

I was chagrined at the amused derision in which the wives and significant others held their men who sought answers to a mystery in the neighborhood. "Very funny!" I trumpeted, returning her good-natured grimace. "No. I didn't learn much, except that no one, not even the folks who've lived here longer, seem to know anything about them either. One of the guys was guessing at their name, but he didn't seem to know anything for sure. That tall man—what's his name—the one who lives in the painted brick house down the road? He evidently thinks that they came here from New York City, but isn't certain about that either."

"Yeah, I heard that, too."

"So wait a minute! You're giving me crap about the men kicking the issue around and yet you girls spent time talking it up, too? Nice!" After she threw a pillow at me and feigned embarrassment, I added, "Well, to tell you the truth, one of the neighbors has even gone to the courthouse to try to get their name from the tax rolls. But they, whoever they are, don't own the house."

Janet dived onto the bed and looked at me intently, knotting the eyebrows above her small flickering eyes in her best Nancy Drew impersonation. She whispered in a voice drawn straight from some 1940s radio crime drama dripping with mystery, "I know! It's scary. But isn't it exciting?" When she settled back to normal, or what passes for normal with Janet, she went on, "Jeff's wife was telling us about what he'd done. According to her, the house is owned by some corporation no one's ever heard of. So I guess they're just renters. Some folks do rent on Belvedere Road, you know." After a moment more of considering the problem, she added, "But they sure take care of that yard like it was their own. To be renters, I mean."

I kissed her brow, wrinkled in concentration, good night. Rolling over and pulling the covers up to my ears, I gave the conversation one last parting shot. "Some renters do take care of their yards, you know. Even on Belvedere Road."

That was almost two years ago. I've found that many of life's mysteries resolve themselves in the fullness of time. This riddle about the reclusive neighbors did not. Not by itself, that is. In the intervening time, no one came to know them or, as far as we were aware, even to speak to them. Nothing changed until about a month ago.

About three o'clock one morning, we were awakened by gunshots ringing out somewhere in the neighborhood. When we were finally beyond that fog from initially awakening, Janet wasn't sure what the noises were, but, having been in Iraq (the first time we went there), I knew what I'd heard. After telling Janet to call 9-1-1, I threw on a pair of jeans and a T-shirt and grabbed the handgun from my bedside table. I eased out to the front yard, uncertain of what I might find there. Nothing stirred in the dim illumination of the street lights, but I could hear the distant sound of a car's engine as it barreled down Belvedere Road.

"Roy!" The voice was a stage whisper. I turned to find Bob standing between our houses, a short-barreled revolver at his side. "Do you know where they came from?"

"No, but it was close. I know that." We were quietly walking toward each other.

As Bob was agreeing with me about the proximity of the blasts and we were confirming that neither of us had fired any shots, we heard police sirens approaching from a distance. Bob looked at his gun as if he'd forgotten he had it in his hand. He got my attention and nodded toward my gun, raising his slightly. "We'd better get these back inside before the po-po get here. Don't want to be standing in the dark at the scene of a 'shots fired' call with a gun when they arrive."

"Oh. Yeah." I swallowed hard just thinking for a moment about the tragic events that could ensue from such a scenario. We went our separate ways for the time being. I was replacing my gun and explaining to Janet that I had no idea what had happened or what was going on, when we heard the first police car arrive. By this time, Janet was dressed, and we moved as unobtrusively as possible to our front porch. Three police cars were scattered about the road in the vicinity of our yard and the yards on either side. Officers, with service weapons drawn, were in positions at various spots around them. I decided that our best option was to go back inside. That's where an officer found us when he knocked on the door a short time later.

He was canvassing the neighborhood for possible witnesses. After answering his questions and telling him what we knew, I also explained that I'd initially gone outside with my weapon, for which I had a carry permit. My concern was that some well-intentioned neighbor might have seen me outside with the gun, mention it to the police, and have it lead to other issues. The officer asked to look at the weapon. When I agreed, he accompanied me to our bedroom, where I pointed out its location in the drawer of the bedside table and stepped back. I've been around enough weaponry in difficult situations to know better than simply to open a drawer and pull out a gun with an officer standing there, no matter what my intentions might be. The officer looked the gun over and replaced it, thanking me. I breathed a sigh of relief, grateful that it hadn't been confiscated as evidence. As we walked the hall back to the living room, he explained that my gun was a revolver and they would be looking for a semiautomatic handgun of a different caliber. I surmised that shell casings had been found inside the house where the shooting occurred.

"So you've found where the shots were fired?"

"Yes sir. In that house right across the street," he indicated, pointing toward the home of the reclusive couple.

"Are they okay?" Janet piped up. Her voice quivered with sudden emotion.

"I can't say at this time, ma'am. The EMTs are in there right now, and we're waiting for the detectives."

My curiosity was aroused. "Can we go back outside, officer?"

"Sure. Just stay out of everyone's way and better keep to this side of the road."

When we returned to the chaos that Belvedere Road had now become, we saw little clusters of our neighbors here and there, staring in disbelief. Bob and Rose were in their yard but walked to where we stood. Bob spoke first. "Something, huh?" I was surprised, supposing the prosecutor to be in his element with this kind of occurrence.

Janet voiced the thought. "This must be old hat to you, Bob, though not normally in your own neighborhood." As an afterthought, she added, "I hope."

Bob gave Janet a gentle nudge and laughed. "You've been watching too much television, Janet." Despite what was going on, he was obviously in a teasing, playful mood. "Assistant district attorneys don't get called to scenes like this as a matter of routine. That only happens in the movies or on the tube. In reality, we only see this stuff through crime-scene photos and in case reports. Nah. It's new and exciting to me, too." He turned serious and looked at me. "Did you hear what happened?"

I nodded in the direction of "witness protection's" house. "The canvassing cop said that the shooting occurred in their house. That's all. Not who, not why. How about you, Bob?"

"Same here."

After a few minutes of gawking, Bob perked up. "Hold on a second." Without anything more, he walked toward the road and some men in street clothes gathered at the trunk of what was, evidently, an unmarked police car. "What is it, Bob?" Rose called after him, but the question went unanswered as she stayed with Janet and me, waiting.

Bob stopped short of the road and appeared to call quietly to one of the men. We heard words being spoken but couldn't make them out. A man turned and walked to Bob, shaking his hand as he approached. After a brief conversation, they shook hands again, and our neighbor returned to us.

"Well, part of the mystery is solved anyway. The couple that lived there was shot to death. And their name was Buffington, by the way. Tony and Connie."

Janet immediately began to sob quietly. "Those poor people," she repeated several times through her tears. She didn't know them, had never even spoken to either, yet she wept for them. Her compassion for others is one of the many reasons I love her. All I could do was hold her as she wept quietly.

A couple of days later, Bob told me that the investigation revealed there was no apparent motive for the killings: no robbery, no sexual assault involved, no drugs, and no apparent forced entry to the residence. Nothing.

One Saturday morning several weeks later, Bob walked through the open door of my carport-converted-to-garage as I worked on the engine of a reluctant lawn mower. "Knock, knock, Roy."

"Hey, buddy, come on in. What's up?"

He hesitated. "Have you seen Joe lately? I thought I merely kept missing him, but I went by his place again, and it looks like nobody's been there for a while. I could still see some furniture when I looked through the windows, though."

"No. Haven't seen him for about three weeks." I stopped to think for a second as I wiped my grease-stained knuckles with a streaked chamois. "In fact, it was the day after the shooting I saw him last. He seemed to be ducking into his house in a hurry at the time. I figured he was busy ... or just shy. He always acted pretty timid for such a big bruiser. And from New York City, too. Those folks just don't come across as too introverted that much. At least not to me. You need something from him?"

"Nah, just asking. Strange, Joe just disappearing without any word, though. And his furniture's still there. But, as we learned from across the street, you never can figure some people. I just hope he's all right." Bob looked around and lowered his voice. "Anyway, I have some more information on the Buffingtons. Now that they're dead, there's no harm in telling you. But you've got to keep this between us."

I must admit that my curiosity ran wild at the mention of their name. "Okay. Give."

"You're not going to believe this, but I learned today that they actually *were* in the Witness Protection Program."

I know I gasped audibly and spoke louder than I meant to. "You have *got* to be kidding me!"

While glancing around us again, Bob moved his hands up and down, palms down, to quiet me. "No. I'm as serious as a heart attack. The night of the shootings, I saw a detective I know at the car in the road. That's why I walked over. But there were several other men there in plain clothes, and I'd never seen them before. Now I know that they were with the U. S. Marshals Office. My detective tells me that's why there was no apparent motive. The idea is to show the killing for what it was—retribution. Then the word gets around everywhere and chills those folks in the know, who are inclined to be talkative with the authorities."

I lowered my voice. "Wow! I can't believe it! And after all the joking we did about that! Who could have known?" We stood quietly, thinking about the situation. After several beats, a thought occurred to me. "But, Bob, what blew their cover? They never spoke to anybody that we know of! They were as quiet as a church mouse peeing on cotton and as low profile as they could have been. The neighbors said they'd never seen them in the local supermarkets or department stores. So nobody even knew when or where they shopped!"

"Maybe they tried so hard to maintain a low profile that they stood out instead. Maybe they tried too hard. I dunno, Roy. Nobody does. We may never know."

Another couple of beats passed.

"Yeah, well, I hope Joe is okay, too. Funny, just disappearing like that, though. He seemed like an okay guy—" I stopped short as crazy thoughts raced through my head. Apparently, similar ideas struck Bob at the same time. We stared hard at each other in the next instant, each studying the other's face, trying to read the other's thoughts. Neither said a word.

We snapped back to the reality of the instant, momentarily tossing aside the notion we'd both possibly entertained.

"Well, I'd better head back and get some of my 'honey-do' list done. See ya."

"Yeah, Bob. See ya later." I went back to fighting with the mower.

When I didn't hear his footfalls on the pavement after a couple of steps, I looked up. Bob had paused just before he reached the garage door and stood, his head back, looking up. I started to give voice to my thoughts but resisted the temptation. Then, as if whatever he'd been contemplating had passed or maybe he'd simply thought the better of speaking about it, Bob merely looked down, shook his head, and continued walking away.

I later heard from Mr. Catchings that he saw a truck from one of those rent-to-own stores picking up Joe's unpaid-for furniture. And the house turned out to be a rental.

I never saw Joe again. And, to my knowledge, neither did Bob. Neither of us has ever mentioned the Buffingtons or Joe since that day in my garage.

PRINCESS PAMELA AND THE BLIND HOG

We were having our typical Saturday evening dinner with our customary group of friends, referred to by my wife, Pamela, in her normally haughty way as "the gang," when I decided I could take no more of my life with her. I had to end it. One of us *had* to go. Divorce was not an option open to me. Suicide was out of the question. I enjoyed life away from Pamela too much, *and* I was a coward. Watching my wife in full evening dress sip her after-dinner coffee with her upraised pinky, gaily tossing her head back as she laughed in her frivolous manner, I decided to kill her. Understand that my cowardly tendencies related only to bringing about my own demise. I held no such trepidations about helping Pamela shuffle "off this mortal coil," as the Bard so aptly put it.

The act of killing Pamela itself, I decided, would not be problematic for me. I was very angry, very determined. My loathing for my wife knew no bounds. In addition, it should be easy enough to get away with. Simply put, the end *must* look like an accident. And, if "murder" *did* enter the minds of the authorities, there ought to be a multitude of others with reason enough to want her dead. I certainly wasn't the only person out of whom she had kicked the intestines. Pamela's self-important, cavalier airs had infuriated and injured any number of people I could name. Heaven only knows the figure to which such a population would swell if one added the people about whom I was not even aware. She always seemed to waltz through life, oblivious of the pain and suffering she caused others. Some of her uncaring ways merely annoyed many people. Others had been hurt to a significant extent. Although she pretended to be unaware of the harm she caused, Pamela frequently appeared calculating and intentionally hurtful in her actions and words. The dinner that night was a prime example. During a lull in the conversation, Pamela offhandedly commented on seeing one of our mutual friends with another woman, not his wife, somewhere out of town. Raised eyebrows and whispered conversation ensued.

As I watched her self-satisfied expression, I realized that she was still the raven-haired, high cheek boned beauty with skin pale to the point of translucence that I'd fallen in love with those years before, but she had to go. Those beautiful gray eyes that had enthralled me and enchanted all who were caught in their range had lost their appeal for me. The time had come to end it.

"You realize, of course, Pamela, that your unnecessary comment tonight is going to cause yet another painful episode in the lives of four of our friends." We were driving home, and I could no longer bear being silent about her actions. She ignored me. Undeterred, I prodded her, "Pamela?" Pamela. She was always "Pamela." "Pam" was too pedestrian for her. "Pamela" was indeed appropriate. In my view, the shortened version may have imparted too much in the way of true warmth and fun to a person incapable of either characteristic. Although the urge to use the latter name to annoy her often pressed me, I avoided it to keep a civil air between us. Why *that* was important to me, I have never fully understood. It would, however, prove invaluable now that I'd decided to kill her.

"Whatever do you mean, Gerald?" she asked, her dismissive tone clear. Gerald. She never, ever used the shortened form of *my* name either. I've been known to one and all as Jerry my entire life. But Pamela has always used my given name. It preserved her tone of refinement. The couples in our "gang" often smiled at me when she used it. I merely fumed inwardly, yet grinned in return.

"You know very well the comment to which I'm referring. That remark about Henry Chastain being seen upstate with Emily Thompson outside the bed and breakfast inn. How could you be so careless? You know full well that the tongues will wag that juicy morsel around until it somehow reaches Bonnie Chastain and George Thompson. Then there will be hell to pay. Four more lives in chaos because you must repeat things you've heard."

"I did not *hear* it, Gerald. I *saw* it with my own eyes when I was antiquing with Janet last weekend." Pamela stared out her window at the passing city lights in an effort not to look in my direction. Nonetheless, in the reflection in the darkened car window, I glimpsed that evil smirk she often wore when she had knowingly said or done some cruel thing. "Besides I cannot help the loose tongues of others." On her countenance showed the recognition of the incongruity of her statement. Nothing more was said about the matter by either of us. I took solace in the thought that, as of this evening, the population with a motive to kill Pamela had increased by four.

Attempting to reason with Pamela was an exercise in futility. There would be no permutation of her character. As I saw it, one very important fact would make it easy for me to get off scot-free with Pamela's murder. No one, not even my wife, had any inkling of the extent of my unhappiness or of any marital strife between us. No "other woman," as the pulp fiction writers put it, waited in the shadows. No large life-insurance windfall, which might arouse the suspicions of the authorities, would be waiting for me after her death. All these years, I have simply seethed in silence. Though I am not a Donald Trump, I have always made a very comfortable living. Throughout our marriage, Pamela has been provided everything she's wanted and been free from the need to seek employment. None of the usual motives for murder were present. The only dilemma I now faced was the manner with which to complete the task. The "how" occupied my thoughts constantly for the next few weeks. For years I've read and enjoyed the genre of murder mysteries, never contemplating that I would someday need to implement the methods used by fictional characters to achieve their ends. Above all else, the key was not to get caught. As a result, I dismissed one means after another by which to dispatch Pamela. And I never ventured near the trap of Internet research that so often snared real-life killers.

Inauspiciously, Pamela, through her typically careless ways, provided a means by which I could rid me of her for at least some period of time. One day several weeks after that Saturday night dinner, while returning home from luncheon with one of the "gang," Pamela ran a red light, struck another vehicle broadside, and killed its unfortunate driver and sole occupant, one Mr. Hector Garcia. Mr. Garcia's older, dilapidated subcompact was no match for Pamela's mammoth, luxury SUV. Unlike Garcia, Pamela was completely unscathed by the mishap. As luck would have it, Pamela later told me, she had been on her cellular telephone at the time of the accident, no doubt relaying to another of the "gang" some juicy bit of gossip derived from her noonday repast. More significantly, she had imbibed several martinis during her meal. Although Pamela was examined by EMTs at the scene and judged to be physically all right, she was found by the police to have been driving under the influence of alcohol, was arrested, and summarily carted off to jail, charged with vehicular homicide, a felony in our state.

I was at my office at the time of the accident. On learning of Pamela's arrest and, more important, determining to my chagrin that she'd sustained no life-threatening injuries, I contacted my attorney, Chuck Weatherington. After hearing about her predicament, Chuck reminded me that he only practiced civil law, and, while he could recommend several criminal lawyers who could handle the case, he would not be able to help with her defense. He did tell me that the maximum penalty for Pamela's transgression was fifteen years in prison. Further, he speculated that, this being an election year, I could expect the district attorney, who was seeking reelection, to prosecute Pamela, a drunken driver responsible for the death of another, wholeheartedly. Finally, he recommended that I call an attorney as soon as possible to arrange for bail and for Pamela's release. Chuck even offered to place some calls for me to obtain an attorney on Pamela's behalf. Thanking him for his offer, I told him I would make the necessary arrangements.

However, before I telephoned any of the lawyers Chuck had suggested to me, I experienced an epiphany. This turn of events suddenly redirected my thoughts about how to relieve me of Pamela. Fifteen years imprisonment seemed entirely inadequate for a crime involving a death. But I was forced to deal with what little prison time the law would allow. If I could appear to be supportive of Pamela in her plight, while surreptitiously ensuring her incarceration, I could be seen as the loyal husband yet rid me of her for a time. Who knows what might happen if she were imprisoned? Inmate-on-inmate murders occurred with regularity, according to the media. She might be killed by an annoyed, less-understanding fellow inmate, thereby saving me the trouble. At the very least, I would have more time to plan her "accidental" death upon her release, should that distasteful eventuality arise. Besides, I believed that any attorney Chuck might recommend would certainly be very capable enough and highly motivated to do a good job at defending Pamela. I could have none of that.

Instead of calling to secure Pamela legal representation, I telephoned the detention center to determine when her first court appearance might be scheduled. The less-than-sympathetic person with whom I spoke told me that she would go before a judge early the next morning for what was called an "initial appearance," but that I could see Pamela at the jail that afternoon. I left my office and drove to the county lockup. Checking in with the jail staff for my visitation, I studied the people in the lobby area waiting for their inmate visits. If *they* were any indication of the types that awaited Pamela on the "inside," I felt certain that she would never survive incarceration.

When they brought Pamela to the visitation area, she looked lost and haggard despite her best efforts to appear to rise above her current surroundings. After only several hours of confinement, a fair amount of Pamela's self-importance had faded from her demeanor. However, in my presence, she seemed to regain some measure of that proud luster. She was happy to see me but was very disconcerted that I had not appeared with a lawyer and a bond with which she could be released from the "hellhole." Pamela appeared to be quickly gaining an intimate knowledge of the vernacular of the criminal element.

Her rather loud demand to know why Charles, as she always called him, was not present brought an admonishment and mild threat from a nearby female deputy sheriff. Pamela was aghast at her treatment at the hands of such "unrefined" people but calmed herself. After explaining that Chuck dealt only with civil matters and that I was in the process of securing her a criminal defense attorney who, in turn, could arrange for her release, I informed her of what I'd been told about her court date the next morning. Pamela was mortified at the thought of spending a night in such horrid conditions among the unwashed masses of our county's "penal system." She made it clear that I was to have an attorney for her at her court appearance. My heart leapt with joy at the disheartened look on her face when I told her that I was doing my best. When visitation ended, she was taken away, clinging pitifully to assurances of my efforts on her behalf.

At home that evening, I focused on researching the Internet for information. Our telephone rang incessantly, which told me that the news of Pamela's mishap had made the rounds. I ignored it while I roamed the cyber highway for facts I felt might help me.

The next morning found me sitting in a courtroom well before the time set for the call of Pamela's case. I intended to set my objectives in motion by dealing directly with her prosecutor. Approaching what was evidently the district attorney's table in the courtroom, I asked the man standing there whether he would be handling the Pamela Sutherland case. He glanced up from a file folder and nodded toward a woman standing nearby. As it turned out, Pamela's case was assigned to a fervent young assistant district attorney, who evidently held a particular vendetta toward well-to-do people driving in an intoxicated state. She made that abundantly clear when I approached and spoke to her.

After she abruptly kept me from moving past the rail that separated the public seating area from the well of the court, she admonished me that only court personnel and officers of the court were allowed beyond that point, except by explicit invitation of the judge. I regained my composure and asked, "Are you the prosecutor in the Pamela Sutherland case?"

The young woman eyed me warily and said that she was.

"I'm her husband—"

She threw her hand up to silence me. "Stop right there, Mr. Sutherland. I suggest that you get your wife an attorney as quickly as possible. Then I will speak with him or her about the case."

"See here," I retorted quietly, "my wife is a very prominent woman in this community. We both are well known and very well respected. And I happen to know the district attorney personally."

In truth, I had only met the district attorney once, briefly, at a chamber of commerce meeting some time back. I seriously doubted he could recall either me or the event itself.

As I'd hoped, the prosecutor was astonished and irritated at my presuming to sway her with name-dropping. Moreover, she did not share my desire for a hushed conversation. "Well, with all due respect, Mr. Sutherland," she pronounced loudly, "maybe you should go talk to my boss, because I have a job to do. My job is to prosecute your wife to the fullest extent of the law. And I don't believe for one second that the district attorney would expect anything less from me!"

Her response in the open forum of the courtroom embarrassed me, but I ingested my pride and pressed on to achieve my end. In quiet tones, I asked her about a bond while hinting broadly that, despite our "wealth," Pamela would never think of leaving the state or the country although she could very easily do so. "A very low bond is certainly in order. In fact," I asserted, "she should be released on her own recognizance." Thank you, Internet. "That would be most appropriate in this case." I overreached, as those in the legal profession are fond of saying. My effort did not go unrewarded.

"Excuse *me*, Mr. Sutherland! A man was killed by your wife while driving under the influence of alcohol! Surely, you can understand that! I *will not* be on record as allowing your wife simply to sign her name and walk away from the jail and not pay *some* amount of bail money to ensure her return to this courtroom! The idea of an 'own recognizance' bond is out of the question!" The assistant district attorney's ire had been sufficiently aroused by my blustery attitude. Goal attained: one antagonized state's attorney. Passing up the temptation to spit the word "allegedly" back at the young woman and thereby incurring more of her wrath and histrionics, I simply "sulked" away quietly under the glares of those who'd heard at least the prosecutor's side of the exchange. Seated, hidden in the back of the courtroom, I used all my self-control to refrain from smiling broadly at my success. Periodically, a heavyset woman, seated in the row in front of me, would turn and glance askew at me as if I were some being recently dispatched from an extraterrestrial mode of transportation.

At the appointed time, the judge took his place on the bench. When the inmates were finally led single file into the courtroom, I hardly recognized Pamela. She looked as if she had not slept at all. Without makeup, her face showed an age and weariness I'd never seen. The ill-fitting jail clothing in which she was dressed did nothing to help her appearance. Looking miserable, Pamela spent the entire time clutching her elbows. Gone was the brief recapture of her arrogant bearing I'd seen at the jail the day before. As she turned her gaze away from the judge and tried desperately to find me in the crowd, one of the sheriff's deputies leaned toward her and spoke quietly. She pulled back from him as if insulted by his very presence. She ignored him and continued to scan the packed courtroom. Discreetly, he grabbed her arm and firmly turned her attention to the judge who was addressing the group of prisoners. I could see Pamela's shoulders shaking as she cried softly. Not even her sad, beleaguered appearance could arouse any sympathy in me. Truly, my heart had hardened and my course was set with respect to her.

Moving across the group, the judge spoke to each inmate individually, advising them of the charges against them, of certain rights, and of the absolute need to be represented by counsel, either retained by them or appointed by the court through the public defender's office. When he reached Pamela and asked whether she had retained counsel or needed to have one appointed for her, she hesitated and tried again to quickly search for me. When the same deputy moved slightly in her direction, she quickly turned back to the judge and blurted, "My husband will hire an attorney for me, I'm certain! He should be here!"

The judge scanned the gallery beyond Pamela and asked whether her husband was present. To keep Pamela from panicking, I stopped utilizing the aforementioned stout woman as a shield from being seen by those in the front of the courtroom, rose, and spoke up, "I'm here, your honor! I'm Mr. Sutherland!" While the heavyset woman's eyes followed me closely, I stepped forward as I spoke. "I'm sorry, your honor, but the acoustics back here are terrible. Yes, I will be hiring an attorney for my wife. I simply haven't been able to do so before now. I would like to ask about a bond for my wife."

As I'd hoped, the young prosecutor rose to the bait. "Absolutely not, your honor! These are very serious charges here! And, with the financial means available to this defendant, there is too great a flight risk!"

"All right, Ms. Winkler. That will do for now." Turning his attention from the prosecutor to me, the judge continued, "Mr. Sutherland, I suggest you obtain the benefit of counsel for Mrs. Sutherland as quickly as possible and let them make the appropriate motion for bond. I'll hear from both sides at that time."

Having thus dismissed me, the judge quickly moved on to the next inmate. Afterward, when the prisoners were led away, I could hear Pamela still sobbing. Initially, I didn't understand why the courtroom crowd continued to grow despite friends and family members leaving after each inmate had been addressed. When Pamela's group was moved out, I thought the court session had finished. However, before I could leave, the judge began calling another calendar, this one for an upcoming trial term. With nothing else pressing to do, I decided to stay and watch the proceedings. Possibly, I thought, I might find exactly the type attorney I had in mind for my "dear" Pamela.

The prosecutors announced that a number of guilty pleas had been negotiated, and the judge decided to proceed with those before going to the scheduled calendar. The defendants and their attorneys were summoned to the front of the bench. As the judge, prosecutors, and defense attorneys methodically proceeded with the business at hand, I couldn't help noticing one defense attorney in particular who represented several of those pleading guilty to the crimes charged. However, it was not his adversarial skill that caught my attention: it was that a few of his clients, as shown by their demeanor and words, seemed less than enthusiastic about accepting his advice to plead guilty. Several of them seemed to resent his very presence as their court-appointed lawyer. One young man actually recoiled in apparent revolt when this attorney whispered something to him and had to be "calmed" by the deputies. Moreover, his clients' sentences seemed a tad harsher than those of the other defendants charged with similar crimes. He appeared to stumble through the proceedings. In general, he impressed me as only marginally proficient at what he was doing. I studied him more closely. He was a flaccid-cheeked, baggy-eyed middle-aged man sporting thick eyebrows, a shaggy salt-and-pepper beard, and the expression of one who has lost something of some vague significance and has no idea of where to begin looking for it. One could probably find more trustworthy looking characters in a mug book. He stood before the bench, his clothes in total disarray. His shirt, mostly untucked, and coat of some indefinable checked pattern were wrinkled despite being stretched over a ponderous belly. The tie he wore looked as if it could provide a soup of some unknown composition if placed for a period in a vessel of boiling water. In short, he looked like an unmade bed. From the court proceedings, I learned that his name was Edward Easley.

When the judge took a brief recess, I approached the front of the room, but, before I could get his attention, Easley disappeared into what appeared to be an inmate holding cell adjoining the courtroom. I then diverted my line of travel to the prosecutors' table or as close as I could to it without breaching the "sacred decorum" of the court. The young lady I'd spoken with earlier was putting case files in a box on the table. She glanced sideways in my direction, stopped what she was doing, heaved a deep sigh, and abruptly said, "Mr. Sutherland! I've already told you that I am opposed to a bond for your wife! I'll not discuss the issue with you any further! You need to hire an attorney!"

"I understand that, Miss," I said quietly. "I *am* going to hire an attorney. I merely want to ask you if you would recommend Attorney Edward Easley for my wife's case. I—"

As I spoke, a hint of a smile crossed her lips, but she held back as she interrupted my inquiry, becoming stony-faced once again. "Yes, Mr. Sutherland, I know Mr. Easley. I've had many cases with him. But the law prohibits me making a recommendation about any particular attorney."

With her last words, the older assistant district attorney with whom I'd initially spoken and with whom she shared the prosecution duties in the courtroom, approached the table. His gaze at me told me at once that she'd told him of our earlier exchange. Expecting possible difficulty, he intervened. "Any trouble here, Lynne?"

"No. No trouble at all. Mr. Sutherland here was just asking if I knew 'Easy Eddie.' He wants to hire him for his wife's case."

Giving his younger partner a look of stern disapproval, he quickly turned to me and said, "Mr. Sutherland, we cannot recommend an attorney to you. The decision whether to hire Mr. Easley is strictly yours to make." Returning to his partner, he quietly added, "Easy there, 'Miss Vicious.'"

With that, they shared a knowing glance and smiled at some "inside" joke as I turned to walk away. That bit of banter sealed my decision. The Columboesque Mr. Easley was my man. A short time later, Easley reappeared in the courtroom. As the court was still in recess, I again approached the rail and tried to get his attention. Finally, he turned and walked to where I stood. "Yes, sir? Can I do something for you?" Easley's breath was brutal, and his clothing smelled of ancient cigarette smoke and sweat. His voice was like sandpaper.

"Yes, Mr. Easley, is it? I'd like to speak with you about my wife's case." I introduced myself and gave him a brief explanation of the situation, including Pamela's incarceration.

"And she's charged with vehicular homicide? That's a pretty serious charge, Mr. Sutherland." He frowned thoughtfully. Knowing the allegations against Pamela, he seemed hesitant.

"Of course, you *can* handle such a serious case, can't you, Mr. Easley?" I asked, feigning a genuine concern for his ability. Removing my checkbook from my suit pocket, I tried to sweeten the deal, "Within reason, money is no object."

On seeing my checkbook, his eyes revealed a spark of avarice, and he quickly moved on, "Oh, certainly, Mr. Sutherland! I was simply reflecting on the severity of the charges your wife faces. It's just a big case and may involve a lot of work. I can handle her case, no problem." His demeanor reflected less confidence than his words. Nonetheless, he adopted a bold manner when it came to his fee. "I'll need a ten-thousand-dollar retainer," he muttered, his eyes trying to gauge my reaction to such a sum.

I was taken aback at the fee he sought. Considering what I'd witnessed of his abilities in court that morning, it seemed an exorbitant figure. And although ten thousand dollars was more than I wanted to part with for an inept defense of Pamela, it seemed a small price to pay to rid me of her. Nonetheless, as I wrote Easley a check, I asked, "Do you think this will cover the full representation, Mr. Easley?"

"Oh, one can never tell what surprises may lie around the corner, Mr. Sutherland." When I apparently turned ashen, he quickly took the check from my hand and added, "But this should cover the whole case, including a trial if necessary, nicely. *If* that changes, I'll be sure to let you know immediately."

When I inquired about a business card, he fished around in his pockets and finally produced a somewhat dilapidated one from his coat. As he handed it to me, he asked for its return once I'd copied his address and phone number from it. Lacking a pen with which to copy his business information, I borrowed Mr. Easley's similarly well-worn writing implement, which was decorated with the name of a local motel. My confidence in Easley's inability was growing steadily.

Reading his card, I was struck by the rundown area of town in which his office was located. "I see that your office is in the old Belvedere Building. That's a pretty rough section of town nowadays."

"Well, most of my clients come from the rough part of town, Mr. Sutherland." Leaning closer to me, he confided, "It will be a nice change of pace for me to represent someone like your wife." Plucking his card from my hand, he added, "Now, the first order of business will be to get a bond for Mrs. Sutherland and get her out of jail. She may have to be subject to house arrest, surrender her passport, and—"

Fearing where this was leading, I cut him short. "Mr. Easley, can we talk in confidence?" Because Easley's presence was required when court reconvened, we then quickly adjourned to a nearby bench in the hallway crowded with attorneys, police officers, and witnesses involved with other cases. I did my best to look devastated. "As much as I love my wife, I hate to say this, but Pamela needs to stay in custody."

Easley carefully walked the thin line between advocating firmly on his client's behalf and not losing the check I'd just given him. "Please understand, Mr. Sutherland, that I will be representing your wife, not you, and it's her best interests I need to be looking after."

I glanced around, and then leaned toward Easley, speaking in hushed tones as if imparting some great confidence. "Rest assured that I, too, am concerned about Pamela's 'best interests,' Mr. Easley. And I say this with that in mind. Look, I love Pamela deeply, but I know her better than anyone. She is a careless and a, dare I say it, sometimes stupid woman. She is self-absorbed and can be conniving on occasion. Pamela requires, shall we say, 'special handling.' I'm afraid that, if she's released, she'll do something silly, say something inane that will come back to hurt her case in her sentencing or at her trial, if we should later have to go that route. I really need you to believe me about this, Mr. Easley. After all, she's charged with running a red light while driving under the influence. In confidence, she was probably talking on her cell phone at the time. A man is dead as a result, and she has no remorse," I pleaded. I'd been studying his face as I spoke. He was listening intently and appeared to be making sense of what I was saying. I paused, giving him time to digest my arguments thus far, before continuing. "Besides that, one more thing occurs to me, Mr. Easley. Just between us, Pamela has a tendency to dress up for every occasion and to put on haughty airs, if you know what I mean. If you do have to go to trial, wouldn't she make a more sympathetic defendant if she's kept from her fine clothes, the beauty salon, and her makeup?"

Easley sat back, looked at me with a mystified expression for a moment, and then replied, "I think I see your point, Mr. Sutherland.

You certainly know her better than I do at this juncture. Let me go talk with her, and then I'll call you. Fair enough?"

Eager to bring our close dialogue to a swift conclusion owing to, among other things, his breath, I stuck out my hand and concluded, "Yes, thank you. Please, please keep me in the loop."

"That I will do, Mr. Sutherland. But what do I tell Mrs. Sutherland if she asks about a bond?"

I smiled in amused contempt. My choice of attorneys was yet again confirmed. Here was her counselor seeking my advice about how to deal with his client. "Simply tell her that the odds are very much against her being given a bond. Add that it will serve only to antagonize the judge and the public, who read the newspapers and who will be sitting on any jury she may have, if you ask for a bond under the circumstances of her case: a man is dead at her intoxicated hands."

Easley studied me through the appearance of a perpetually hung-over countenance and nodded his agreement, if not his understanding. With a handshake and a reminder to Easley that I'd be waiting for his call, we parted. As I walked out into the bright mid-afternoon sunlight, I realized that Mark Twain had been correct when he said that "lawyers are like other people—fools on the average, but it is easier for an ass to succeed in that trade than any other. To succeed in other trades, capacity must be shown; in the law, concealment of it will do." Easley apparently excelled in the concealment of it.

I returned to my office very confident in my choice of attorney, but still concerned to some extent that my charming Pamela may yet be able to manipulate the seemingly malleable "Easy Eddie." Until I heard from him, my mind could not focus on work, so I called it a day at three o'clock. I spent the rest of the afternoon at home, sipping a lovely Bordeaux, and contemplating my existence without

Pamela. Whether from the wine or from a satisfaction with the recent turn of events, a feeling of contentment enveloped me. I even allowed myself to take a few of the phone calls from our friends. All offered compassion, whatever assistance I might need, or companionship, at least one of which, it occurred to me, came from a female friend with questionable motives. All of these I graciously declined in the best somber, heartbroken voice I could feign. I was doing just fine, thank you. Regarding the latter "offer," I thought that, if doing away with Pamela was in the offing, I could ill afford any dalliance at this point.

"Your wife is disconsolate in the extreme, Mr. Sutherland." Several days had passed. Easley and I were walking through a torrential rain from the parking lot to the visitors' lobby of the detention center. The downpour only added to the misery of having to spend unwanted time with Pamela, pretending that I cared. With our respective umbrellas constantly bumping each other, Easley struggled to walk close enough to be heard above the clashing thunder as I affected concern. I'd found myself doing a great deal of "feigning" lately. "I feel that a visit from *both* of us might help her attitude," he cantered onward.

Later, inside one of the small attorney visiting rooms, we were seated across from Pamela who slumped on the other side of a wire-reinforced window. Our efforts to meet with Pamela were rewarded with a freezing glare and stony silence. The stark whiteness of the painted cinderblock walls only added to the coldness of Pamela's reception. She was angry, arrogant, and defensive by turns. I tried to break the tension by asking whether there was anything I could do for her.

"There certainly *is* something that you can do, Gerald! Get me out of this hellhole! I'll tolerate no more stalling about this! I want answers *now*, Gerald! I'm living in horrid conditions among filthy cretins! And they are procreating!" she exclaimed with some *hauteur*.

Although taken aback by the forcefulness of Pamela's riposte, I couldn't help taking pleasure in and adding to Pamela's unhappiness, while trying not to tip my hand. "Procreating? Here in the jail?" I asked incredulously, glancing at Easley. "Are there conjugal visits here?" I exclaimed in mock horror and with a stern look.

Before Easley could respond, Pamela folded her arms across her chest in revulsion. "Don't be disgusting, Gerald!" I was rebuked. "Of course not '*in here*.' But their families come trouping through the visitors' area with their stair-step children in tow. They *are* subhuman, there are *more* of them than there are of *us*, and they are *breeding*, Gerald!"

A disconcerting thought suddenly came to me. I suspected that Easley always met with Pamela in an attorney visiting room, segregated from the general visitor's area. "How do you know what people come to the visitor's section? Has anyone besides Mr. Easley come to see you, Pamela?"

"Well, some of the 'gang' has been here to see me, thank God. I don't know how I could survive without my *dear* friends. *You* certainly haven't been a constant source of comfort." Pamela saved me the effort of making some inane excuse about not visiting her as frequently as she thought I should by shifting her fierce look from me to her lawyer who she regarded with pursed lips and an expression of disapproval. "Now, Mr. Easley, what have *you* done for *me*? I'm *not* impressed with your efforts thus far! I want out *now*!" she trumpeted.

Easley, responding to an attack on his professional competence, gathered himself and quickly retorted, "I *have* been working diligently on your case, Mrs. Sutherland. And I—"

"Well, I certainly cannot see any effort from in here!" Pamela bristled in a tone of icy contempt. She was making a mistake, I thought, quarreling with her defender, but she'd never been one to worry about what impact her words might have on others or, in return, to herself. "Please elucidate!"

Pamela's counsel was obviously upset at having to respond but held his righteous indignation in check as he went on undeterred, "As I was about to say, I have investigated the facts of the case and feel that this matter should be taken to a jury since the prosecutor will not listen to anything I have to say and is being hard-lined about any plea negotiations." Inwardly, I was smiling at the thought of twelve fair-minded citizens judging Pamela's actions in this case. Easley continued trying to reason with Pamela. "It is my considered opinion that the case for the defense has some significant merit."

Oh my, yes, I was thinking when Easley dropped his bombshell. Your 'considered opinion' and five dollars will get you a cup of plain, black coffee at Starbucks.

"To that end, I have filed a demand for a speedy trial." He beamed with a glow, like a child waiting for approval after a recitation.

I failed him in his expectations. "You've done what?" I was stunned as my mind tried to wrap around what I'd just heard. Was this the effort of an incompetent or had Easley actually found some glimmer of hope on which to pin a trial? Certainly, I did not believe one could find optimism in light of the facts as I'd heard and understood them. The suspicion I saw in Pamela's eyes as she stared angrily at me caused me not to voice my thoughts.

"I did a good thing," Easley said, childlike, almost pleading. "I filed a speedy trial demand." His answer was a shade less confident than he intended. He looked at me and continued hesitantly, "It's a right guaranteed by the Sixth Amendment of the Constitution."

"I'm familiar with the document *and* with the concept, thank you." I was stunned.

Pamela quickly returned the conversation to the center of her universe: Pamela. "What exactly does that mean for *me*, Mr. Easley?"

"It means, my dear lady, that the prosecution has to try you very soon or the case must be dismissed. It's a compromise tactic, my dear Mrs. Sutherland, for you staying in custody pending your trial, which should be forthcoming very shortly." Easley could kowtow with the best.

Pamela was obviously not paying attention to her attorney. "And if they don't try my case soon?" she challenged Easley with a tenor of frosty disdain.

He gave me fleeting look, and then leaned toward the window and raised his voice as if Pamela were some distance away, rather than just not listening. "If your case is not tried within a set time period, the law requires them to dismiss your case. Or the judge will do so. Even if they do try the case, I feel very good about our chances!" Again, Easley's demeanor reflected less confidence than his last words.

Pamela momentarily stared at Easley as she digested his words. Then she began nodding vigorously and smiled broadly. "Excellent, Mr. Easley!" She seemed to relax, and he sat back, pleased with himself.

Because the die had been cast and not wanting to miss an opportunity to appear ever the caring husband, I added, "See, Pamela, I told you I'd find the best attorney I could for you!"

Thus emboldened, Easley pressed on. "In preparation for the trial, I want the names of several character witnesses for you, close friends, who can testify that they don't believe you'd *ever* drive under the influence and have *never* seen you do so."

Although still fairly confident in my choice of attorney, a sick feeling washed over me. What had become of the defense counsel I'd watched in court that day? That lawyer with all the eager self-confidence of a rabbit caught in a snare? These thoughts were racing through my head as I asked, "I don't mean to be argumentative, and surely your optimism comes as fabulous news to Pamela and me, but what about the police who examined her at the scene of the accident and pronounced her as 'driving under the influence'? Surely they will testify!"

Easley merely smiled and advised us that he was preparing for that. Beaming with a newly found self-confidence, he would say nothing more. He concluded our meeting by informing Pamela that she would be dressed in "street clothes" for the trial. The jurors would not be allowed to see her in inmate clothing. Easley explained that he wanted Pamela to look as ordinary as possible. Over Pamela's objections, he told her she *would* wear a plain black suit, a white blouse, and no makeup. Ignoring all her protests to the contrary, he insisted that her hair was to be neat but plain. No arguments allowed. He instructed her to show no response during the proceedings, except for the well-timed sign of grief at the mention of the deceased. Easley expressed the opinion that tears would be a nice touch. He went on to explain that he had learned Mr. Garcia was alone in the world, so there would be no grieving widow or fatherless children sobbing, playing on the tender mercies of the court or the jury. Finally, he reminded Pamela of something that he must have told her during a previous visit: *he* was her only friend and confidant and she was to speak to *no one else* about her case. "I'll be back soon. And often," he told her as we stood. Suddenly, Easley seemed far from out of his element. And Pamela seemed more satisfied than I would have expected. Evidently, she had even accepted her plight of remaining in jail until the trial. Hopefully, both were overconfident about Easley's ability to extricate her from her predicament.

"I still don't understand why the hell you filed a speedy trial request!" I was striding back to my car, trying desperately not to show my anger and frustration. Easley was loping beside me, trying his best to keep pace in the pouring rain.

"Demand. Not a request, a demand, Mr. Sutherland. I explained all that back there. It was a compromise for Mrs. Sutherland sitting in jail. From meeting with your wife, I came to the conclusion that you may be correct in your assessment of the 'dangers' of her getting a bond. But she was quite insistent on getting out. So I compromised. I thought you'd *both* be pleased, but I feel the need to remind you that it is your wife I represent, Mr. Sutherland."

We had reached my coupé by this point. As I opened the car door, I turned to him and, playing the apologist, sighed. "I understand, Mr. Easley. Please forgive me. All this is simply so foreign to me, so upsetting. We both have the utmost confidence in you. I just hope you know what you're doing." As I drove away leaving him standing in the rain, his pants soaked from the knees down, I watched his face in the rear-view mirror, looking for any sign of recognition of my true feelings about all this, hoping I'd not overplayed my hand. Despite his sudden attempted foray into the realm of "legal genius" and my "reassurances," the dulled-eyed look of uncertainty he'd exhibited in court that first day had returned. Maybe this appearance of competence was merely a momentary anomaly on his part.

As a result of Easley's speedy trial demand, Pamela's trial was scheduled to start a few weeks later. As the date approached, an odd sort of bonding evolved between Pamela and her attorney during their meetings, two of which I attended. They were now allowed to meet in an attorney conference room at the jail. Here, no glass partition separated them, and they huddled together, speaking in hushed tones. I merely sat off to the side and observed this form of "dance" between the two. Easley started calling my wife "Princess Pamela."

Although I took this as a comment on her haughty mannerisms, he earnestly meant it as a compliment. Pamela obviously delighted in his references, giggling like a schoolgirl every time. For her part, Pamela truly looked upon Easley as her "rescuing knight," hanging on his every word, her adoring eyes reluctant to leave him. Likewise, he enjoyed the attention this sophisticated, attractive woman lavished on him. Her genuine interest in him and in his work on her behalf buoyed him, gave him renewed energy as he went about his preparations, which belied his look of a perpetual hangover. Despite all the interplay between them, it seemed to me an exercise in futility owing to the overwhelming evidence against Pamela. During the meetings that I attended, Easley never revealed much about his plans for Pamela's defense. He only spoke in broad terms about the character witnesses he'd scheduled on her behalf and the general nature of a trial. Virtually nothing was mentioned of what, if anything, his investigation had revealed.

This, I thought, was because there was nothing about which to speak. He had no plan of attack. My confidence in the weakness of Pamela's defense, and in the man presenting it, remained. I felt akin to an old crone knitting beside the guillotine, waiting for the blade to drop and the crowd's cheers to rise.

"Here are Pamela's clothes." I handed the requested clothing to Easley, who, in turn, gave them to a female deputy. We were standing in the courtroom early on the first day of the trial and jury selection was to begin in an hour or so. Easley turned back to me, as I continued, "I'll bring a different blouse, along with clean underwear, every morning."

"Good. Very good, Mr. Sutherland." I remained "Mr. Sutherland" to Easley who continued to hold me at arm's length, as they say. Perhaps I'd unintentionally given him too much insight into my true feelings about my wife and her trial. While we stood together briefly, I noted that Easley had maintained the same high level of "sartorial splendor" for this trial as he'd displayed every occasion since I'd met him. In the pretrial atmosphere, he was fidgeting nervously like a children's party clown with Tourette's syndrome. Nonetheless, Easley went on hesitantly, "I'll need you to sit in the gallery just behind your wife and me. The jury needs to see your concerned face every day. By the way, if you see or hear the name of anyone in the jury panel you know or know of, please tell me immediately. Getting the right jury is always important, but it could be most crucial in this case."

I reluctantly agreed and, with some time before the court proceedings were to begin, went to a nearby café for a cup of coffee. There I encountered a few women from the "gang" who were attending the trial, supporting Pamela and me. A couple of them were to be character witnesses for my wife. I bought a round of café lattes for the group. As I was paying, I noticed Ms. Winkler, the prosecutor in Pamela's case, was also there getting a "prebattle" pick-me-up. She was standing at the other end of the counter with a baby-faced, diminutive police officer, who looked as if he'd be better suited making undercover arrests for underage drinking at a middle school sock hop than driving a patrol car. He had the appearance of someone who constantly thinks his authority is about to be challenged and doesn't intend to stand for it.

When she met my glance with an icy glower across the small coffee shop, I knew at once that her attitude toward me and my wife's case had not changed since our earlier meeting. Good, I thought as I smiled, I need her fired up and ready to convict.

"Look who I've brought with me!" I'd returned to the courtroom with the "gang" in tow and was trying to regain some of Easley's confidence in my position regarding Pamela. Pamela was already dressed in her black suit and seated at the defense table, looking respectable and confident but uncharacteristically plain. She was huddled with Easley, who turned and smiled as he saw us approach. Ms. Winkler and the policeman, who I later learned was the arresting officer in Pamela's case, came into the courtroom almost immediately behind us. She pushed past us as our friends spoke to Pamela across the rail under the watchful eyes of the sheriff deputies. Winkler moved quickly to the prosecution's table as the bailiff announced the judge's entry and called the courtroom to order.

After a few preliminary matters, including the sequestering of the witnesses outside the courtroom proceedings, the prospective jurors were sent for and jury selection began. Easley soon returned to his old form. He stumbled through the selection process hesitantly, somehow completing the task, although the procedure seemed glacial.

During her opening statement to the jury, Ms. Winkler glided around the courtroom as easily as a professional skater, unlike Easley, who, during his opening remarks, appeared as graceful as a hog on ice. Pamela's confidence seemed to drain away like bathwater. Ms. Winkler smiled at his apparent ineptitude and, occasionally, would cast a smirk in my direction as I sat in the gallery behind the defense table. Even the jurors could be seen smiling at each other when he periodically gave the impression he was at a loss. His disheveled form only added to the sad picture. I was very pleased.

The first person called to give evidence for the State was the sole eyewitness to the accident, a certain Mrs. Eleanor Godfrey. A large, middle-aged woman, with unconvincing blond hair, blue eyes the size of silver dollars, and red cheeks like those of Santa Claus in the old Coca Cola magazine advertisements. Heavily weighed down with makeup, she wore an assortment of colored scarves and bright costume jewelry. Mrs. Godfrey approached the witness stand with a strut intended to derive the most from the unaccustomed attention her presence there evoked. Once sworn in as a witness, Ms. Winkler guided her carefully through her testimony, leaving the jury with a clear picture of Pamela's careless actions, at least from Mrs. Godfrey's perspective, which led to the untimely death of Mr. Garcia. The witness had been sitting in her car in a left-turn lane at the intersection. Her left-turn traffic signal was red, but, according to her testimony on direct examination, the light for the traffic traveling from her direction and going straight through the intersection was green. Mr. Garcia's small red car drove into the intersection from her direction where it was struck broadside by Pamela's SUV. Mrs. Godfrey described the "horrible" crash in very emotional terms, dramatically dabbing her eyes at the appropriate times. After the collision, she further related, she had called 9-1-1 on her cell phone and stayed to speak with the responding police officer. Ms. Winkler confidently turned the witness over to opposing counsel for cross-examination.

As Easley rose to question the witness, his forehead glistening with perspiration, he made a futile effort to smooth his crumpled suit. I noted that the crooked knot of his skinny tie had slowly fallen away from his collar as the day wore on. The witness turned her focus to Pamela's attorney, eager to continue her part as the center of attention. Easley moved toward the witness with the majestic deliberation of a pachyderm and started his questioning of Mrs. Godfrey as if uncertain where to go with this damning testimony but intent on asking something of her in order to appear to earn his fee. In due course, he asked her what first brought her attention to the crash itself.

She squirmed slightly in her seat, glanced at the prosecutor, and responded, "Well, first I heard this horrible noise. Then I looked up and saw this small red car spinning away from the SUV. Counterclockwise, I think it was spinning." After a brief motion with her hand to reenact the scene in her mind, she concluded, "Yes, it was counterclockwise."

Easley paused, inclined his head, and smiled faintly. "Now, Mrs. Godfrey, I don't think you mentioned 'hearing a noise,' and *then* 'looking up' to see the accident when the prosecutor was questioning you a moment ago." As he so stated, he turned and gave Ms. Winkler a fleeting look of puzzlement. He then returned to the witness. "Is that your testimony about what you saw at the scene of the accident? You first heard a noise, and then looked up to see the spinning car?"

"Well, yes, but Ms. Winkler didn't ask me that here today, sir." Mrs. Godfrey was clearly defensive at this point. For their part, the jury showed a distinct interest in this bit of information.

"So, Mrs. Godfrey, what exactly were you doing when you *heard* the crash?" Easley had stumbled, no doubt unwittingly, onto a kernel of hope. And, like a bulldog, he wasn't going to let go easily.

"I was looking through my purse for my cell phone. It was ringing, you see, and—"

"In that case," Easley put it to the witness, "you were *not* looking at the traffic light in front of you, were you? Honestly speaking, you have *no* idea whether the light Mr. Garcia passed through was green, yellow, or even *red*, do you?"

Mr. Godfrey looked to Ms. Winkler for assistance. None forthcoming, she resigned herself to her own answer. "Well, it was green when I started looking for my phone!" Pleased with her response, she smiled at the jury. They did not return the favor.

I could not believe what I was hearing! While I realized that this was only the first witness, the trial was not supposed to happen this way! I could only hope that Winkler would return on redirect examination with some case-saving questions. Easley sat down and patted Pamela's arm. For her part, Pamela seemed not to be following the significance of what had just been said. Perhaps she was still dreading, whereas I was still counting on, the testimony of the arresting officer.

"About how long were you looking through your purse for your phone before you heard the crash, Mrs. Godfrey?" Ms. Winkler was trying to rehabilitate her eyewitness.

Mrs. Godfrey's defensive posture had grown as she felt the glow of her star's spotlight fade with the impact on the jury of her uncertain testimony. "Well, surely for no more than a minute!" A minute! With that blow, the prosecutor subsided to her chair. She clearly had decided to cut her losses.

When Mrs. Godfrey left the witness box, it was with obvious relief. And much of her testimony would be repeated later in Easley's closing argument to the jury. After a couple of other peripheral bystanders testified, the judge recessed court for lunch. Easley whispered briefly with Pamela as the jury filed out of the courtroom. When the last juror had disappeared, sheriff's deputies ushered Pamela to an awaiting cell with defense counsel in tow, still talking to his client.

Just before returning to court from the noon recess, I was briefly able to capture Easley's attention away from the others as he was dopplering down the old marble floor of the courthouse hallway. I had to know where we stood now. Before I could formulate a question that would not betray my despair about the testimony thus far, Easley slapped me on the back and waxed effusive, "That Mrs. Godfrey certainly didn't hurt Pamela one bit did she, Mr. Sutherland? I feel very good about the case now! Reasonable doubt, Mr. Sutherland! Reasonable doubt! *Onus probandi*!" Easley hurried away toward the courtroom, leaving me with unanswered questions, unhappy prospects, and uncontrollable frustration.

The first officer who responded to the scene of the wreck, the one I'd seen in the coffee shop with Ms. Winkler, was next called to testify. The assistant district attorney led him through the events of that fateful day, ending with his arrest of the unrepentant Pamela for driving under the influence. Surely, I thought, these inescapable facts were enough to harden the jury against Pamela. Again, a confident Ms. Winkler turned her witness over to the defense attorney.

"How long had you been on the police force at the time of this accident, Officer Hoffman?" Easley was examining the witness with more confidence than he had shown in any part of the trial thus far.

"About eight months."

"And did you have any law-enforcement experience before that?"

"No, sir."

"Any military experience?"

"No, sir."

"No military police experience then." The words formed more a statement than a question. "Now you testified on direct examination that you completed your academy training as prescribed for certification as a law-enforcement officer in this state, right?"

As the officer nodded, uncertain of where Easley was going, the judge instructed him that he was required to answer aloud so the court reporter could make a record of what was said. "Yes, sir," he replied to both the judge's instructions and to Easley's question, his voice booming as he leaned toward the microphone at the witness stand.

"Other than the routine class or two at the police academy, have you had any specialized training in making 'driving under the influence' assessments or arrests?"

"No, sir."

"How old are you, officer?"

"I'm twenty-four years old, sir."

"And prior to the date of this accident, how many 'driving under the influence' arrests had you made?" Easley was evidently determined to beat the word "accident" into the jury's thought process.

Officer Hoffman hesitated and looked to the judge for a second. When the judge proved to be unavailable for any referrals, the officer responded somewhat defensively, "This was my first DUI arrest, sir."

"Please tell the jury, Officer Hoffman, what assessment process, what roadside sobriety tests you used to determine my client was driving under the influence of alcohol at the time of the accident."

Again, Easley had succeeded in arousing defensiveness in a witness. "Well, she admitted that she'd been drinking. *And* I could smell alcohol on her breath. Also, she was obviously glassy-eyed and unsteady on her feet. So ... none."

"Fair enough, officer. Now let's just stop for a second and consider each one of those things you just said led you to her arrest for drunk driving. You say she said she'd had a drink. Did she say how many drinks?"

"No."

"One drink? Three drinks? Ten drinks? What?"

"Objection, Your Honor!" Ms. Winkler was on her hind legs trying to salvage her case. "Asked and answered!"

"Your Honor, this officer has made a claim against my client that is at the very heart of this case. The jury has a right to know how he reached his conclusion and *if* that conclusion holds up to the light of day!"

"Objection overruled. Answer the question, Officer Hoffman."

Suddenly, I found that I'd hired Perry freaking Mason! Easley pressed the witness. "Did my client say how many drinks she'd had that day, officer?"

Hoffman was becoming more frustrated. "No, sir, she only said she'd had a drink with her lunch," he grumbled.

"*A* drink! *One* drink! And speaking of which, in your limited training related to drunk driver assessments, did you learn that food intake can dramatically reduce the effect of alcohol on a person's faculties?" Here, I supposed, Easley was falling back on his personal experiences.

"Yes, sir, I did, but she was unsteady on her feet!"

"We'll get to that in a minute. First, tell the jury how many drinks it takes before you can smell alcohol on another person."

"Well … ."

"Yes?"

"Well, I guess, depending on what they were drinking, that could vary."

"So possibly only *one* drink would give off the odor? But that would not necessarily be enough alcohol to impair someone, right? Did Mrs. Sutherland say what she'd had to drink?"

"No, sir."

"And as you just testified, it would be guesswork, without more information, to try to determine whether that amount of alcohol, whatever the amount, was sufficient to impair someone anyway, right?"

Hoffman remained silent but turned a particular shade of violet. The jury was very attentive.

"Let's move on, officer. You said my client was unsteady on her feet, right?" Not waiting for the obvious answer, Easley continued, "Now she'd just been involved in a serious automobile accident, right?"

"Yes."

"Have you at least investigated other automobile accidents in your vast eight months on the force?" A suggestion of sarcasm filled the air between the two men.

"Objection! Argumentative!"

"Objection overruled, Ms. Winkler. Mr. Easley is entitled to a thorough and sifting cross-examination. You may continue, counselor." The judge gave a hint of a smile as he spoke. I suspected that he was relishing the exhibition of newfound abilities in an attorney who had stumbled through court appearances before him many times.

Easley simply stared at the officer for a long minute. Hoffman turned over the question as if it were an unfamiliar article. Finally, he relented. "Yes, I've investigated car accidents."

"Fine. Now, it's not unusual for a person involved in such an accident to be stunned, glassy-eyed and/or unsteady on their feet immediately following such an episode, is it? Especially, if they've hit their head during the accident?"

"Well ... no."

"And so such manifestations do not have to be related in any way to the consumption of alcohol, do they, Officer Hoffman?"

Hoffman was showing signs of losing his temper. He glared at Easley and answered through gritted teeth. "No!"

"Before you summarily arrested my client and hauled her away in your patrol car or at any time thereafter, no one else with your department confirmed your assessment of Mrs. Sutherland as being under the influence, did they?"

The officer begrudgingly muttered his response in a low tone. "No."

"I'm sorry, Officer Hoffman. I didn't hear your answer." Easley coarsely prodded as he glanced at the jury.

"No!" This time, the answer was nearly shouted by the red-faced policeman.

Here, Easley paused to let the obvious defensiveness of the officer envelop the jury. Continuing with a more gentle thrust and parry, the defense counsel calmly moved on. "Now, Officer Hoffman, one final question. Did you or, to your knowledge, did anyone else administer a Breathalyzer test on Mrs. Sutherland the day of the accident day to determine whether she was, in fact, intoxicated?"

"No, sir." Hoffman had accepted defeat.

Easley sat down wearily. Watching his repose, one might have imagined him as Hercules in the midst of his enormous tasks. At this point, Ms. Winkler made no attempt to rehabilitate Officer Hoffman. As the somewhat discredited policeman sulked away from the witness stand, she called her next witness. However, one look at the jury showed that the prosecution's case has breathed its last gasp. The jury seemed to fall into a state of somnambulism during the two-day completion of the State's evidence, which only provided further confirmation of the few innocuous facts to which previous witnesses had testified and which inadvertently offered the additional tidbit of the unfortunate Mr. Garcia's illegal presence in this country. Easley's witnesses for Pamela held her to be a good, caring person of upstanding character. It demonstrated either how little people really know about each other or in what low regard they hold an oath to tell the truth.

As much as I hated him for it, I had to admit that Easley clearly and concisely summed up the case in his closing argument, hammering home two salient points. The first of these was that the chief "eyewitness" for the State had not really witnessed anything except the aftermath of an unfortunate *accident* because she'd been digging around in her chaotic handbag. The second point defense counsel fervently articulated was that the police officer in question was not capable of factually representing nor was anyone else able to show beyond a reasonable doubt that Pamela was actually driving under the influence of anything.

Whether through the efforts of Mr. Easley, because of their reaction to an overzealous officer, or owing to the current community attitude toward illegal immigrant personages, the jury returned a "not guilty" verdict in short order. As Easley and Pamela hugged each other in celebration and Ms. Winkler stormed off in total disgust, my world crashed around me. Pamela was released from custody immediately. And, in the course of time, we found ourselves at an obligatory celebratory dinner with the esteemed defense counsel, who modestly acknowledged that "even a blind hog can find an acorn once in a while!"

Now I'm sitting here, peering across the top of my wineglass, seething with anger, watching the two of them revel like schoolchildren let out for the summer. I realize I've returned to square one. But now I'm trying to decide whether I'm going to kill only Pamela or Pamela *and* her lawyer.

THE 3000 EYES

People say that being in Washington, D. C., in August is like standing in the breath of a very big dog—very hot, very humid. Please allow me to share with you a story about one such day in our nation's capital. The following is not a story that you have ever read about in the newspapers or heard about on the radio or seen on television. It took place in those heady, shiny days of our country before the attacks of September 11th. You will not recognize the story, because it represented a failure of our government to look after its own on more than one level. As such, it was a source of shame and embarrassment to those involved and was, thus, buried. And please do not ask me *how* I know the story.

The Coast Guard lieutenant remembered that axiom about late summer in Washington as he rode the escalator taking him from the relatively pleasant subterranean environment of the Metro subway system to the blast-furnace surface world of Washington. This August was worse than usual. As the escalator approached the early-morning glare and the stifling air, he reminded himself that he *had asked* to be transferred to Headquarters in Washington. He also recalled how the lieutenant commander, who was responsible for officer assignments, had laughed aloud until he'd realized the junior officer was serious about the request. After all, no one *wanted* to be assigned to Headquarters. The lieutenant, determined to work his way into a legal billet after going to law school on his time, paying for it with his money, knew such an assignment would never happen if he stayed in Coast Guard duties in the hinterlands. So he reminded himself that this weather was "self-inflicted."

When the officer reached the street level, each breath in the oppressive heat became a distinct displeasure. On the bright side, as they say, his plan had succeeded. Soon after arriving in Headquarters, he'd "browbeaten" the legal billet officer into giving him an assignment as a "law specialist." The Coast Guard didn't have that sexy "JAG Corps" label, made popular and seemingly exotic by movies and television. Even so, the lieutenant considered it a great privilege to be designated a "law specialist" in the U. S. Coast Guard. So he endured.

Entering the building where he had worked for the last seventeen months, separate and aside from the Headquarters building itself, held little difference from the outside as far as atmospheric conditions were concerned. The outward coolness of modernistic glass and marble buildings can certainly belie the oppressive conditions inside. Maybe a foreboding of what the day had in store should have come over him at that point, but everyone else waiting for the elevator at 7:30 a.m. was suffering from the cruel heat, too. So no such thoughts entered his mind.

In his office, what laughingly passed for central air-conditioning barely belched enough air, all of it warm, to pass for a bad fan. In less than an hour, the lieutenant was perspiring profusely and what was left of his thinning hair was matted down. The young officer felt as if he'd been born in the uniform clinging to his body. Even opening the door leading directly to the hall from his small, windowless office didn't relieve the sultry environment. He finally capitulated and closed the hallway door for the sake of privacy, leaving the other door to the main office reception area open. Thank God, he thought, this job didn't require any serious physical work. As an attorney in the physical disability evaluation system, he provided legal counsel to people, or evaluees, as they were called, whose fitness for duty or, in the alternative, whose disability level owing to some impairment was being assessed. Strictly a desk job.

The day was fairly routine, awash with forms, phone calls, scheduling hearings, and decisions for evaluees. The lieutenant had lost track of time when he looked up through his door to the outer office and realized the lights there were off. The rest of the office staff had left for the day. Because he always arrived about half an hour after everyone else, he stayed later. While finishing a letter, the officer heard the front office door being opened and closed quietly. The cleaning people are later than usual, he thought. He continued trying to complete the correspondence so he could leave to catch his commuter train at Union Station.

Suddenly, he realized he wasn't alone: a motionless form stood in the shadows just outside his door. After the opening jolt, he relaxed, but only for a moment. Initially, he didn't recognize the face, half hidden by the shadows. As the woman, wearing a denim blouse and dark-blue slacks, eased into the light of his office, the facts of the case washed over him like the tide over a beached conch shell. The young enlisted girl, older than her years, had been one of his early disability cases. A childhood of abuse and confusion, and then one bad experience in the service after another, including a broken marriage, had led to serious psychological problems. Very serious. These emotional problems were compounded by her unshakable, yet unfounded belief that the service had ignored her and cast her aside when she most needed support. Maybe it was no large matter to most people. However, to her, the issues were cause enough for much very bitter, pent-up anger. The lieutenant had learned all of this when he'd served as her legal counsel in the disability proceedings.

Despite her slight size and deceptively quiet nature, those weeks dealing with her had not been the most comfortable of his life. A seething anger always drifted immediately below the surface of her persona. The officer recalled thinking her volatile personality was like a brain aneurysm, concealed but just waiting for the wrong word, the misunderstood intention, the stress of which could likely bring about fatal results. Walking on eggshells had never been his strong suit, but he'd managed while working with her. And he remembered getting lost more than once in those steel-gray eyes—icy pools—that, more often than not, seemed those of a corpse. More than once, he'd caught her looking through him as one does a pane of glass in a window to the scene beyond. Oh yes, she'd been a difficult 3000 series case, the 3000 referring to that section of the disability code relating to the series of psychological diagnoses. Some ugly stuff in that volume. And, psychologically speaking, she'd been a classic case of ugly issues. She had long since been discharged from the service and, so far as the lieutenant knew, remained under continued psychiatric care. What she needed most was protection from the things in her head.

So, here she stood at his office door in the early evening with probably not another soul in the building, much less on that floor. He found himself grasping at hope in the thought that possibly some custodial folks were still around. But, notwithstanding the optimism of that idea, he could not shake his uneasy feeling about the situation. Calm down, the lieutenant told himself in a respite of relief. After all, you'd been her counsel … on her side, and the disability board had been very generous in its findings. The mental roller coaster he'd been riding in those few seconds came to a shattering stop when he finally focused on her eyes.

After swallowing hard, he struggled to quickly recall he name. "Ms. Lamar?" Brittany Lamar. Yes, that was it. No response. Just a vacant glare. The roller coaster started a downward run again. His sweat (he'd graduated from perspiration) now seemed completely unrelated to the temperature of the office. "Brittany?" He was trying again, allowing an informal address he normally never used with a client.

The officer sensed something deep inside her stir. She blinked, stepped into his office, sat in the chair across the desk from him, and stammered, "Hello, again, lieutenant."

After an awkward moment of silence, he asked whether there was anything he could do for her. No response. Then, before he could ask again, she made some unintelligible comment.

"Excuse me?"

She looked disoriented. "I said I've come to collect what the service owes me."

That roller coaster ride slowed slightly as a short-lived measure of relief came over him. Evidently, she was confused, but, then, so was he. What was she doing in Washington? As well as he could recall, after her discharge, she was to return to her parent's farm somewhere in the Midwest, near a little town called Belvedere, if he remembered correctly. A very good Veterans Administration hospital, where she could get continued psychiatric care, was in a larger city near their home.

"No, Ms. Lamar, you don't understand. You see, the——." He never finished the sentence. The sudden blaring of a siren from the fire station across the street made her start. She bolted from her seat and ran to a window in the outer office. From his desk, he could her where she stood, and he could see those eyes in a frantic search for the source of the alarm. For a moment, the lieutenant's mind shouted a warning that he should get the hell out of there through the door into the hallway. But logic laughed off the idea of any danger. Certainly, he told himself, this is only a confused and lonely woman. Nothing more. He felt foolish for his anxiety.

When she returned to his office, something about the forsaken look in her eyes made him immediately regret the decision to remain. She had a ghostlike serenity about her. Unearthly, yet menacing. That roller coaster sped up.

"You were sayin' that I don't understand. Well, it's you who doesn't understand, lieutenant. You and all the others." As she spoke, she pulled a gun from a purse the lieutenant had not noticed before that moment. Now, despite being in the military, the lieutenant did not have a vast familiarity with handguns, but the one she held looked deadly enough. The weapon was larger than a derringer yet smaller than a howitzer. But only slightly smaller. And she knew how to handle guns, all kinds of guns. She'd learned that much growing up on a farm. Despite his mind's furious pace, he recollected reading that in her service record during the disability proceedings.

For the first time that day, he could feel the sweat rolling down the hollow in the small of his back. The officer tried to swallow without success.

"What're you doing, Ms. Lamar?" The words nearly died in his throat.

"Like I said, I'm collectin' what I'm owed. Where are the others?"

"What others?"

"The ones who are usually here, messing with people's lives."

The roller coaster accelerated even more. The lieutenant decided it would be best not to argue with her, if at all possible. "Gone for the day. They're gone for the day. You can't expect—collect what?" He tried not to sound panicky, but knew he'd failed.

"I'm owed something for all the grief and pain the service has caused me. Use a person, and then throw 'em away. It's just not right! So now I'm gonna collect something ... some satisfaction, maybe, if nothin' else! I ... you—you!" Her rage continued to grow until she was nearly incoherent. Just as quickly, she was calm again. "I'll start with you, and then get the others later." Despite his fear, he watched those eyes and realized that they never changed whether she was angry or serene. They remained the same cold and vacuous steel-gray. She continued calmly. "What's the diagnostic code for a bullet in the brain, lieutenant?"

That roller coaster was now in free fall. Sheer terror rose in the officer's being. But calm reasoning had to be the best approach. He tried to steady himself. "Look, I've tried to help you all along. Do you remember how many hours we worked putting your case together for the medical board? Why do you want to hurt me? Or the others? You need help. I'll do all I can to get it for you. Please just put the gun down. You can't gain anything by this. You can't get away with it."

She gave him a lopsided half-smile, but her eyes never changed. She stopped smiling and became stone hard. "Don't even waste your breath, lieutenant." As her stare intensified, she continued, "If I *had* a mind, you *might* be able to reason with it."

His sweat felt cold. Suddenly, the room was chilly. Someone or something had pushed her over that edge she'd been dancing along for some time. And he knew the time had come for him to die.

"Get up," she said, motioning with the gun. "I want the others to find you when they come back. Then they'll know I'm here. And I'll be back for them, too."

"Please listen … ." He went silent as the rest of his words failed him. He was terrified beyond anything he could have imagined—no apologies offered.

The lieutenant moved on wobbly legs around his desk and into the outer office. She followed closely and turned on the lights.

"Stop!" she screamed suddenly. His heart almost did. He'd made no abrupt moves, no effort to get away, so why the hysteria on her part? No motive is required of a 3000 series, he reasoned.

"Sit here," she said, indicating a chair with the gun. She was calm again. Somewhere in his soul, he made a vow never to get near a roller coaster again if he lived through this. Slowly, he eased into the chair, never taking his eyes off the gun.

"Try to understand this is nothin' personal," she explained.

His throat and mouth were dry as he pleaded. "Look, I've always sort of thought of *my* death as a 'personal' thing, you know?"

"But you're part of *them*, and the doctor said *they're* killing me." As she finished the statement, she calmly raised the gun, extending it at arm's length, and pointed it at his forehead.

As he looked up, the young officer thought those eyes, those damned unearthly, gray eyes would be the last thing he'd ever see. A scream welled up in his throat. But before he could utter a sound, the front office door opened abruptly, and the room was filled with muted hip-hop music. A custodial worker appeared with a trash bag in his hands, earbuds embedded in the sides of his head. Without so much as a second's hesitation, Brittany turned, raised her arm to the level of her shoulder, sighted down it, and fired in one swift motion. The bullet struck the worker squarely with devastating results. The wall behind the man became a splatter, and then a smear as his shattered body fell against it and slid to the floor. It happened in a nanosecond.

In that instant, the lieutenant used a leg sweep to knock Brittany's legs from under her. She spun and fired as she went down. The impact of the bullet tearing through his left shoulder was followed by a searing pain. He almost passed out. A footrace between fear and anger began in his brain. At the same time, he fell to the floor, hitting hard enough to empty his lungs. Somehow, he managed to scramble on top of the sprawled woman, while grabbing desperately for the gun. Another gunshot near his head left him momentarily deaf. Even though he couldn't hear her ravings, he knew them from her eyes, which never left his as they struggled for control of the firearm. It seemed as though her howls, the mournful screeches of a thousand lost, forgotten, maniacal souls, were emanating from her eyes.

Their struggle seemed interminable. The perspiration that drenched his hands made his efforts to control the gun all the more difficult. Sweat also obscured his vision. Suddenly, he realized the gun was between their heads, pointed in his direction. Despite his adversary's unexpectedly astonishing strength spurred on by madness, the lieutenant managed to turn the gun slowly in her direction. As if she realized what was happening and was determined to steal the moment, Brittany stopped screaming, smiled slightly, and pulled the trigger. The force of the gun's blast into her neck nearly severed her head from her body. She went limp. But one thing never changed, even in death—her eyes. They were no more vacant in death, than they'd been in life.

He didn't know how long they lie there eye to eye—those damned eyes—in the fleeting light. He was too exhausted to move. Eventually, building security found them, someone having reported the shots being fired. An ambulance was called, and the lieutenant was patched up "like new," at least physically. Everything's fine now, except … except now he can't concentrate during the day or sleep at night. He keeps seeing those eyes of hers—those frosty pools in which you could drown. They're everywhere he goes. Sometimes he cries when they press too close, when they come in the night. Their pain and anguish are his now. Their emptiness, too. But no one understands. The young officer was relieved of his duties and told to rest. But he knew what they were saying: that he's a 3000 series, that he's deranged somehow. And, if you see him wandering the streets of Washington, he will tell you her eyes *are* there. He *can* see them. She *is* with him now. Always.

Contact the author at
Tom.Woodward71@gmail.com

Made in the USA
Charleston, SC
18 December 2012